laugh

the last laugh

TRACY BLOOM

Bookouture

Published by Bookouture in 2018

An imprint of StoryFire Ltd.
Carmelite House
50 Victoria Embankment
London EC4Y 0DZ

www.bookouture.com

ISBN: 978-1-78681-292-6
eBook ISBN: 978-1-78681-291-9

For Gemma

This is not about you but it is because of you.

Forever missed.

Prologue

Somehow our bodies move as one, bouncing up and down to the beat, singing our hearts out, beer sloshing out of stubby bottles, broken plastic glasses crackling under our feet, air guitar solos occasionally breaking away momentarily before being brought back in the fold by hugs and kisses and the joy of feeling as one under the glorious champagne supernova that is the sky. There's me in the middle of it, high on someone's shoulders, long sun-kissed hair cascading down my back, smiling inanely down at Mark's face bobbing up and down below me.

I'm so high.

Not because I couldn't have dreamed of a better way to spend my twenty-fifth birthday, not even because of the quantity of tequila slammers I've inhaled.

I'm just high on life.

At least I managed it once.

Chapter One

Twenty years later…

'Table for three?' asks the waitress, standing guard next to a cardboard cactus at the entrance to the restaurant.

'No, four.' I turn around. 'Where's Ellie?' I ask Mark.

'You really wanted to come here?' he replies with a look so disdainful I whisk my head back round towards the waitress, ready to apologise for my husband's rudeness, but she's busy handing George a colouring-in menu and a pot of crayons.

'He's a very short fifteen!' I say, thrusting my hand out to intercept the handover. It's not George's fault he's still waiting for a growth spurt, but it might help if he didn't hide his face in the depths of a hoody if he wants to avoid being mistaken for someone in need of artistic distraction during a meal. I am too eager in my protectiveness, however, and send the pot of crayons flying out of the idiotic waitress' hands and all over the blue and white mosaic tiled floor.

George grunts.

Mark tuts.

The waitress gasps.

No one helps as I bend down to pick up the broken colouring sticks.

'What's Mum doing on the floor?' I hear Ellie say as she emerges from whatever cover she was using to avoid being seen dead with her family.

'She knocked the crayons out of her hand,' I hear Mark reply with a sigh.

I can see the yellow one has rolled next to his foot ready to cause a potentially serious incident. I leave it there.

'Sorry about that,' I say, standing up and handing over a pile of broken coloured wax into the hand of the waitress. 'He's just a bit short,' I add, pulling George's hood off his head to reveal the back of his neck, which is bright pink.

'Would you like to follow me?' asks the waitress, grabbing four enormous menus as she escapes down the length of the restaurant towards the back.

I chase after her to ask if we could actually sit near the front. I need to be able to see the cactus fairy lights, you see. And I want to be near the bar where it's livelier. Where I can sit and watch other people enjoying themselves even if I'm not.

'We're not actually serving food in that area,' she replies as she carefully lays the enormous menus on a table in a dark corner with no view of anything.

'But *I* would like to sit there,' I say defiantly, looking round to see if there is any vague chance Mark will step in and back me up. Mark, Ellie and George have not even registered that I have moved, all engrossed in their phones or, in George's case, his own mortification.

The waitress looks at me and puts her hands on her hips. Yes, her hips.

'We are only serving food in this section,' she says.

I stare back at her. Part of me wants to give up now, go home and write the night off as a bad idea. But it's my birthday. I want to at least attempt an enjoyable meal with my family before... well, before things may never be the same again. Before I break the news to Mark on the twentieth anniversary of us getting together that, well... there might be something wrong with me. Catastrophically wrong with me.

'I want a table where I can see the cactus fairy lights,' I tell her with what I hope is an air of authority.

'Yeah.' She shrugs.

I realise I am in a stand-off in the back of a Mexican restaurant.

'You let us have a table at the front or we will leave,' I demand. My voice wobbles slightly, which may have given her the upper hand. I hold my breath.

She looks at me and sighs – yes, sighs.

'I'll have to go and ask the manager if we can open up another section,' she says, strutting off and leaving me standing on my own.

I quickly gather up the enormous menus and begin a fast walk back up to the front of the restaurant. I'm thinking that if we're seated before the waitress gets back she won't be able to do anything about it.

'What is Mum doing?' I hear Ellie ask for the second time that night.

In my haste to win the race I have not spotted that the other three members of my family have finally deigned to join me and are walking in the opposite direction down the next aisle.

'We're sitting at the front,' I say, barely slowing up. 'Quick, this way,' I shout over my shoulder.

'But someone might see us if we sit there,' I hear Ellie cry.

By the time Mark, Ellie and George join me, I've bagged, in my opinion, the best seat in the house. Back to the wall, right at the front, facing the bar, I can see everything going on. That is, until we all pick up our menus, blocking all of the view and a big chunk of light.

'Why on earth did you want to come here?' grumbles Mark from somewhere behind two layers of laminated card. 'We could have gone to Sebastian's. I said I'd treat you all. You don't even have to book to come here. I can't remember the last time I went to a restaurant where you could just turn up. Can you imagine if you did that at Sebastian's?'

I remember the last time I'd agreed to go to Sebastian's with Mark. It was his firm's Christmas do. The lack of food (overblown and insipid) and terrible company (men: overblown, women: insipid) had led to an overindulgence in champagne on my part. When I loudly whispered into Mark's ear that the only way the night could be salvaged was by a visit to a karaoke bar he'd given me a horrified glare followed by a large glass of water.

'Do not drink any more champagne,' he'd angrily whispered. 'This is not the time nor the place to get drunk.'

But it's a Christmas party, I thought. If there is any time and place to get completely pissed, surely it's now. I watched as Mark leaned forward over his vanilla and basil posset with a hint of lavender foam to ask the Chairman's wife about her plans for the holiday season. I leant back, sulked and never said another word. No one noticed.

The atmosphere between us was somewhat frosty for several days afterwards until he announced we were at the point in our marriage where we should no longer bother with Christmas presents. I declared I'd already purchased his and so he begrudgingly agreed we should do it one last time. The next day I went out and bought him a karaoke machine. He bought me a SodaStream.

The enormous menus effectively prevent any eye contact until a waiter, thankfully not the scowling one, appears to take our order. All that can be heard is Mark huffing at the thought of nachos being the peak of today's culinary experience. We even place our orders from behind our temporary barriers. I hear Mark ask for a chicken burrito like he's agreed to eat regurgitated frogs' testicles. Ellie asks for a taco salad but without the tacos, and the only indication that George has successfully ordered is the lowering of the menu and a wordless jab of the finger at an item, followed by a tremor of panic when the waiter asks how he wants his steak to be cooked.

'Do you want it medium rare?' I ask George.

'For goodness' sake, Jenny,' snaps Mark. 'Make him ask for it, if that's what he wants.'

George doesn't raise his eyes from the menu but I know he is wounded.

'Medium rare, please,' he whispers without looking at the waiter.

Then suddenly our barriers are whipped from us and we are all caught like rabbits in the headlights from the glare of our nearest and dearest.

'Drinks?' the waiter asks chirpily. Clearly he's already completed the course on how to smile at a customer – unlike his colleague.

'I'll have a lime and soda,' answers Mark before any consultation can take place.

'I'll have a large Chardonnay,' says Ellie.

'You will not,' cries Mark.

'All right then, a small one,' she replies.

I smirk.

'It's a school night and you are seventeen,' says Mark, looking at me as though I made the request.

'Perhaps we could share a bottle?' I say.

He doesn't say anything, just shakes his head in wonder.

'I mean, you and me could share and perhaps let them have a small bit,' I say.

Mark looks at the waiter.

'These two will both have a Diet Coke,' he says, waggling his finger at Ellie and George.

'I'll have a margarita,' I jump in.

'It's only six o'clock, Jenny,' warns Mark.

'On the rocks or frozen?' the waiter asks, looking right at me with a smile. I like him.

'Definitely on the rocks,' I reply, grinning back. 'It's a special occasion.'

I watch him cast his eyes around our party. Ellie has her elbows on the table, phone held at eye level, the screen illuminating her face as she taps away furiously. George has his head staring down in his lap, the air of concentration giving away the fact he has also turned to his phone for company. Mark is stroking his own phone, which is on the table in front of him, as though to reassure it of his constant presence.

'And what is the occasion?' the waiter asks, struggling to keep hold of the slippery menus clamped under his arm.

'It's my birthday.' I swallow. We share a look. I could burst into tears but I hold them back. I stupidly bought cheap mascara that doesn't mix well with tears, and I can't cry yet.

My gaze goes to the cactus fairy lights above the bar. I love them. They are so stupid and pointless but so bloody happy. How can you not smile at the sight of cactus fairy lights? There's a couple sitting on high stools sipping fluorescent pink cocktails. Clearly not married. He's trying really hard to entertain her and she's trying really hard to be entertained. They are all smiles, hair flicks, body part touching and eye contact. Maybe it's the promise of potential sex that is the only reason why people make eye contact these days, I think as I pull my eyes back to my fellow celebrators. Or to deliver bad news. I shudder.

I wonder how Mark will look at me when I tell him later that I've been prodded and poked to investigate my defects. What will he say when I tell him I need him to come and hold my hand when they deliver the verdict on what they have found? That it could be bad, really bad. They might say the C-word. How will my husband look at me then, I wonder.

Mark gets up out of his bright green chair and wanders off, murmuring into his phone. George and Ellie… well, you can guess what they are doing.

The drinks arrive. The margarita looks magnificent. I thank the waiter as he places it in front of me, then thank him individually for everyone else's drink as they fail to acknowledge their arrival.

Mark takes his seat again and puts his phone face down on the table. It buzzes immediately, its glowing underside making it look like a mini rectangular UFO. Thankfully he ignores it and gulps down half his lime and soda. George and Ellie sip on their Cokes without tearing their eyes away from their screens. Mark picks his phone up again.

I sigh and lift my glass to my lips and mutter, 'Happy birthday, Jenny.'

Chapter Two

'Tell you what, shall we play "Would you rather"?' I say after several minutes during which the only words spoken have been me requesting the delivery of my second cocktail, following my explanation to Mark that it's happy hour so it's technically a free drink.

Ellie turns to look at her father.

'What's she doing?' she asks him.

'You remember we always used to play "Would you rather" in restaurants when you were little,' I say. 'George was brilliant at it. He always thought of the best ones. It was hilarious.' I nudge his elbow and he grunts.

'What was that one he said when we were at Watford Gap Services? He was sat there eating fried chicken and he just came out with it. Something like, "Would you rather fight ten chicken-sized hamsters or a hundred hamster-sized chickens?" That was it, wasn't it, George?'

'Zombies,' he mutters out of the corner of his mouth.

'Oh that's right,' I say, nodding encouragingly. '"Would you rather fight ten zombie-sized hamsters…"'

'No,' interrupts George, shaking his head.

'Jenny, please,' says Mark, but I refuse to look at him.

'What do you mean?' I ask George.

'Other way,' he mutters.

'Right, got you.' I clear my throat. 'So, would you rather fight ten chicken-sized zombies or a hundred zombie-sized chickens? Anyone?'

Utter silence and blank stares from Mark and Ellie.

'Really, what is she doing?' Ellie asks Mark as though I'm an exhibit in a zoo.

'I'm trying to have a conversation with my family,' I spit out in frustration, tears hovering dangerously close to the cheap, unable-to-deal-with-any-kind-of-moisture mascara.

'About zombie-sized chickens?' asks Ellie.

'No!' I exclaim loudly enough for Mark to look around in embarrassment. 'Chicken-sized zombies. Don't you remember that was the answer? We all agreed. We discussed it for a very long time and, after a family vote, we decided that you would have more chance against chicken-sized zombies than zombie-sized chickens. It was a conversation where everyone had their say—'

I pause to look pointedly at George.

'Everyone had an opinion, everyone joined in. We were just… talking,' I say, falling back in my chair with the sheer exhaustion of trying to get through to someone, *anyone*.

No one says anything.

Thankfully, the nachos arrive.

Chapter Three

'Do you remember my twenty-fifth birthday?' I murmur after we have eaten our main courses largely in silence. The shadow of tomorrow is looming over me and I'm miserably attempting to remember happier times to somehow lighten the mood.

'What?' says Mark.

'My twenty-fifth birthday,' I repeat. 'I was just remembering it.'

'The one where you got the sack,' he states.

'The one where we got together,' I reply.

'I nearly didn't come.' Mark says this as if it is no great revelation. That if he hadn't come it would not have dramatically changed the course of both of our lives.

'But… but it was the hottest ticket in town surely,' I splutter. 'A holiday rep's birthday party in Greece on a private beach. How could you not be dying to go to that?'

'Oh I was. But you were all so wild and crazy.' He casts me a small smile. 'I really had no idea why you invited boring old me. Besides, I couldn't get my head around your theme, to be honest.'

I drop my knife and fork on the table and push my chair back in amazement.

'*It's a Knockout*, you mean!' I can hardly believe my ears. 'It was utter genius.'

'What are you talking about?' asks Ellie. Clearly my outburst over the nature of my birthday party twenty years ago has fought its way through the cyber-babble.

'Only the best birthday party of all time,' I tell her, determined to share a piece of my misspent youth, in stark contrast to the pathetic excuse of a birthday I seem to be experiencing now. 'When I was a holiday rep in Greece.'

'Please, no stories of nakedness or shagging or anything,' she replies, reeling in horror.

There were most certainly both of those going on at the time but they are not the aspects I want to dwell on with my daughter.

'My boss, Clare, refused to give me the night off so we planned this epic party instead for all the reps after we'd finished work.'

Ellie looks vaguely impressed.

'We did *It's a Knockout* on the beach!'

Ellie looks blank.

'People in stupid costumes going over obstacles whilst getting fired at with foam machines and water guns,' Mark informs her. 'It was a TV show from the seventies.'

'Me and my mate Karen pulled in favours from all over to set it up,' I tell Ellie excitedly. 'We wangled a private bit of beach from one of the hotel owners and we had twelve inflatable banana boats, fourteen ringos, twenty sumo suits, three water cannons, five foam guns, a smoke machine and a massive drum of custard. Oh, and a karaoke machine as well as Dave on his decks. Have you ever seen twenty people dressed as sumo wrestlers playing British Bulldog whilst being pelted by custard pies?'

I lay this down before her with utter confidence that she hasn't and that I am absolutely certain it is the best fun ever. End of.

Ellie stares back at me and I watch as she tries to work out how to turn this dream night against me.

'At about four in the morning Karen brought out this enormous birthday cake with twenty-five sparklers on it and everyone went mental,' I babble on. 'I mean, they went crazy, and then all the lads got me up on their shoulders and I was bouncing up and down and everyone was chanting my name like this – "Jen-ny, Jen-ny, Jen-ny, Jen-ny, Jen-ny" – and then Dave put Oasis on and we were shouting the lyrics to "Cigarettes & Alcohol" at the tops of our voices.'

I'm pumping my fist in the air and singing Oasis like I'm right back there in 1996. And I am, just for a moment. I'm twenty-five again. I can smell the sea and the sand and feel the cigarette smoke prickling my eyes and I'm laughing my head off, six foot off the ground without a care in the world, Mark hovering somewhere below, adding an extra romantic frisson to the night.

Then I'm back in 2016, sitting in a Mexican-themed restaurant, aware that Ellie and George are staring at me in horror whilst Mark looks around to make sure no one else is observing the spectacle he clearly thinks I'm making of myself.

I lower my fist.

'Like I said, best night of my life.' I bite my lip.

'Then all your mates threw you in the sea,' adds Mark.

'Yes,' I say. 'And *you* rescued me.'

'Well, what could I do? You were a damsel in distress.' He smiles at me again. A flicker of memories of happy times flashes between us. The smile fades fast. Is he thinking the same as me? That we haven't managed to make many of those lately.

'They left me lying there in the water,' I tell Ellie and George. 'Your father came over and offered me a hand up.' I stop.

'And?' asks Ellie.

I glance over to Mark. He's shaking his head and looking down at the dessert menu.

'Well… the rest is history.' I clear my throat.

'You shagged, didn't you?' spits Ellie.

Mark's head jerks up to look at me in an accusing manner.

Yes! I want to cry. Yes, yes, yes and it was glorious!

'How long had you known each other?' she demands when both of us reveal our guilt by failing to answer her question.

Mark shakes his head again, then shrugs as if to say, 'You got yourself into this one, you can get yourself out of it.'

I close my eyes and mentally count in my head.

'Nine days,' I say when I've worked it out.

'Jenny!' gasps Mark. 'You could have lied.'

I shrug – I don't see the point. Ellie clearly can't decide whether to be impressed or horrified and George's chin is back in the top of his sweatshirt. Honestly, he's like a tortoise.

'All the lectures you give me about respecting my body and saving myself for the right person and you sleep with someone you've known for *nine days*!' says Ellie, staring at me accusingly.

I note she is not blaming her dad for our promiscuity. Oh no. And she has the audacity to call herself a feminist.

'We were twenty-five,' I shrug again. 'And we, well, I at least, just knew, somehow, that it meant something. That we were going to stay together.'

Mark isn't looking at me. His head is bent low as he studies a picture of some churros. I spot the beginnings of a thinning patch of hair on the top of his head and it feels like another lifetime since we began our lives together on that beach.

Chapter Four

I first laid eyes on Mark at Corfu airport on the 17th June 1996. It was just before midnight, I was tired and I still had to get fifty-three overexcited holidaymakers into seven different hotels.

His particular crowd were going to be the difficult ones to handle, I could already tell. I'd closed my eyes and gripped my Sunseeker clipboard as they approached me. The noise they were making was unbelievable and I'd prayed they'd walk past me to harass some other poor rep from another company waiting for the latest batch of lilywhites to arrive.

'Well, if this is the standard, then we are in for a bit of all right, aren't we, boys?' said a stocky lad, draping a drunken arm around me.

'Trust you to grab the first thing you lay eyes on,' said another. 'We haven't even got to the hotel yet.'

'You can never start too soon,' replied his mate. 'We only have fourteen days and I intend to pack as many in as I can, if you know what I mean.'

He squeezed my shoulder several times as he said this and I could clearly feel the sweat from his armpit on my bare skin.

I removed his hand deliberately and applied my authoritarian voice.

'Right, can I have all your names please, and then you can take your luggage over to the coach in bay fifteen.'

'Aye, aye,' continued the rather short but very round lad, 'she's already asking my name. I'm in here, boys,' he said, laughing.

'Enough, Stubby,' said a tall slim man, stepping forward to stand between me and this appropriately nicknamed idiot. 'Please let me apologise for my so-called friends. They don't get out very often. You lot,' he shouted, turning to the rest of the group, 'bay fifteen *now*, off you go.'

To my amazement, with some mumbling and gentle ribbing, they all shuffled off.

'I'm Mark,' he said, holding his hand out. I looked down at it and realised he wanted to shake my hand. Something which, in my three years of being a holiday rep, had never happened in an airport. I looked up as he shook it vigorously. He was smiling with his mouth and his eyes. I was smitten.

Throughout the following week I'd be hurtling here, there and everywhere but, if he was ever present on one of the trips I was running, or if we bumped into each other in one of the bars along the beachfront, then he would always insist on buying me a drink. Not to get me drunk and get in my pants, which was of course an occupational hazard, but just to show his gratitude for the job I was doing. Which I guess still had the effect of him getting into my pants by day nine, but there you go.

'A Design for Life' by the Manic Street Preachers always reminds me of those early days of low-level flirting. Mark liked to talk to me about his design for life. He was training to be an accountant whilst working for a building firm. He came from a working-class background and so university just hadn't been on the radar, but he was determined to get to a 'graduate-level lifestyle', as he called it.

'I want to be the Finance Director for a medium to large private company,' he explained, as we shared a goldfish bowl full of margarita. 'You need to be in finance, it's the only position in a firm that knows exactly what is going on,' he continued, as one of his mates danced topless on a podium next to him to The Prodigy's 'Firestarter'. 'If you can get a job like that then you can make all sorts of things happen. Help grow the firm, get some shares, sell to an investment company, or go for private equity. That's how you make serious money.'

I nodded in awe as if I knew what he was talking about.

'Sorry, I must be really boring you,' he added. 'I know I can be really dull about this stuff sometimes. It's just I find it really interesting and people have to remind me that not everyone does.'

'No, no,' I insisted. 'It's nice to hear someone talk about how much they love their work. Most people are here to escape a job they hate and refuse to talk about it or, worse, have a good cry about it on my shoulder at four in the morning.'

'I don't know how you do it,' he said. 'Did you always want to be a tour rep? Was that your plan?'

I told him I only planned as far as which resort I wanted to work in next season. I wanted to travel the world one resort at a time. That's why I had become a tour rep. The only trouble was that the places I really wanted to see, like Africa and India, weren't on the typical Sunseeker circuit. And what I did was very poorly paid so I was mostly stuck in Europe until I worked out how to get myself to some more exotic far-flung places.

'I really want to see the world too,' he told me earnestly. 'But I'm going to do it when I can do it properly. After I've made my fortune.'

'Well, I'll drink to that,' I said. 'Maybe one day I'll see you in Bali. Watch out for me walking by with my backpack as you're coming out of your five-star hotel.'

I remember wishing I had a bit of his forward planning. I was more a live-in-the-moment, fly-by-the-seat-of-my-pants kind of girl.

I had things I wanted to do but no idea of how to get there. He was the exact opposite. I'd never met a man like him before. A man with a plan beyond how many girls he could pull that night. He was the Clark Kent of Corfu in a sea of wannabe playboys.

By halfway through his holiday he'd made no move. None of the usual flicking of hair or touching of knees or even wearing my best pulling top appeared to be working. In desperation, I told him about my birthday party, swearing him to secrecy as I didn't want word to get out and there to be an influx of gatecrashers. I told him it would just be other reps and no other guests, hoping this might give him the hint I was interested. But he just nodded and calmly wrote the details down on a piece of paper, not committing either way whether he would come.

That night, when Karen whispered in my ear that Mark had arrived, I whisked round at speed, my heart pumping like a steam train. I'd forgotten I was holding a water cannon at the time and instantly soaked his crotch. We both collapsed laughing and I think I knew then how the party was going to end.

We laughed a lot that night, I remember. By the time we got to the kissing part in the early hours of the morning, my cheeks were aching with laughing and smiling so much. I was leaning against a palm tree and I thought I was going to burst with happiness. Never had a night gone so well. The party, *my* party, had been amazing, everyone said so. And to put the cherry on the cake, here I was, under a palm tree, being kissed by moonlight by a man I had totally fallen for whilst George Michael sang 'Fastlove' in the distance.

A romance with that kind of start had to end well, didn't it?

Chapter Five

'I wonder what would have happened if you hadn't have got the sack?' asks Mark, looking up from his dessert menu. He says it as though he is musing on the destiny of an old school friend, rather than the woman he ended up marrying and who bore his two children.

'So why did you get the sack?' asks Ellie. 'For sleeping with a guest?' she sneers.

Mark laughs. 'Christ, there wouldn't have been any reps there by the end of the season if that had been a sackable offence,' he says. 'They were all at it.'

I ignore him. 'I got the sack because my boss found out about the party and fired me for inappropriate use of company property. I think someone also told her that a picture of her face had been taped to the back of the urinal,' I add. 'I knew it was Dave but I couldn't let him take the blame.'

'She came crying to my hotel room that night,' added Mark with a sigh.

'I didn't know what to do, I was upset.'

Mark had been so kind, so caring. He'd sat and listened as I sobbed out Clare's cruel cutting off of the job I loved. He told his mates to go out without him and we sat on his balcony, drinking a bottle of ouzo, whilst he tried to plan my new future for me. My new design for life.

He put the 'Do-Not-Disturb' sign on the door whilst we made love in that desperate passionate way you do when you feel that the only thing good in your life is the person in your arms. And that is pretty much where we stayed for the next four days, only leaving the room to buy food and alcohol and to carry Mark's roommate's mattress next door so he could bunk up with two others in the crowd. Not a popular decision but, to my delight, Mark didn't seem to care.

On the morning that he was due to leave, Mark went out for coffee and when he came back, he sat on the edge of the bed looking nervous. This is it, I thought. This is the 'It's been nice, have a good life' speech.

Instead he'd turned to me, his knee twitching up and down at speed, and said, 'Come home with me.'

I nearly spat my coffee across the room.

'I've worked it out,' he continued. 'I have a spare room. I was going to rent it out to a lodger so I can pay off the mortgage quicker but I'd have to advertise and you're never sure who you're going to get, are you? I mean, you don't have to sleep in it, you can sleep in my room of course – if you want to, that is – but you could come and live with me. What I'm saying in a stupid roundabout way is that I really like you and I'd really like you to come and live with me. If you want to, that is. I mean, you might not want to. I know I can be a bit boring when I start banging on about work and I've got nothing to really offer you. In fact, I've no idea why someone like you would ever leave all this to come with me, but the thought of not seeing you again—'

He stopped abruptly and looked down at the floor, his left knee still bouncing up and down.

'Or you could see it as a stop-gap if you want,' he said, looking back up, 'until you sort yourself out. No pressure.'

I couldn't believe it. Here was a wonderful man handing me a life on a plate when I thought I'd lost everything. I knew there was no way I would get another job as a tour rep with a decent company, given how I'd been fired. But now Mark had come riding in on a white charger, offering me a new life with a home and maybe even a plan. Who knows, maybe we would even end up seeing the world together one day?

'Yes, oh, yes,' I gasped, flinging my arms around him. Moments before, my life had been one massive question mark and now I had a roof over my head, and I was pretty sure that meant that I also had a boyfriend as well, didn't it?

He hugged me back.

'Really?' he said when I finally let go of him. 'You really want to?'

'Of course,' I grinned. 'I like you as well,' I said. 'A lot.'

I think we both blushed a little then. The tentative significance of our words, and our decision, sinking in.

I wonder how I would be feeling about what I was facing tomorrow if I had lived another life entirely since then. What if Mark had walked away after those four passionate days without a backwards glance? Would I have hung on and eventually bunked up with a waiter or a barman or another tour rep? Is there someone out there, a total stranger, who, if I had turned a different corner in life, would be sitting next to me tomorrow, clutching my hand and waiting for the verdict on my future?

I look back to Mark. My chosen path. I've purposefully not told him what's going on so far, which might appear strange but I cannot seem to say the words out loud. I cannot even bear to hear them. I've tried. I've stood in front of the mirror and formed the words in my head and attempted to force them out of my mouth but nothing comes out. I just stare and stare and stare at myself and think, is this really happening? If I don't actually say the words then maybe it isn't, maybe everything will be all right.

But there will be words spoken tomorrow. Out loud. I can feel myself flinching at the mere thought of it.

'I need to talk to you about something later,' I say quickly to Mark.

'Is it important?' he asks, waving at the waiter for the bill. 'Can we do it tomorrow night? I'm going to have to drop you home as it is and go back to work. The auditors have demanded some more figures,' he says, throwing his credit card on the table. 'I shouldn't be here at all really.'

'But Mark, it's really important,' I say.

He looks at me with a pained look.

'This deal is important, Jenny. You don't seem to get that. Let me get this deal done and then you can talk to me about anything you want.'

The waiter arrives with the bill and the card machine already in hand. Mark raises his eyebrows as he checks the total then plugs in his card. He's already up and out of his seat before the waiter has printed out his receipt.

'Come on then, you lot,' he says impatiently. 'I need to go back to work so I can pay for this overpriced fast food.'

I look at the cactus lights.

Chapter Six

'You ask,' I tell George.

He shakes his head vigorously at me.

I let out an exasperated gasp and look at my watch. I'm going to be late. This wasn't supposed to happen. I was supposed to arrive a picture of calm serenity with my supportive husband on my arm. But no, here I am in the Co-op, down the third aisle, desperately seeking some ingredient I can't pronounce that George has failed to warn me he needs for his Food Technology class.

'*You* ask,' I demand, glaring at him. Come on, George, I think. I really don't need this today. Surely today you can open your bloody mouth and ask someone a bloody question, I want to scream.

He shakes his head even more vigorously and looks terrified. His therapist has told me that losing my temper with him will have an adverse effect. I should try and be calm and patient. I look at him and I am almost envious. He has a label that allows him to behave this way. A lady in a white coat told us he suffers from anxiety. It's official. The fact that I am unofficially anxious today is irrelevant. I do not have the label and therefore I will be the one embarrassing myself in front of a shop assistant, unable to pronounce whatever this ridiculous food substance is.

There's a man lifting boxes of quick-cook rice off a trolley and onto a shelf. I dash over to him.

'Do you have any quin-oh-ah?' I ask as though I'm speaking in my second language. I can already hear the sound of George shaking his head vigorously behind me. I've said it wrong, I know I have, and embarrassed him and made him *more* anxious. Well, it's his own fault. If he'd asked himself in the first place, or had the decency to point it out before I did the online shop, then we wouldn't be in this predicament, would we?

'Pardon?' the man replied.

Oh God, I'm going to have to say it again.

'Quin-oh-ah?' I repeat. 'It's a grain apparently.'

He frowns. 'I don't think I've heard of that.'

George coughs. 'Keen-wa,' I think he says to the floor.

'What did you say, George?' I demand, dipping my ear closer to his mouth to try and hear.

'Keen-wa,' he repeats.

'Keen-wa?' I say to the man. There is a pause. I see a trip to Sainsbury's looming, a late mark on George's register and my date with Doctor Death cancelled.

'Ah yes,' he says. 'Follow me.'

'How do you say it again?' I ask as I snatch the packet with 'Quinoa' written in large letters across the top.

'Keen-wa,' he replies.

'Ridiculous,' I tell him and turn and take a fast walk to the checkout.

I spot Ellie waiting by the door as I literally throw money at someone, anyone, just so we can get out of there. She's with Phoebe, her so-called 'bestie'. 'Beastie', as George and I refer to her when Ellie is not around. It makes him smile knowingly at me, which makes it so worthwhile. Phoebe is an evil piece of work, and it horrifies me to know Ellie has the poor judgement to hang around with her. She's a viper in a stupid little black trilby hat that she thinks makes her look cool and edgy and above every other mortal on this planet as she casts her judgemental eye over all she surveys.

'We're gonna walk,' announces Ellie as I approach, thrusting change into my wallet.

'You'll be late,' I bark back. 'I said I'd give you a lift, seeing as we had to go to the Co-op, so hurry up.'

'That's okay,' shrugs Ellie.

'What is?'

'Being late.'

'No, it isn't!'

'Chill, Mum,' says Ellie, smirking at Beastie. 'We'll just put our watches back five minutes…'

'…and say we had no idea we were late, Mr Barrowman,' interrupts Phoebe in a sing-song voice, pushing her cleavage towards me, fluttering thick, perfectly mascaraed eyelashes and smiling from expertly lined lips. 'Works every time,' she continues, snapping her head back and staring at George until his chin disappears into his neck.

'Suit yourself,' I say to Ellie. I don't have time for the teacher manipulation strategies of Year Twelve girls.

I grab George's arm and depart at speed, praying the school-run traffic will have died down and there has been no major outbreak of disease overnight leading to a higher than normal demand for the pitiful number of car parking spaces at the hospital.

★

'Mr Randall is running a little late,' the receptionist at the Oncology Unit tells me as I pant out my name, having run down what feels like twelve miles of identical corridors. 'He was called on to a ward early this morning. I'm so sorry.'

She smiles ever so kindly at me. She knows, I thought. She's seen the notes already; she knows it's bad. That's why she's so apologetic. I resist the urge to grab her round the neck and shriek, 'Just tell me!'

'That's okay,' I smile sweetly back. 'Roughly how long do you think he will be?'

'He's about forty minutes behind at the moment, I'm afraid.'

'Okay,' I nod, although it isn't. It's far from. I turn and find a seat and sit down, smoothing out my suede skirt. I brush my hand across it; this way and that, making it switch from dark brown to light tan in an instant. It calms me, like stroking a dog. It had been the right thing to wear, and I'm glad I dug it out. I knew I'd kept it somewhere as I pulled all sorts of memorabilia out of the fitted wardrobes in the spare room.

I would never have thrown it away, even when my waist expanded as a result of two pregnancies and too much Nutella. I'd bought it with my first paycheck after I moved back to the UK and in with Mark. I'd felt so mature. For the very first time I had money in the bank, I lived in a real house, I had a boyfriend who had a real job where he had to wear a suit, not just shorts and a suntan, and I could walk into Miss Selfridge and buy whatever I wanted. On learning I had blown most of my earnings on a skirt, Mark didn't entirely agree that I had matured, but he soon saw the benefit when I invited him to feel the quality, especially around the posterior area.

I smiled to myself. The skirt hadn't stayed on long. Whenever I wore it after that he'd raise his eyebrows and we would exchange a knowing glance. We both knew that soon enough he would be 'feeling the quality' again.

This morning I'd known it would fit me, even though I hadn't been able to wear it for a very long time. I'd lost weight recently. As a cover I'd told Mark I was on a diet but, then again, I'd been on a diet ever since 1996, when I returned to the land of pastry, decent chocolate and Chinese takeaways. He hadn't actually noticed that for the first time in twenty years the diet was apparently working.

Maybe that would have been the opportunity to tell him that it was the 'you may have a terminal illness' diet that was finally doing the trick. That I stood in fear on the scales every morning, not from potential weight gain but from seeing the numbers fall steadily and slowly in a way I had dreamed they would for so many years.

But no, he never commented. Not even when I stood in front of him this morning in the brown suede skirt that I last wore in my twenties. The skirt he couldn't get off me quickly enough then. I'd stood there as he gulped down coffee at the breakfast bar, wringing my hands and building up to saying, 'I need you. I need you to come with me.' But George had come hurtling in and stuffed a book under my nose, pointing vigorously at the word 'quinoa'.

'Got to go,' said Mark, brushing past me into the hall. 'Bye.'

The front door slammed and he was gone.

I'd blown it. Missed my chance. Missed my chances. The hundred or so times when I'd been on the verge of sharing with him but either couldn't bear to say the words out loud, or the moment was interrupted by the ring of a phone or the arrival of a message or the demand of a child.

You must think this is a sorry state of a marriage if I couldn't share with my husband that I had been having tests for cancer. Perhaps you are right. Maybe you are thinking that, if you were me, you would *have* to tell him. You would make him listen. He's your husband, for

Christ's sake. He should be sitting there right now next to you, gripping your hand ever so tightly so you know you're facing this together. You are not alone.

Well, that's how we would like to think all people facing terrible news would be. That's what we assume. We'd never expect a married mother with two children to be sitting there being asked to wait another excruciating forty minutes to see how long she is going to live – alone. But it happens. I know this because it is happening to me.

I get through the next fifty minutes (as it turns out) by making up stories about the other people in the waiting room with me. It's something I used to do to distract myself at the airport whenever there was a severe delay on an incoming flight.

There's a sweet little elderly lady, virtually bent double in her chair next to her evil plotting daughter who has taken charge of all her mother's medical appointments, much to the delight of her busy but clueless siblings. They'll be sorry when it comes to the reading of the will and the solicitor hands over the keys to the family home and a red savings book with over a hundred grand stashed away to the daughter who successfully managed to infiltrate her mother's dying wishes.

Then there's a couple, in their early sixties. They are the male and female version of each other. They've been married so long that they even look like each other: similar haircut, same dress sense, similar glasses perched on the ends of noses. They are a match. It wouldn't surprise me if, when they met, they'd both said, 'Snap,' knowing they had found their pair and that the rest of their lives would proceed in perfect partnership. Until now. It's her that's ill, I think. He has his hand over hers and is looking around in dignified yet defiant silence. He will protect her. He will stop this dreadful thing happening. He has her. She calmly looks far into the distance, knowing she is not alone.

My phone buzzes in my bag. I instantly start to scrabble around in it whilst deflecting the disapproving glances of my fellow loiterers. Eventually I find it after chasing blindly after a packet of tissues, a lipstick and a room card key from a hotel in the Lake District from two years ago. It's one of my favourite possessions. A reminder of a wonderful night away with my husband. I need that right now.

I glance at the screen whilst trying to find the silencer button. It's a text from Mark.

Will be late tonight – more numbers needed – don't wait up

I stare at it. I switch my phone off and throw it back in my bag.

Such a bummer that I might have cancer just as my husband is approaching everything he has planned and dreamed about. The company he works for is about to be bought by a private equity firm. Whatever that means. Well, I know exactly what it means actually. It means that Mark's 'design for life' has gone perfectly to plan. He passed all his accountancy exams then got a job with a medium-sized engineering firm, where he worked his way up to Finance Director. He relentlessly negotiated share options into his package and now an investment company is buying them out, and apparently Mark gets a huge wedge of money.

How much, I don't know. He won't tell me. He says he doesn't want to jinx it but I've seen on our home computer that he's been browsing the Porsche website so I think we are talking some serious cash. He doesn't really seem excited though. He's tense and distant, but then he has been working all hours. I've hardly seen him in six months. I've hardly even had a conversation with him in six months. I don't ask him about work because I don't understand it. He starts talking and my eyes just glaze over. It's like he's speaking in a foreign language. The only time work is discussed is in the context of why it is keeping him away from home for such ridiculously long hours, leaving me to take most of the strain of parenting two teenagers. I try and talk to him about the kids and he seems to think they are fine, that right now his focus has to be on crossing the line with this damn deal.

'Jenny Sutton,' a nurse calls out. She is holding a folder of notes and she looks harassed. Overworked. I scrabble around to pick up my bag and walk towards her. She heads left towards a corridor and I fall into step beside her. She says nothing. Clearly she doesn't know what to say to me because it's bad news. She knows. Of course she knows. She looks harassed because she knows what is about to happen to me.

I'm about to mention the weather as I normally would when thrown into the awkward company of a complete stranger but I stop myself. She won't be expecting small talk from me. No need for the usual pleasantries.

She turns a corner and opens a door into a small office. There's a desk with a chair behind it and two in front. A computer. Some shelves. A window with a blue blind. And that is it. Nothing else. This room belongs to no one. It's faceless and lacking in any human touch whatsoever.

'Mr Randall will be with you shortly,' announces the nurse and shuts me in the magnolia box.

I look at the back of the door and weirdly there is an eye test chart hanging on it. I can hear my breathing. I wish I were having an eye test. I sit down and look back at the chart. I start reading the letters, seeing how far down I can get. All but the last line. I put a hand over my left eye and try again. Same result.

I put my hand over my right eye to see how that one fares and that is how Mr Randall finds me when he enters the room. Mouthing a 'W' with one hand over an eye like a dyslexic pirate.

I pull my hand down sharply and cough. He closes the door quickly but then it seems to take about three years for him to walk past me and take the seat behind the desk, where at last I can get the full view of his face and watch his lips start to move.

I feel like Sherlock Holmes as I watch him take this epic journey before my eyes. My heart is now pounding at a phenomenal rate and I have clocked that he is wearing a suit, a navy suit that he has had for some time for the hem of the trousers is slightly frayed. His black shoes are extremely shiny, military shiny. Perhaps he was a soldier at some point but he smells nice. I can smell aftershave, which strikes me as not what an ex-serviceman would wear for work somehow. Maybe he just has a wife who likes to clean his shoes or maybe, when you are a consultant, you just get the junior doctors to lick your shoes clean.

He's sitting now and looking at me. He has a kind face. Is it kindness or is it pity? He's running his hand through his hair and now his lips are moving. Now he is speaking and I must listen: the moment has come to listen to the impossible words.

'Do you have someone with you?' he asks.

I shake my head. I'm doomed.

'In the waiting room?' he prompts hopefully.

'No,' I reply. 'I came alone.'

I watch a look of panic flicker across his face and then he coughs to cover up the fact his mind is thinking rapidly about what he should do next. It isn't the sort of news he's used to giving to someone alone, clearly. My heart starts to beat even faster.

'Well, I'm afraid it's not good news.'

'Right, right,' I say, nodding my head rapidly to reassure him that it's perfectly all right to tell me this without someone gripping my hand to keep me upright. I can stay upright all on my own. Look at me, Doc, I can do this.

'The scans show that, as suspected, you do have a tumour in your cervix, but there are also signs that it has spread to your bowel.'

I cannot speak but my head is now nodding so determinedly that I must look like one of those stupid Churchill's dogs you see in the back of cars. The doc is still speaking but I cannot take in what he is saying. It's as if I'm on a plane and my ears are popping. All sounds are muffled and incoherent and time has been suspended whilst my insides adjust to a new air pressure. But I'm not adjusting to a new air pressure, I'm adjusting to a whole different dimension.

The doc's lips have stopped moving. He's looking at me expectantly. I realise I've stopped nodding like a dog and now I'm shaking my head rapidly. The quick change in direction is making me feel dizzy.

'Do you understand what I'm saying?' he asks.

My head never pauses, just carries on shaking. I'm aware my hands have joined in too. The doc puts his fingers through his hair and I can see rapid thoughts flicking across his eyes again. He gets up and walks round the desk to take the chair next to me and takes my hands in his. I stare down at these strange hands holding mine. Clean smooth hands. Safe hands. It will all be all right now, I think.

'You have some decisions to make,' he says slowly, making sure that I am looking at him.

I nod. Churchill is back.

'I would recommend chemotherapy, in your case.'

He didn't say surgery. Why didn't he say surgery? I want it out, I just want it out. I want surgery. I need to ask him why he's not sending me straight to surgery to cut it out but I can't speak. I think I'm going to be sick. He's wrong, I think. He meant to say surgery. He's missed the fact that he can cut it out. I need to tell him he's wrong. That he needs to send me down to surgery *now* to cut it out as quickly as they can. But if I ask him about surgery and he says no, then what does that mean? I don't want to ask him in case he does say no. No wouldn't be a good answer would it?

'What about surgery?' I manage to whisper.

'No,' he says.

I'm on that plane again and my ears are popping. I'm about to enter another dimension.

'The way in which it has spread would make surgery very difficult…'

Difficult, you are saying, but not impossible. That's what he said, wasn't it? I look around for back-up to confirm that I heard him right but I have no back-up. My back-up is staring at a spreadsheet somewhere in a glass building on a business park. He can't hear from there.

'Chemotherapy is probably your best option at this point in time.'

'But will it get rid of it?' I ask, searching his face for the right answer. The hint of a smile, a lack of concern, anything.

He looks down at our hands for a moment so I can't see the look in his eyes and presumably so he can't see the look in mine. He looks back up.

'It's unlikely at this stage,' he says quietly.

The head-shaking is back and the rest of my body is joining in.

I want to ask him what he is saying, what he means, but I am too terrified of the answer.

'Chemotherapy is likely to prolong your life but it is unlikely that it will get rid of your tumours.'

Now I am in a freezer, my whole body numb. I pull my hands away from his and lean back in my chair.

'How long?' I pray for the look of surprise on his face. A look of shock to indicate that I have totally misunderstood. But it doesn't come.

He leans back and folds his hands in his lap.

'It's virtually impossible to say,' he says with words that toll the final bell. 'Any answer I give you will be inaccurate but, if pushed, I'd probably say between eighteen months and two years. But it could be longer, could be shorter.'

'But there is a small chance that the chemotherapy could get rid of the tumour?' I ask.

I have to ask something. I can't leave his previous answer hanging out there for scrutiny. It's blinding.

A small smile plays on the edge of his mouth. He must hear it every time – the desperate cling for hope.

'There is a very small chance,' he replies. 'But it is very unlikely.'

What a terrible word *unlikely* is. Ugly and vague.

'Can I make a suggestion,' he says, leaning forward and putting his hands on his knees in a motion that clearly states we need to move on from the whole finding-out-I'm-dying thing. 'Why don't you ring someone to come and fetch you? Go home. Let all this sink in and then come back and see me in a couple of days. But bring someone with you. Do you have a husband, Mrs Sutton?'

I nod.

'Call him and ask him to come and fetch you. I'll set you up with an appointment and we can decide on your treatment plan together. I can talk it all through again with him. Two sets of ears are often best in this situation. It's hard to take it all in on your own.'

I'm looking at him but I'm not listening to him. For some reason all I can hear in my head is the crowd at my twenty-fifth birthday shouting, 'Jen-ny, Jen-ny, Jen-ny, Jen-ny.'

Chapter Seven

Twelve pounds fifty! Twelve pounds fifty to park whilst I find out I'm dying! Utterly outrageous. The NHS should be funding an entire hospital, given how much it costs to leave a car whilst you absorb a death sentence.

I look up at the parking charges displayed on the board as I wait for the machine to regurgitate my ticket. Over seven hours I've been here. I've already had seven hours of this. Seven hours spent trying to understand the incomprehensible whilst sitting in my car with my head on the steering wheel or walking laps of the hospital grounds. Somehow I couldn't leave. The minute I leave, my new life will have to begin, and I have no idea how to live that life. That terrible life.

Of course I'd tried to ring Mark. Five times in fact. But each time it had gone straight through to voicemail. I left a message three times. A short, 'Hi, it's me. Ring me as soon as you can.'

I'd tried to keep my tone light so as not to worry him, which may seem ridiculous given this was one of the most worrying pieces of news I could possibly give him. I'd tried to think of what could be worse. Something wrong with the kids of course would be infinitely worse. That had given me some respite from trying to face up to the simple fact that I was dying. At least it's not one of them, was the only thought that could stop me from going to the edge of the cliff and looking death full in the face.

I just couldn't do it. I just couldn't make my brain focus on it. I approached it with caution, then at the last minute would veer left into something I could get my head around. Much easier to focus on the fact my kids are safe and well. I held that fact close to my chest like a security blanket, a buffer, for a good hour until the dark thoughts crept back in.

I'd rung in sick to work. Why I hadn't just taken the day off I have no idea. Some vague hope that I wouldn't need it. That I would be strolling back in, relief written all over my face.

I bet you're wondering what happens to sacked tour reps from the nineties, aren't you? Where does one go with a vast experience in organising ridiculous cultural outings that no one wants to go on unless the majority of the time is spent eating and drinking? Or with my ability to be a surrogate agony aunt to countless fall-outs and squabbles that occur when you put a load of childish human beings in one place. Where could one possibly take such skills?

It's obvious, isn't it?

An old people's home.

A combination of my unique talents and requirement for flexible working hours led me to become Activities Coordinator at Shady Grove Retirement Home after I had had the kids. So I'm still a tour rep really, just for out-of-control geriatrics rather than out-of-control twenty-somethings. But there's no way I can face out-of-control anything today. I'm out of control myself.

By six o'clock I can't put off leaving the hospital any longer. I will go to Mark. Who knows when I might see him if I don't? If I go now, the office should be quiet and I can break it to him gently and then I won't be alone. Yes, that's a good idea. Better there than at home, where George or Ellie would have to be addressed before we have time to properly contemplate what we will tell them.

I text the kids to say I will be home late. A single *x* back from George and nothing from Ellie. No doubt she will use it as an excuse to hang out at Phoebe's in her five-bedroom mansion with double garage that has electric doors housing the Mini that Phoebe's father's already bought for her, ready for when she passes her test. A fact that arises all too frequently in our household.

Mark has hinted that he might buy Ellie a car if this deal comes off, to which I reacted badly. He spoils his daughter, leaving me to be the bad cop in order to somehow try and keep her feet on the ground. His extravagance with her and my constant efforts to pull him back have driven a wedge between me and Ellie that he fails to feel any responsibility for.

Still, soon he will be able to buy her what he likes without me harping on about her needing to understand the value of things. How will that turn out, I wonder. How will *she* turn out, I find myself thinking with a terrifying lurch. For too long now I've hoped she's just going through a spoilt brat phase. Now I will never get to see if it was just a phase. Never get to see if she grows up to be the strong, determined woman I know is in there somewhere. The thought causes me to shake violently. I cannot think about my children's future yet. Not now. I must save that for later when I pray it will somehow be less terrifying.

I park in front of Mark's office. Thankfully the car park is virtually empty. The firm moved to this brand new building, barely distinguishable from the rest of the business park, just two years ago. It's shiny and masculine and full of white male ego and empty of any imagination. I walk through the huge glass doors and into a double-height lobby, where black leather sofas seat the minions coming in from the outside world to beg an audience with the powers that be at *Brancotec – Suppliers of Precision Technology for Precision Machines.*

A security guard sits behind the ten-foot-long reception desk sporting the company logo.

'I just need to speak to my husband,' I gabble. 'He's working late. I know where his office is.'

'Name?' drawls the man.

'Mark, Mark Sutton. Oh, do you mean mine? I'm Jenny Sutton, his wife.'

The guard looks me up and down slowly, assessing whether I'm capable of industrial espionage. His decision that I'm not comes in the faintest flick of the head towards the stairs and the offer of a plastic card, which I presume I need to get onto the floor where my husband works.

I scamper towards him and grab the card before he remembers that industrial spies can come in any shape or form, including that of a scatty-looking middle-aged woman.

Mark had very proudly shown me around the new building when they first moved in. He'd beamed as he'd guided me into his office on the third floor with all the other directors. Right on the end, a corner position with windows overlooking the back of the factory and the car showroom next door. We'd hugged each other in that very office. An unspoken moment between us to acknowledge that life at that point was most definitely going to plan.

I'm slightly out of breath when I get to the top of the three flights of stairs. I pause to get my bearings then recognise the double doors that lead through into the directors' wing, complete with boardroom, kitchen, a full array of large green plants serviced by a specialist office plant supplier, and two toilets. No urinals apparently. Is that a perk of being a director? I remember asking Mark. You don't have to get your knob out in public. I don't remember his reply.

I show the plastic card to a square cube mounted on the wall and miraculously hear a click. I push the doors open into the inner sanctum. All is quiet. All the offices I can see appear to be empty but I know Mark is here because his car is in the car park.

I walk down towards the end of the corridor to find him. I can see his office door is shut. My heart starts pounding. I'd rehearsed, somewhere around four o'clock, on about my fifth lap of the hospital grounds, how I would tell him. Sitting down was key, I'd thought. Make sure he's sitting down and then announce I had something important to say. If he looked worried, if he started to panic, then I must talk quickly. Think of the most efficient way to get the words out. I'd just say whatever came into my head, I finally decided. Just blurt it out. If I was lucky I'd get it out before I started crying. More than likely I'd cry immediately and then it would take a good fifteen minutes to gather myself and say the words aloud. I'd even thought of writing it down, walking up to him, bursting into floods of tears and shoving a note in his hand explaining why I was crying. But I didn't know what to write. No, just blurt it out and let him put me back together again. That's all I was capable of.

I swallow and put my hand on the door handle. Taking a deep breath, I push it down. I peer in. On first glance his chair is empty behind his desk and I'm about to withdraw when a movement in the corner of my eye catches my attention. I look up to the left towards the window that overlooks the factory at the back of the building. The movement that my eyes had automatically tracked is my husband's buttocks as he bends over someone's backside, pumping away over the low filing cabinet.

Chapter Eight

I run.

I turn and flee, running down the stairs so fast that at any moment I'm likely to trip myself up and fall all the way into the stairwell. I might break my leg.

This reminds me of one of George's 'Would you rathers'. Would you rather have no arms or no legs? No legs had been my choice, I remember as I career into the bannister on the first floor, virtually blinded by my own tears. Hurtling down the last flight, I consider a new choice.

Would you rather find out you have cancer or that your husband is having an affair? Oops, sorry my mistake! There is no 'Would you rather' about it. No choice whatsoever. Congratulations, you have hit the jackpot. You don't have to choose, you get them both.

I remember George once demanding I choose between two impossibles. He was probably about ten. Would you rather have twenty Twixes or ten Mars Bars had been his challenge. I told him I couldn't choose. It was quantity versus quality as far as I was concerned and I couldn't pick between them, I wanted both. Well, now I had both. No choice available. Two catastrophes in one.

I run across the lobby and out the double doors, fumbling in my bag for my keys. All I can think about is that I have to get as far away as possible. The image of them standing there, oblivious to their audience, is burning into my brain. Snippets of detail pop in and out of my mind. Mark's buttocks looked good, *really* good. It must have been a really long time since I had cause to peruse his backside from that kind of distance and it was impressive. Smooth and creamy without a single blemish or rogue hair. Has he been doing something to keep it in tip-top condition for his new conquest, I wonder.

Not that she could admire it from her position. Her view was of the back of the factory and his was of the back of her head and her long blonde hair. Of course she was blonde. She had to be, didn't she? Such a cliché. And she was wearing a blue skirt pulled up round her waist. I shake my head violently to try and rid myself of the all-too-vivid image. I look up as I fumble the keys into the lock, worried they have seen me and that Mark is coming after me, having hastily pulled his trousers up.

I can't face him. I can't face him now. I thought I didn't have the words to tell him about my illness; I certainly don't have the vocabulary to deal with my devastation at discovering the person who I have never needed more to be strong and supportive is actually weak, pathetic and a cheat.

I back out of the parking space at speed. I have no idea where I'm going but it has to be anywhere away from here.

Chapter Nine

'Fuck off, Alanis,' I shout at the top of my voice. Ever since I hurtled out of the business park driving my green Mini (original, by the way) way too fast for its delicate little frame, Alanis Morissette had haunted me from 1996. What was it that she was so angry about in that song? I thought there was a line about a cheating husband in there somewhere until I go through the lyrics in my head and realise it was actually about thinking you've met the man of your dreams then learning he already has a beautiful wife.

'Just bloody unlucky,' I scream. 'Not ironic at all and nowhere near as bad as this.' I realise I'm hitting the steering wheel in anger and that I really should stop before I have an accident and kill someone. Now wouldn't that be ironic, I think.

I pull into a random side street and park outside a bungalow.

'Bastard, bastard, bastard, bastard,' I rage, using both hands this time to strike the unfortunate steering wheel. In some ways it's a relief to let some emotion out. The cancer news has left me numb, unable to conjure up any type of reaction. The affair news, however, now that is something I can really throw everything at. Tears, rage, head banging, you name it.

After I have shouted and screamed at the speedometer for a good few minutes, my mind drifts towards the piecing together of the backstory of Mark's new status as adulterous husband. Late nights at work. Numerous overnight stays in London meeting with the investors. Too preoccupied to talk. Too tired for sex. Too busy for a night out together. Too frequently annoyed by my presence. Too much new underwear being bought. I'd congratulated him at the time, when he came home having made a special trip to John Lewis. I was impressed that he'd finally realised that it is not in the wife's job description to buy their husband's pants.

All this hyped-up behaviour had been explained away by the huge effort required to sell Brancotec and his pivotal role as Finance Director. The perfect cover for an office affair. Sell a company, have a shag. Who knows, maybe she, whoever she is, had a whiff of the money that is coming. Maybe that's why she was prepared to pull her knickers down over a filing cabinet. The promise of a fortnight in Barbados after the deal has been done and the wife ditched. Only he didn't even have to ditch me now, did he, just wait until…

How come he gets all the fucking luck and I get all the shit? I scream.

My phone buzzes in my bag. Perhaps it's him texting to say he's going to be home even later because he's not quite *done shagging yet!* I scrabble around in my bag and fish it out.

If only it had been Mark texting.

Chapter Ten

*DON'T FORGET IT'S MY BRIDGE NIGHT. I NEED TO BE
GONE BY 7.*

'You have got to be kidding me!' I shout at the phone. 'You have
got to be kidding me!' I shout louder, throwing it back in my bag and
turning on the ignition.

The three-point turn is a disaster and I see a lace curtain twitch
in the bungalow I'm parked outside. I wave as I depart on my way to
my next hell.

You'd think your mother would be the one you would run to in
such a situation surely? A mother would have to be the absolute pits of
the earth to not be the one you could flee to when your entire world
has just collapsed. It's a truly sad state of affairs if you have a mother
you cannot imagine will provide any words of comfort to a daughter
who has just received the most devastating news about her health and
found her husband having sex in his office.

As I drive, breaking the speed limit yet again, in the direction of my
parents' house, I think about sitting my mum down and breaking the
news to her that I'm sorry but she will not be able to attend her bridge
night tonight. I need her to console me because I've got cancer and
Mark is having sex with another woman. I try to imagine her response.

Best possible response: 'Oh dear. Can we talk about this after I get back, only Margaret and Roy are relying on me?'

Medium-level response: 'Well, I always thought Mark was too good for you.'

Worst-level response: 'At least it's you and not your brother going through this.'

You think I'm kidding, don't you? You don't think anyone's mum could be like that. Well, I've known her for forty-five years and, believe me, none of these responses would come as a surprise.

To say we never bonded is an understatement.

To say I'm a total and utter disappointment is an understatement.

To say that she's obsessed by my high-achieving but smug bastard younger brother is an understatement.

To say, however, that despite the utter shame of having a daughter whose career peaked with being named 'Sunseeker Tour Rep of the Season, Corfu 1995', she is perfectly happy for me to act as general dogsbody to do whatever her bidding, whenever she wants it. Of course she couldn't possibly ask Antony as he's too busy chopping people's legs off somewhere under the guise of 'apparently' being an orthopedic surgeon. Something I refuse to believe he is capable of since he famously fainted at school whilst dissecting a frog and split his head open. Something I enjoy reminding him of on the rare occasions we see each other. We speak on the phone twice a year when I call to remind him it's Mum or Dad's birthday. I always remember his birthday and I always send him a card with a frog on it. He never remembers mine.

My rhythm is on hyper-speed now. I'm breathing heavily and looking warily around as if trying to spot where the next blow will come from. I mount the pavement and park on the verge outside Mum's perfectly neat, four-bedroom house in the deepest darkest depths of suburbia. She'll have a go at me about that later. Apparently the gardener complains about the ruts my tyres cause. I suspect he doesn't complain at all. I suspect she'd prefer it if I parked on the drive so the neighbours are less likely to spot what she believes to be a ramshackle excuse for a car that her excuse for a daughter drives.

I don't pause. I'm straight out of that car and heading for the front door, my brain no longer capable of preparation of any kind. I'm living in the moment, literally. I'm totally incapable of seeing, thinking or planning what might happen next. Stuff is just going to happen whatever I do. That's what I've learnt today. Stuff is happening to me and I have no control over it. So I give up trying to plan or organise anything in my head because there is no point.

The front door is open even before I reach it.

'I thought you weren't coming,' announces my mother from the hall, pulling leather gloves on in the manner of someone preparing to strangle me. 'You will not believe the day I've had,' she continues, casting her eyes around for her bag and never once looking at me.

'Your dad's not had a good day. I left him alone for five minutes whilst I put the smoked salmon on the blinis for tonight's game and he was gone. Looked for him everywhere. Rang Roy, he wasn't there. Rang your Auntie Pauline, he wasn't there. Do you know where he was?' She finally looks at me as she picks her keys off the hall table.

I shake my head.

'In the utility room!' she exclaims. 'I didn't even realise he knew we had one. He certainly never went in there when he was working.

Never. He once asked me where the shoe polish was and I told him it was in the cupboard next to the washing machine. I watched him go all round the kitchen opening every cupboard door looking for the washing machine. Can you believe it? That's what my generation has had to put up with. Men who didn't even know where the washing machine was. You don't know you're born, young lady. Really. I bet Mark knows where the washing machine is, doesn't he? And I bet he even knows how to use it.'

She says this in a way that makes me feel it's my fault that Mark can work a washing machine and it's something I should feel guilty about.

'*And* I've seen him load the dishwasher,' she says, prodding a finger accusingly in my chest. 'Your dad's had his tea. He's just watching *Tom and Jerry*. His tablets are on the chopping board in the kitchen. If you put him to bed around nine thirty, he'll be okay then. I'll be back by ten anyway. No need for you to hang around.'

She brushes past me and bangs the door behind her. I can hear her heels tapping up the path at speed. I breathe out. I realise I have been holding my breath the whole time. Poised to speak. Poised to get some horrible truth out in the open in the hope that my mother will listen. At least listen.

I push open the door into the living room. I'm about to walk in but stop myself at the sight of the pristine light cream carpet. I slump down on a chair and kick off my shoes. Entering the living room in outdoor shoes leads to a fate worse than death in this house.

I pad into the room feeling my feet sink into the sumptuous pile. Dad is staring at the TV, the light from the screen reflecting off his glasses. I can just about make out Jerry hitting Tom over the head with a mallet. Dad is smiling and it makes me smile.

'Hi Dad,' I say, my smile out of nowhere becoming a weak watery one. I can feel myself sinking, as though the carpet is swallowing me up. He looks up at me and smiles back.

'Jenny,' he says.

He said my name. He recognises me. Today of all days. For once he said my name.

I can't help it. I fall into his arms and he holds me like he used to when I was a child. His arms are around my back and his cheek rests on the top of my head. I bet he hasn't held me like that in over thirty years. I bet I wouldn't let him. Oh, how I wish I had. How many moments like this have I missed being embraced by my father's love?

'What's the matter?' I hear him say into my hair. 'Did they push you over in the playground again?'

I raise my head to see the look of concern in my father's eyes.

'Something like that,' I reply, trying to stop the tears, realising the pointlessness of attempting to explain any different to his dementia-addled brain.

'Well, you just stay here,' he says. 'You're safe here. No one can get you here.'

'Thanks, Dad,' I say, leaning into him again, closing my eyes and pretending that he's right. I'm safe here.

Chapter Eleven

I don't feel myself when I wake up the next morning. I have longer than the usual momentary confusion about what day of the week it is and how I feel about that. Is it a work day? Have I prepared everything? What are Ellie and George doing today? Has Mark already gone to work? Can I hear the kids moving about? Do I need to go and shout at them? Why is it so quiet? Is it the middle of the night? Why do I feel like shit? Shit, I have cancer. Shit, my husband is cheating on me. I feel like shit because I have cancer and my husband is an adulterous shit-bag and possibly because I took two sleeping tablets last night.

I try and lift my head off the pillow but it is as if some hideous bully has his steel-toecapped boots resting on it. Is this how my dad feels every morning, I wonder. I hope not. I've never been a fan of my mother giving Dad sleeping tablets so that she gets a good night's sleep. He takes enough medication as it is and who knows what hidden side-effects they have that he isn't able to articulate to us. Typical of Mum, however. If there was a tablet that kept him semi-conscious at all times I think she would give it to him. She has a somewhat Edward Rochester approach to his care, keeping him imprisoned behind net curtains away from human eyes and avoiding all discussion of him outside the home. He may as well be dead.

I hope he had a lively night without the suppressants my mother feeds him and he led her a merry dance. No doubt I will hear all about it later and it will all be my fault. Which it is, of course, as I slipped his sleeping pills into my bag rather than into him. Serves her right for not taking just one moment to ask how her daughter was. To ask how her day had been.

I inch my way around until my feet are on the floor. I blink rapidly, hoping the fog will clear. Hoping I am waking up from some hideous long nightmare, meaning yesterday never happened.

But the clock by my bed says 9.34am, which means yesterday must have been real. I would never sleep that late unless I had sleeping tablets and I would only do such a thing if something terrible was preying on my mind and actually something, no, two terrible things, are. So the fact I am waking up at 9.34am confirms that yesterday did actually happen.

I trudge slowly downstairs in a stupor. I go straight to my mobile in a trance, just like I always do. Every morning. As though all my non-existent friends on the West Coast of the States will have been messaging me overnight with urgent news. I look at the screen.

On my way home.

That came in from Mark late last night. I don't even warrant an explanation. Or even an enquiry as to why I rang him five times yesterday. How long will it be before all communication ceases?

I scroll down to see a predictable flurry of communication from my mother.

7.15am – Had a terrible night with your father. Did you let him finish those Maltesers? Will you come this morning so I can go shopping – 9.30?

9.01am – Are you ignoring me? I know you are not at work until this afternoon. I really need a new outfit for when I go to Antony's. See you at 9.30.

9.09am – Missed Call

9.31am – Roy said he will come and sit with your dad which is really inconvenient for him. I feel terrible. You must give him your apologies next time you see him.

I can't help it, I press delete. My mother is so off-radar today. I refuse to communicate at all.

One last message came in a few minutes ago.

9.34am – Don't forget Nourish at 10. Looking forward to celebrating your birthday – Zoe xx

Oh shit! I stare at the text. That's a depressing text if ever I saw one. It makes my eyes heavy with the gloom of it.

For a start, Nourish? WTF!

Since when has Victoria sponge with a two-inch wedge of butter icing in the middle been nourishing? It may as well be called Fatten, or Eat More Lard. Just because you put a cream scone on an earthenware plate and provide a plethora of distressed mismatched chairs to sit on doesn't make everything that passes your lips healthy, including saturated fats. Believe me, I know. I have tried all approaches to eating saturated fats without gaining weight and eating it in healthy hippy-style coffee shops does not work. Nourish is a bog-standard café trying to be cool but it doesn't fool me. My friends, however, clearly yes, since they have deemed it the ideal location to party on down for my forty-fifth birthday.

And as for the ten o'clock meeting time? So insulting. Ten o'clock is the 'I haven't really got the time to spare you despite the fact it's your birthday' slot. I'll fit you in for a quick forty-five-minute flat-white then I can pat myself on the back for being a good friend and go on my merry way to my essential Pilates class, which I'm more than willing to give a good hour of my valuable time to.

Jesus, this really has to be the shittiest birthday of all time. The best they can come up with is to 'celebrate' my birthday with a coffee in a crap café. Who are these people?

Oh yeah, they are my friends. Well, the friends thrust upon me by my children by mere virtue of being the mothers of their misguided friendship choices at the age of four. The random group of women I happen to have first experienced being a school mum with. Somehow our joint experience of managing children of the same age has glued us together into an awkward, slightly dysfunctional group that never quite gels into the easy banter of a crowd that have come together through sheer affection rather than convenience. I remember going through a phase of dreaming that Ellie had been born a year earlier. From the looks of Facebook, the mums of that year had much more fun together with their sneaky lunches out and joint birthday parties and girly weekends away in someone's aunt's cousin's cottage in Padstow. If only Ellie had been born in 1998, then I too could have paraded my awesome social life with my friends on social media. But instead I'm in the 'hot chocolate at Nourish' crowd and hell will freeze over before I post that on Facebook.

'Happy birthday,' announces Lisa, when I walk in, her eyes flicking up from her laptop opened up on a rickety 'vintage' table that no doubt has a 'vintage' wobble as well.

She is dressed as usual in head-to-toe designer Lycra that matches. Yes, matches! It's very different to the stuff I throw on for my once-a-year amble into physical exercise, which usually consists of black leggings with holes at the knees and a faded fun run T-shirt from five years ago. When Lisa's not buying Lycra or talking about entering a marathon without ever actually entering one she's running a huge corporate empire from her spare bedroom. Actually she trades on eBay but you'd think she was doing a daily audition for *The Apprentice* the way she goes on about it.

'Happy birthday,' echoes Zoe, pulling out a chair next to her. 'I got you a hot chocolate with cream, as it's your birthday. I assumed organic?'

See what I mean? This place is seriously screwed up. They load a hot chocolate with cream and then ask if you'd like an organic healthy twist on that. Wrong, all wrong.

'So, have you had breakfast in bed this morning?' Zoe asks, looking me up and down as if to say, it looks like you've come here straight from bed. I've pulled my brown suede skirt on again but my top lay crumpled on the floor all night and there was nothing else half-decent ironed so I've come crumpled. Zoe has the uncanny knack of making every pleasantry feel like you've failed in some way.

I'm about to say no, and point out that actually it was my birthday two days ago so today would not warrant a breakfast in bed anyway, before I remember that we are only here today because Zoe had a prior engagement on my actual birthday. She claimed she had a meeting with her accountant but we all know she was having another colonic irrigation session because Lisa's sister works at the clinic. I look into Zoe's eyes to see if they are bloodshot, something Lisa reckons is a sure sign of recent colonic treatment. But then again, Lisa is the person who claims that she once slept with Jason Donovan backstage whilst he was in *Joseph and the Amazing Technicolor Dreamcoat*. You do have to take what Lisa says with a pinch of salt sometimes.

'Has Mark treated you then?' continues Zoe.

I look at her. This could be a classic leading question from Zoe. A question designed not to praise my husband's gift-buying powers but as an opportunity to reassure herself that the presents she receives from her own husband are way better. Oh yes, I want to reply. He treated me to a view of his bare backside yesterday, humping some blonde. Oh, and by the way, I have cancer.

'I keep dropping hints about my birthday to Geoff,' Zoe shares with everyone when I don't answer. 'I left a Sunday supplement open on a page listing the most romantic hotels in the Cotswolds.'

I raise my eyebrows at Emma as I always do whenever Zoe ever mentions Geoff in a romantic context. I actually like Emma, I really do, and feel we could actually have a laugh if she just let herself go a bit, but in the main she's… what is she? Well, she's a worrier. She worries about everyone and everything and one day she will have a nervous breakdown if she doesn't just learn to chill out a bit.

'Oh, wouldn't that be lovely?' replies Emma, nervously fingering the mini-shortbread on her saucer as she glances round the rest of the table to see if anyone else has eaten the free scrap of biscuit provided with all hot drinks. When she concludes that all her companions have shown restraint, she withdraws her hand sharply as though someone has tapped her on the wrist and told her not to be so greedy. 'Did Mark take you out, Jenny?' she asks to deflect the attention away from her hungry fingers.

'We went to the new Mexican in the Intu Centre.' I cough. My voice sounds strange. As though I am listening to someone else. Is that me talking normally as though the two landmines that have detonated in my life haven't happened?

'Oh, how lovely,' nods Zoe. 'It looks so much fun,' she adds, by which she means if you're six years old and like being distracted by primary colours.

'I like the cactus lights,' I shrug defiantly. 'And the nachos were the best I've ever eaten around here.'

'I can get you cactus lights,' interrupts Lisa before anyone has the chance to be in awe of my achievement of finding the best nachos in town. 'Give me one second and I'll get you a price. They'd look great in your kitchen, seriously.'

We all stare at each other whilst Lisa strokes her mouse pad trying to track down light-up plastic plants.

'How's Ellie getting on with Mr Partridge?' asks Heather, who unsurprisingly is trying to move us away from the cactus lights.

I turn to look at her and find myself sitting up straight in my chair. All conversations with Heather have a *Mastermind*-like quality to them, with Heather playing the role of merciless question master whilst you quake in your boots, praying you might get at least one answer right. The specialist subject is always same: our children's education. I think she is actually incapable of having a conversation outside of this subject area. I know she is a very intelligent woman. She has a PhD in something or other but she must be too clever to earn a living, and definitely too clever to be a housewife, so she's left with the ongoing analysis and monitoring of her children's schooling so that they can end up too clever for anything as well. Unfortunately her attentiveness and inside-out knowledge in this area leaves me feeling like a complete failure when it comes to my own children's education.

'Who's Mr Partridge?' I ask before I swallow, my eyes wide. I know I'm feeding her obsession but I cannot help it, I have no idea who she

is talking about. She looks at me like I don't know my own children's
birthdays.

'He's standing in for Miss Ryan whilst she goes on maternity leave,'
she says, firmly awarding me a U in her mind for my parenting skills.

'Oh,' I say.

'You know Miss Ryan who's taking them for English Lit?' she adds.

'Ah ha,' I cry. Yes, I actually say, 'Ah ha,' such is my pride in my
revelation. 'Ellie isn't doing English Lit,' I announce, looking around
triumphantly. 'She nearly did but decided on History instead.'

'Oh,' replies Heather. 'Megan said that Ellie swapped to English
Lit. Apparently she wasn't enjoying Russia in the Age of Absolutism
and Enlightenment 1682–1796. She told Megan it was boring and
she would prefer to be reading *Feminine Gospels* by Carol Ann Duffy.
Which I think I would if I had the choice. The study of feminism is so
much more relevant and enlightening than eighteenth-century Russia
to a young girl, don't you think?'

The table is silently waiting for my response.

Nothing is relevant, I think, any more.

'There you go, look,' says Lisa, turning her screen round to show me
a picture of plastic cactus lights twinkling merrily at me. 'Do you want
some? Why not two strands, they're only five pounds ninety-nine? Shall
I order you some? When we lived in the States I had two enormous
light-up palm trees on my deck. They were amazing.'

She sighs and leans back in her chair. 'So what about these cactus
lights then?' she says, turning to me. 'Did you say you wanted two sets?'

I stare at the screen then back at my friends.

I don't give a fuck, I want to scream. I want to curl up in a ball and
have someone take me in their arms and slowly draw out of me the
catastrophes that are going on in my life. But instead I'm stuck here

realising I don't think it can be any of you. I've known you all for over a dozen years and I don't think any of you can prop me up.

Take Zoe. Whilst being oh-so-sympathetic, I think you would thrive on the drama of finding yourself elevated to the status of the poor woman outside school who has the friend with a terminal illness. I can see you now, taking on the role of gatekeeper to all the other mums regarding any information on my health. As my 'closest friend' you would drip-feed anecdotes to all those who enquire with sad watery eyes and lap up the praise when they congratulate you on how good you are being to me. I'm sorry, Zoe, but it would be all about you and I couldn't bear to watch that.

And as for Lisa?

She'd retreat.

I can already hear her saying, 'Move away from the nearly dead person. There's nothing to see here.' Lisa really only ever wants to be somewhere better. Never content, a three-year stint in America with her husband's job has spoilt the rest of her life. Stateside she presided over four thousand square feet of all-expenses-paid real estate in a perfectly pretty suburb of Connecticut. Top of the tree with a lifestyle to match. She has never got over the comedown of an over-priced semi on a noisy main road purchased merely for school catchment purposes. Her online trading obsession is just one of the many ludicrous plans she hatches that she somehow thinks will transport her back to the land of drive-thru Starbucks and ridiculous gun laws. Her friend being ill would be a dose of reality she just wouldn't want to face and yet another reason why this country is shit. Clearly, living in the UK has given me cancer. She would settle her conscience by deciding we were never that close, and others were far better equipped to support me in my hour of need, as she backed away into somewhere I didn't have to be addressed.

Emma surely? Nice Emma. Sweet, lovely Emma would step up, wouldn't she? She'd be there by my side, mopping my brow, a shoulder to cry on. She wouldn't mind me calling her in the middle of the night when the gloom was thick and choking. Emma is my wingman on this. My prop, my support.

No, I don't think so.

I fear she'd collapse under the strain. I'd spend my time propping her up. Telling her not to worry, it's all going to be fine, as she weeps on *my* shoulder. I'd be staring my fate in the face every time I saw her, because her inability to put up a brave front, even for my benefit, would feel like constant visits from the Grim Reaper.

So am I left with Heather as my confidante? The least warm person in our group. The woman who insists on playing Education Top Trumps with me every time I see her. It's not life and death, is it, your children's education? Except, for Heather, I suspect it is.

'Why don't we buy Jenny the cactus lights for her birthday, seeing as she loves them so much?' I hear Zoe say.

Our eyes meet over the vintage sugar bowl with one leg missing. I love those lights but I don't want them as a gift for my birthday.

'I meant to get you a little something but nothing caught my eye when I went shopping. It's such a waste of money to just buy something for the sake of it, isn't it?' she continues.

'That's a great idea,' gasps Emma, as though Zoe has worked out a cure for my cancer.

I bet you any money they all reassured each other before I arrived that they hadn't bought me a birthday gift but Emma would be the one worrying about whether they had done the right thing.

'Presents at our age are so hard, aren't they? But if Jenny would really like some cactus lights then that's perfect.'

'Seriously?' is all Heather can say.

'Two sets then,' says Lisa, starting to tap at her keyboard. 'So that will be three ninety-five each including packaging and postage. Shall we just call it four pounds?' she continues, looking up and sticking her hand out in expectation of being paid there and then right in front of me. The birthday girl. Is this what gift-giving has come to? A random mention of affection for something leapt on and instantly ordered on the internet right before your eyes, with contributions collected and pocketed before you can say, actually, what I would really like for my birthday is for you to just take me for a drink and get me drunk so I can tell you how hideous my soon-to-be-extinguished life is.

'What time does the Queens Head open?' I ask as Heather and Emma scrabble around in their handbags for money to give Lisa whilst Zoe impatiently waves a ten-pound note in the air, waiting to see if anyone has change.

'I've no idea,' shrugs Zoe, checking her watch. 'We've not been in since Geoff got barred.'

'Barred!' exclaims Emma. 'What for?'

'Touched up a waitress,' announces Lisa.

'No, he did not!' cries Zoe. 'She bumped into him and claims Geoff came on to her. It's outrageous. Who do these young girls think they are? They can't go around making accusations like that. Geoff's been going in that pub for years and the landlord would sooner believe an eighteen-year-old than him.'

The rest of us share fleeting glances. We have all at one time or another experienced the leering nature of Geoff when drunk. We all cheered inside for the girl who dared to stand up to him whilst feeling ashamed it took a teenager rather than a grown woman to out him as the lech he actually is.

'The Bull then?' I ask. 'What time is that open?'

'About five, I imagine,' says Emma.

'But it must be open for lunch,' I say. I look at my watch. It's ten forty-five. 'I bet it's open at eleven. Let's walk down there now. Come on, it's my birthday. Let's go for a proper drink, not this full-fat organic stuff,' I say, looking disdainfully at my mug.

'What, now?' says Heather, her brow furrowed as though I have just asked some deep philosophical question that may not have been covered on the syllabus.

'Yes, now,' I say and I actually slam my fist on the now even more distressed table. I don't think I can bear to go home without releasing some of what is going on inside me, even if it is to this awkward bunch. The mums on the next table, bouncing red-cheeked crying babies on their knees, look at me and want to say 'Shush' – I know they do.

'Don't you dare shush me,' I want to shout back.

'But… but it's the morning,' says Emma nervously, looking around at everyone.

'Well, I really would love to,' says Zoe, starting to gather up her things, 'but I'm due at Pilates at eleven, and I'm not sure a spritzer would do anything for my core strength.' She laughs her tinkly laugh that she does whenever she is unnerved.

'When did you last have a spritzer?' I ask Zoe.

'Erm, I, er…' she says, putting her coat on as quickly as possible.

'I've never seen you dilute a drink ever,' I say. 'In fact I've seen you in the Co-op, going down the wine shelf, checking to find the one with the highest alcohol content.'

'I do not,' she cries back, looking wildly round at everyone for reassurance. 'I'm checking for food pairings.'

'You're in the Co-op! The only food pairing to do in there is which flavour of Pringles goes best with cheap red.'

'Jenny,' says Emma, putting a hand on my arm.

I know I'm being mean but I'm desperate. Why is it so hard to tell someone, anyone, that you're dying?

'Come to the pub,' I plead with Emma. The smug mums on the next table share uncomfortable glances.

'I… I…' starts Emma.

'Oh, come on, please,' I beg. 'You can miss Pilates just this once, can't you?'

She sits with her mouth hanging open, glancing feverishly between Zoe and me.

'It *is* my birthday,' I state.

Pathetic, a voice says in my head. You are so not handling this situation well. You need to be sitting one-on-one, at home, breaking the news gently and asking for help and support whilst sharing tissues and memories and plans to 'make the most of it'. Instead you're harassing people to play hooky from Pilates to go and get early-morning drunk in the pub.

'We'd better go, Emma,' says Zoe, clearly miffed at my slight on her booze-buying habits. 'We'll miss the start if we don't hurry.'

'Heaven forbid you miss the start,' I say, throwing my hands in the air in an effort to stop the tears coming. 'A whole five calories not taken care of. Call the Fire Brigade.'

But I'm talking to their backs. Zoe has hustled Emma out of the café at a speed usually reserved for exiting young children when homeless Nick wanders in to use the facilities.

'Interesting behaviour,' nods Heather slowly. Oh God, she's gone into 'shrink' mode and any minute will ask me about my relationship with my mother.

'Lisa, pub?' I say hopefully, but she's already gathering her things.

'I have a delivery coming, I'm sorry,' she says. 'And I need to order these cactus lights,' she adds.

'I thought you'd already ordered them,' I say.

'Yes, well, I need to follow it up,' she continues, frowning. 'See you later,' she adds, raising her hand a fraction, and walks out.

'And then there were two,' smiles Heather. 'You don't seem yourself today, Jenny. I think the pub is the last thing you need, don't you? They've got a spiced latte on here. Why don't I get us both one of those and you can tell me all about it.'

'No,' I say, shaking my head a little too vigorously. 'No, I'm fine. I must go, really. I have to be somewhere.'

I get up and leave before she can point out that moments earlier the only place I needed to be was the pub.

Chapter Twelve

I am left with no other option but to go to work.

My choices today are not good.

I could try my mother again but I know we will meet in the hall then she'll swiftly throw on her coat and seize the opportunity to escape from her husband and his Alzheimer's. I can't face trying to tell her whilst she bends down to push her feet into her ankle boots. There needs to be some kind of build-up to giving her the news rather than me trying to babble it out as quickly as possible before she gets to the front gate.

I could go to Mark. Confront him about the office sex. Or do I tell him about the cancer first? Can I bear to watch his face as I tell him about my condition? All manner of emotions could run over it, including the relief that he won't ever have to tell me about the affair he's having. That my cancer has just given him a get-out-of-jail-free card. Can I stand to watch that? Or do I tackle him about his infidelity first, get the truth on that, then watch him squirm as I hit him with the punch in the gut that he's cheating on his wife whilst she's battling with cancer? Watch the self-loathing spread across his face.

It's so confusing. My head can't grab hold of any of it and its consequences. All I know is that I can't face going to his office again. I can't face walking through the building and checking out every blonde woman in a blue skirt to try and work out if it's her. I can't stand there and demand that we go and talk somewhere because I know he won't. He'll make me wait until later and I will have to walk out with my head bowed and sit and dread the moment when his headlights flash in the window and I know the time has come.

So I go to work.

At least it's bingo night at Shady Grove. I don't have to think, just sit there and bark out numbers until I'm interrupted by an incontinence incident or an argument over a winning call. In the past I've asked Sandra if we can organise a trip to go out to the bingo, *proper* bingo, but she says there's too much red tape. Sandra is in charge and what she means by red tape is that it would require her to get off her arse and actually do something rather than watch re-runs of *Peak Practice* on the TV she says is a CCTV screen in her cosy little office. You have to knock on the door before you are allowed in but, if you press your ear to the door first, you usually hear someone complaining of dizziness and a ringing in the left ear during a home visit on a wild and stormy night in a remote farmhouse in the Peak District.

In fact she is just like my boss Clare back in Corfu in 1996. A lazy killjoy. Sandra has given me objectives and sees that as her job done, no more input required. Apparently I need to 'provide a broad spectrum of culturally diverse activities that will stimulate all abilities and provide structure and enjoyment to the daily routine of all residents'. The achievement of this is mainly through the format of bingo, daily armchair aerobics, a weekly tea dance/shuffle around the dining room, the availability of chess, draughts and knitting wool, and the communal daily enjoyment of *Countdown* on the television. In a rush of creativity, however, I have recently introduced a spin on *Countdown* entitled 'Rude Tuesdays'. The first person to come up with a rude word wins a jelly bean. It's amazing how many times you can spell 'piss' on *Countdown*. Jimmy in particular loves it. The letters to the words he shouts out are rarely available but I suspect his ability to shout 'Bugger off' at the top of his voice, several times in half an hour, is doing more for his mental health than the weekly torturous visits from his son, who walks in, picks up the newspaper, reads it and walks out again.

Mark has told me many times I don't have to keep working there, as though he's embarrassed that his wife works with the aged. I think he is looking for something more glamorous to brag to the other directors about, like advertising maybe – or even pornography! Sometimes I catch him sniffing when I get home from work as though he can smell the olds on me. Whenever I come home a bit dazed and upset because one of them has died he always tells me to jack it in. He can't understand why I would put myself through that.

I think I do it for two reasons. One, because it reminds me to be grateful for what I have: my health, my family, my relative youth. Until now that is. And two, because of Maureen.

'I'm dying,' I declare, bursting into Maureen's room unannounced.

'Aren't we all?' she replies from the armchair next to the window. She doesn't even look up from the *Take a Break* magazine resting on her knee. 'What's the name of the youngest sister who died in childbirth on *Downton Abbey*?' she asks, chewing the end of her finger, deep in thought.

'Was it Sylvia?' she asks, finally peering at me over her purple-rimmed glasses. They match the purple scarf wrapped around her neck, but not a lot else. Her outfit, as always, is a riot of mismatched colours and patterns ebbing and flowing over her pillowy frame. She is by her own admission an extreme layerer, often piling vests and cardigans and pullovers over cotton frocks, making her resemble a walking wardrobe. A bold dab of red lipstick and coral pink nails complete the look that declares: 'I'm old and I'm going to look how the hell I like'.

'No, really I am dying,' I say and flop down on her single bed. I lie back, my head hitting her pillow, her flowery perfume instantly engulfing my nostrils. It's comforting. I turn to look over at the array of black and white photographs lined up along the top of a bookshelf and seek out my favourite.

It's right there. A young and very glamorous Maureen grinning out at me, one arm draped around her husband Ray, an Elvis impersonator from Leicester, and one around Frank Sinatra. Yes, *the* Frank Sinatra. Apparently it was taken in the sixties inside the Aladdin Casino in Las Vegas whilst she was accompanying Ray on his world tour. Maureen has lived!

'I'm dying,' I tell young Maureen, Ray and Frank.

I realise this is the first time I have said it out loud. It still doesn't sound like me saying it. It still isn't happening to me. The fact I have failed to get through to anyone else this horrendous fact surely means that it cannot be true.

'I'll try Sylvia,' says Maureen. 'I think that's the right answer but it would make Tess Daly wrong. Oh, and it's got too many letters. Mmmm.'

'Sybil,' I say.

Maureen jerks her head back up to look at me.

'Are you sure?' she asks.

'Yes,' I say, 'I'm very sure. And Mark is shagging someone at work.' I bite my lip to try and fight back the tears that have sprung out of nowhere.

'Oh my God!' exclaims Maureen. A reaction. Progress.

'Oh my God what?' I say. 'Mark or the cancer?'

'Cancer!' she exclaims again. 'Has he got that as well? What are you telling me?'

'No, no,' I say, swinging my legs round so my feet are back on the floor and I can see her face. Not the conversation really to be having lying down.

'*I've* got cancer,' I say. 'Mark's got another woman.'

I watch her face go from shock to confusion to total bewilderment.

'Oh my God,' she says again. She's lost for words. Unusual for Maureen.

'Cancer?' she says slowly.

I nod.

'Since when?'

'I found out yesterday.'

'And Mark. When did you...?'

'Yesterday.'

'Fuck,' she mutters.

I laugh. Despite it all I laugh.

'How long?' she demands.

'The affair or the dying?'

Her eyes flare in horror but she collects herself.

'Both.'

'Who knows?' I shrug, the tears starting to fall now. I look down at my feet swinging off the side of the bed. I don't want her to watch me cry. 'The doctor said maybe two years but he can't be sure. And I've not asked Mark yet. He doesn't know I know,' I say to the floor.

'But he knows you have cancer?'

'No...' I say forcefully, still looking down. 'You're the first person I have told. Well, you're the first person who has listened.'

There is a moment's silence then I can hear her pulling herself forward in her chair. There's huffing and puffing and the tinkling of multiple bangles as she inches herself forward. I can't look up. I can't look up because then I will see the look on her face. Pity, sympathy, heartache, anguish. Whatever it is, it will be the end of me. The look of someone who might care will undo me. I wait, head bent low until she makes it to me, and then I will look at her as she puts an arm around me. Then I will let go.

'Arrgh,' is the next thing I hear. I jerk my head up and watch as Maureen falls to the floor, glasses, magazine, self-propelling pencil scattering everywhere.

'What the…' I gasp as I lunge forward to try and save her but it's too late. She's in a heap, looking a bit pale.

'I couldn't quite reach my stick,' she gasps, clutching her arm.

'Why didn't you ask me to get it?' I say, reaching over to press the emergency button dangling from the arm of her chair.

'Because of the cancer,' she replies with a grimace.

I kneel down next to her and grab her hand, hastily wiping away tears, knowing the nurse will burst in any minute.

'I can still pass you your stick,' I tell her.

'Thought it would ruin the moment if I said, "Can you pass me my stick before I come and put my arms around you."'

'And this is such a better moment,' I say. 'Me with my arm around you whilst we wait for Nurse Hagrid to arrive and give me a severe telling-off for letting you fall.' We both shudder at the thought of the arrival of the towering six-foot-two nurse with eighties rocker hair and a slight moustache. We secretly call her Hagrid, though never to her face, for obvious reasons.

'Don't worry, I'll sort her out,' says Maureen. I can see her wincing in pain and I reach over and press the button again.

'Is that arm okay?' I ask, feeling guilty that my cancer trumps her fall for sympathy.

'I'll live,' she says. 'Oh shit, sorry,' she gasps, realising immediately what she has said. Then she looks at me, tears suddenly flooding her eyes.

'Please don't cry,' I manage to whisper, failing to hold my own tears back.

'But my arm really hurts,' she mutters, and thankfully Nurse Hagrid arrives to take matters in hand.

Chapter Thirteen

Bingo passes by in a blur. I stare blankly back at Harold, distracted by the grey hairs dangling out of the ends of his nostrils as he bitterly calls foul over the winner of the third game. The less I respond, the more agitated he gets, calling on his fellow white male sympathisers to back up his claim that I called thirty when actually the number on the ball was twenty. I have no idea. I might have done. My brain is actually not connected to my body at the moment and so he could well be right.

However, I am with it enough to recognise that this is a common complaint whenever Rita wins. It's possible that this is their silent protest against the fact that Rita insists on pointing out that Clare Balding is a lesbian every time she appears on the TV. I'm sure the less enlightened residents would prefer to ignore Ms Balding's sexuality, but Rita is determined to remind them in a tone that makes it clear she believes it makes Ms Balding even more magnificent than all of them already believe. I suspect Rita would have been a lesbian had there been more openly gay TV presenters around when she was young, to pave the way. But now nothing will stop her celebrating her existence, even low-level prejudice on bingo night.

The prize for winning is a small bar of Dairy Milk. After Harold has ranted for a good five minutes, I walk across the room and hand the chocolate over to Rita. I can feel him pursuing me at a distance (sadly his sprinting days are over); he reaches me just as I turn away from congratulating her and I come face to face with his straggle of nose hair again.

'For you,' I say, pushing another bar of chocolate at him.

He looks down, shock and disappointment written all over his face. This was not the result he was after. He looks up at me in dismay that his protest has not led to the decommissioning of Rita's win. I raise my eyebrows, challenging him to take the chocolate. He doesn't, so I walk away, putting the bar in my pocket as I hear him mutter in disgust behind me.

This time I knock on Maureen's door before I enter. Earlier, Nurse Hagrid had called an ambulance after she'd checked her over, then her six-foot-two wrestler frame had stood looking at me accusingly.

'She found me like this,' Maureen had gasped as soon as Nurse Hagrid had entered the room. 'Stupid me was reaching for my stick and I fell. It was a good job Jenny came in or else I could have been lying here for ages.'

She'd gripped my hand tightly as she'd come out with this lie and I'd gripped it back in thanks. Nurse Hagrid would have had me up in front of Sandra for assault or something if she caught even a whiff of me being in the same room when a resident fell. She hates me. She once told me I was unprofessional because I hadn't done a risk assessment before taking everyone outside for Pimm's and a sing-song on a glorious summer's evening.

I peer around the door now and see Maureen sitting up in bed, her arm in a sling, watching something on TV.

'Oh, no!' I groan, walking in. 'You haven't broken it, have you?'

'No,' she says. 'Just a sprain, said Doctor Pinder. A wonderful man. He told me his father was a butler to Princess Margaret. I could have sat there for hours.'

As she speaks, our eyes search each other's faces. The conversation is white noise as we both battle to know how to start where we left off earlier.

She reaches forward to grab my hand but I am just out of reach.

'Whoa,' I say, pushing her back upright. 'We don't need any more accidents today. You stay where you are.'

'But you need me,' she says decisively, like she has thought about it and actively come to a decision. She sighs in frustration. 'And I've gone and done a stupid thing like this so I can't even put my stupid arms around you.'

'It's okay.' I shrug. Though it isn't.

'Let's get rid of these idiots,' she says, clearing her throat, picking up the remote control and switching off the TV. She has added a layer to her outfit. A pink shawl rests over her shoulders. It looks good against the bright blue wall she insisted on being painted when she moved in because she couldn't bear the abundance beige.

'Beige will be the death of me,' she'd told Sandra, who tried to stop the decorator halfway through the first coat. 'Do you want that on your conscience?'

Somehow Maureen has managed to hold onto doing things her way in an environment that encourages, even demands, conformity. I am in awe.

'So the first thing I need to ask you is, are you sure?' She leans back and pushes her glasses up her nose. She looks like she means business, like she is prepared and she is going to take charge. I feel a flood of relief.

'Am I sure about what exactly?' I ask, determined to answer her questions accurately.

'Are you sure about the cancer?'

I swallow.

I've been thinking about this very question a lot over the past twenty-four hours. Had the doctor really said what I thought he'd said? Had I really taken it in? Had the strange buzzing in my ears and the utter distraction of imagining my life with cancer caused me to miss a vital piece of information such as him saying, 'Just kidding, you haven't got cancer and you are going to be absolutely fine.'

But as I tried to retrace every step of the conversation I knew this not to be true.

'He said I have probably eighteen months to two years.' I concentrate on not letting this sentence undo me as I study Maureen's face for her reaction. A slight nod of the head is all that comes. She holds firm her composure but she blinks more as she processes my answer. She knows as well as I do that it is pretty impossible to misinterpret those words.

'He gave me a time frame,' I reinforce to Maureen.

She nods ever so slightly again.

'So what are you going to do?' she asks firmly, brushing away the emotion to get straight down to the practicalities. I like this. I can handle this.

'About what? The cancer or the affair?' I bat back.

'Jeez, I'd forgotten all about the affair,' says Maureen, raising her good hand in wonder and shaking her head vigorously. Don't lose it now, I silently request. Hold it together. I need you to hold it together. Her earrings stop swaying and she gathers herself.

'Shall we start with the cancer?' she says.

'Yes,' I nod. She looks at me expectantly. She wants me to answer.

'Well,' I falter. What should I be saying? I have no idea, so I say the first thing that comes into my head.

'I've Googled it, how to die, and it was full of climbing this mountain, swimming that sea or becoming a marathon runner and raising millions for charity!'

A look of horror spreads over Maureen's face.

'Sounds like bloody hard work! You can make it more fun than that surely?' she replies.

'It's true,' I tell her. 'A lot of people in my situation seem to raise a huge amount of money for a cancer charity by taking up marathon running or even becoming a triathlete.'

This time I note a minute shake of the head. She looks at me for a long time, unsure how to proceed. She doesn't know if I'm joking. *I* don't know if I'm joking.

'What kind of bloody ridiculous idea is that?' she eventually says, her eyes wide in wonder.

'I know!' I gasp, relieved she has decided I'm joking. 'It doesn't make sense, does it? Who wants to run a marathon with cancer? Surely the fact I have cancer means I have a free pass where exercise is concerned. And why would I raise money to research something I already have? It can't help me now, can it?' I'm gabbling, I know, but I can't stop. 'Besides, do you remember what happened when I did a fun run?'

'I don't remember you doing a fun run.'

'I did. With George. I ended up in A&E with a broken toe because I tripped over at the start-line. Some people demanded their sponsorship money back.'

'So anything athletic is out then?'

I nod. 'Or fundraising. Call me selfish but I don't really feel like being generous to others right now.'

Maureen nods. 'I don't think just because you are dying that you should feel like you have to.'

As she says the 'you are dying' bit our eyes lock. Now she has said it out loud. Someone else apart from Doctor Death. Things are progressing.

'According to Google,' I continue, 'cancer should give me a sudden desire to become an amazingly generous philanthropist, a bit like the nesting instinct when you are pregnant. That didn't happen to me either.'

'Did Doctor Google come up with *anything* helpful?' asks Maureen.

'Well, I should really write a blog,' I say.

Now Maureen might encourage this. She writes a blog. Mainly reviews on books and TV shows, stuff like that. Whilst travelling around the world with her Elvis-impersonating husband she started writing travel pieces and managed to get some published. She doesn't travel any more so she reviews from her armchair. She says the only reason she chose Shady Grove was because they would let her have Sky in her room.

'Would you want to write a blog?' she asks. 'I could help you with that if you like?'

'No,' I declare. 'I'm struggling to tell my nearest and dearest, never mind the entire internet.' This is really hard. 'What would you do?' I ask her. Maureen would do this well, I know she would. Better than me.

'I don't know,' she replies, taking her glasses off and rubbing her eyes. 'Well, actually that's a lie. I do know. I know exactly what I would do but I'm not going to tell you because I'm not you and you're not me. *You* have to decide.'

I want to cry now. I'd been relying on Maureen for something. I'm not sure what but something.

'And then there's Mark,' I say. 'I don't know what to do about that. In some ways it's good. The affair stops me thinking about the cancer and the cancer stops me thinking about the affair.'

Maureen nods. 'That's something,' she agrees.

'And I've totally stopped worrying about George's anxiety and Ellie's bitchiness,' I add.

'Good, good, that's good,' agrees Maureen again.

'But… but… my kids,' I gasp. I suddenly feel as though I can't breathe. The moment thoughts of my diagnosis collide with thoughts of Ellie and George, my mind goes into some form of anaphylactic shock. I can't put the two together. The two repel like two opposing magnets. My brain refuses to make any connection between what is happening to me and what that means in terms of my children, because I know the minute I make the connection the conclusion is too dire, too desperate, too heartbreaking. So for now I avoid the connection like the plague.

'And I no longer feel any guilt at deleting my mother's texts,' I plough on, trying to block thoughts of Ellie and George from my mind. 'I've always wanted to be able to do that.'

'So there are some positives,' says Maureen, grabbing my hand and squeezing it.

'Oh yeah. Could be the best thing that has ever happened to me,' I say as I loll forward onto Maureen's good shoulder and let the tears come.

★

'I also Googled how to tell people,' I say to Maureen about half an hour later when the sobs have abated and she has handed me a real-life hanky, with lace!

'And?' she asks, dabbing her own eyes. I hate that I have made her cry but I'm also really morbidly grateful to see the first set of tears about what is happening to me.

'I started typing it in and I got to "How do I tell someone I have..."
and it automatically predicted I was asking, "How do I tell someone
I have herpes?"'

Maureen screws her face up.

'You know, the sexually transmitted disease,' I add.

'I know what herpes is,' she replies. She shuffles, bristling her
shoulders. 'I went round and handed over a bottle of bleach and told
him never to come near me again. I think he got the message. Was
that on Google?'

I stare at her.

'What?' she asks. 'I used to have sex, get over it.'

'Bleach?' I say.

'Serves him right,' she replies. 'Perhaps you should try it with Mark.'

'The thought of pouring bleach over his...'

'Penis,' adds Maureen helpfully.

'...penis, does have some appeal at the moment,' I admit.

'Well, do it then.'

'It would kill his penis.'

'So, what have you got to lose? What's he going to do? Prosecute?
You've got cancer, the ultimate get-out-of-jail-free card.'

I nod. It's tempting but we both know Maureen is just trying to
cheer me up with the thought of dissolving my husband's adulterous
penis in bleach.

'Well, it doesn't sound like Google came up with many answers for
you,' she announces, folding her good arm over her bad arm.

'No,' I admit. 'It was full of other people's way of dying.'

'Not your way?' she asks.

'No,' I murmur.

She looks at me for a moment then leans forward and grasps my hand.

'We'll find it,' she says.

'What?'

'Your way to die. We'll find it.'

Chapter Fourteen

I know even before I put the key in the lock that Mark isn't home. He would have drawn the curtains and switched the downstairs lights off in a huff by now, shouting at the kids for being so wasteful.

There is silence as I close the front door behind me. I pause, holding my breath. Nothing.

I shout, 'Hello?'

Nothing.

Ellie and George are there but they are not. I have no doubt that George will be commanding some military operation out on the world wide web, fighting some terrible enemy but protected from the real world by headphones blasting adrenaline-surging music into his ears, oblivious to the comings and goings of number three Cheviot Lane.

Ellie will be juggling a multitude of social media channels, sharing her wit and grit with the universe, fuelled by the fleeting reactions of her friends, and strangers who pretend to be friends. The Wi-Fi automatically goes off at nine in this house. Mark and I thought this would encourage family interaction; perhaps we would come together as a unit and communicate before bedtime, but no. The Wi-Fi curfew merely causes a daily panic over the imminent wireless drought, thereby encouraging over-consumption in the hours leading up to it, when no personal communication takes place whatsoever. Other solitary activities are then reserved for after nine. Homework, hair practice, outfit selection for the following day, *Call of Duty* strategy thinking time. This is not a family home, it's more like a student house full of dysfunctional adults who meet in communal areas only to pass on messages or criticise each other's food choices before retreating to the sanctuary of their own rooms.

I throw some pizzas in the oven. We don't normally have pizza until Friday but the thought of cooking, of peeling carrots and potatoes, is too mundane and depressing. My head is so full of drama and despair that adding preparing vegetables to that is likely to tip me over the edge.

I set the timer and sit at the table, staring around me at the kitchen. The kitchen that I have been wanting to re-do for about five years now but Mark keeps telling me to wait until the next stage in his career, when he takes Brancotec to the next level. Then I can have any kitchen I want, he says. Maybe even one in a completely different house. So I've made do with the heavy oak, slightly dated units, the extractor fan that makes a noise like a helicopter taking off, and a single oven.

Occasionally I take a trip to B&Q and run my fingers across granite worktops and pull open silent sliding drawers and marvel at the amazing ways in which you can make an awkward corner cupboard accessible. My favourite features, however, are the multiple ovens. I'm no great chef but the thought of being able to display at least three ovens in a kitchen seems like the ultimate in domestic sophistication to me. It screams successful wife and mother. Something I would have really liked to have been.

The timer goes off and Betsy, our loveable mongrel, jumps out of her basket and stuffs her nose under my arm. She can already smell the leftovers. I shoo her away and in a zombie-like fashion I take out the pizzas and put them on chopping boards. Then I walk to the bottom of the stairs and shout, 'Pizza!' at the top of my voice. I wander back into the kitchen. I can't face eating. I'm not sure whether it's the illness or the stomach-churning emotion. Either way, looking at the array of pepperoni, margherita and Hawaiian (why?) makes me want to gag.

I'll tell them I've already eaten if they ask. This fleeting thought makes me laugh. As if they would question why I'm not eating. My eating habits are not on their radar.

I've already decided today will not be the day that I announce to the family that I have cancer. The minute I tell them I figure a chunk of me is already dead. I will become someone else. The mother with a terminal illness rather than the pain-in-the-arse mum who just doesn't understand me and is out to make my life as miserable as possible. I want to be her for just a bit longer.

After a couple of minutes sitting at the pizza graveyard I get up again and walk to the bottom of the stairs and shout, 'Pizza!' even louder. I listen for sounds of movement. Nothing. I go back to the kitchen and pick up my phone to text my kids to call them for food downstairs. Within seconds there is a thumping on the stairs and George appears, swiftly followed by Ellie.

'You've not cut the margherita with the same knife as the other two, have you?' asks Ellie, sitting down and reaching over to help herself to three slices.

'No,' I lie.

She's eating it before I have answered. She claims to be vegetarian but seems very willing to accept all my deceptions over what has gone into various dishes, when normally she sniffs out my lies like a hound dog. It seems to be an unwritten rule that should her dalliances with meat ever be discovered then she can put all the blame on me. This means she is free to enjoy the odd pork sausage I occasionally tell her are Linda McCartney with a knowing look.

George and Ellie sit and munch in silence. George is trying to hide the fact he's feeding his crusts to a grateful Betsy, who's sitting by his side looking up at him adoringly. I'm happy to watch, conversation beyond me; today the mere presence of my two children feels more meaningful and enjoyable than any of the other million times they have sat next to me and ignored me.

There are maybe half a dozen slices left when Mark arrives home. I'm surprised – I just assumed that he'd be shagging late again and so I wasn't prepared to see him.

'God, I'm famished,' he says, reaching over and picking up a slice and stuffing it in his mouth.

I look for signs of his betrayal. Maybe an untucked shirt or a sheepish look. But he looks exactly the same as he did last week. Impeccably neat and tidy in a navy suit with white shirt and a striped tie. The sight of the corporate him used to get me very overexcited when we first started living together. I'd never had a boyfriend who wore a suit – it seemed so grown-up and mature and so damn sexy. I could hardly keep my hands off him. Clearly someone else now agrees with me.

'I tell you what, the investors wanted their pound of flesh today,' announces Mark. 'I have been through every single page of our five-year strategy. Every page. Still, they seemed impressed, which is the main thing.'

I don't respond. Which is pretty normal actually when Mark starts talking about work. Either I don't understand what he is saying or, to be honest, it's just too damn dull.

He puts his briefcase in the corner and sits down, grabbing a second slice of pizza. I can see George getting agitated at the arrival of his dad as it will mean less pepperoni pizza for him because they both like it best. I watch him eye Mark munching away, oblivious that he is stealing his own children's dinner. I will George to say something but of course he doesn't. He just bends his head low over his plate, observing Mark reach for yet another slice. Betsy jumps up at him in anticipation.

'Get down,' says Mark, roughly pushing her away. I watch as Betsy retreats to the protection of George's side.

'So how did your session with the tutor go today?' Mark asks his son.

George's shoulders shrug in response. 'Fine,' he mutters.

Mark has recently taken the step of hiring a maths tutor for George. Somehow George has failed to inherit his dad's excellent maths genes. Mark waited patiently for numeric skills to emerge so that he could refer to George as a chip off the old block, but they never came. He doesn't consider George's considerable talents with food to be an adequate reflection and so is currently enforcing a strict regime of three sessions a week with a maths tutor. As far as I can tell, this is only having the effect of increasing George's anxiety, making him less likely to pick up any valuable learning.

'What did you do?' Mark presses.

'Simultaneous equations,' says George, making no eye contact as he darts his hand out for the final piece of peperoni pizza.

'Simultaneous equations!' exclaims Ellie. 'Seriously, George, we did those in, like, Year Seven. You're so thick.'

She reaches out and grabs the very last slice of pizza, which is Hawaiian (isn't it always left till last?), and shoves it in her mouth, clearly forgetting there is ex-pig littered all over it.

I'm staring at her with my mouth open, as is George. I squeeze George's hand, allowing him a moment to gather his thoughts. He stands up. He's going to run away, I think. Let her get away with it. I look up at him pleadingly, willing him to just let it out.

'You're eating dead pig, you hypocritical b-b-bitch,' he stutters before he turns and flees the room, Betsy bounding after him. I want to applaud so badly but am stopped by Mark's look of concern for his daughter.

'He doesn't mean it,' he says to her.

'No, he did,' I say, interrupting this father–daughter bonding moment. They both whirl to look at me and I am in the spotlight. 'That is Hawaiian you are eating.'

Ellie looks down at the remnants of pizza in her hand and makes a show of dropping it on the plate like it's burnt her.

'I've eaten ham!' she wails. 'Did you hide it under the pineapple?'

'No.'

'But I couldn't taste it, I swear I couldn't taste it,' she says, looking at her father desperately.

'No harm done,' I say, swiftly getting up and gathering up dirty plates.

There is no response from behind me as I turn to put the dishes in the dishwasher.

'There's probably hardly any pig in the processed stuff they put on those pizzas anyway,' I hear Mark tell Ellie.

'Do you think so?' she replies.

'Sure,' he says.

'Will you take me and Phoebe to Nottingham on Saturday to go shopping?' asks Ellie.

'Okay,' he says.

'There's a bikini I really like in Cruise.'

'Fine,' he mutters. I can tell he's lost interest. He's probably looking at his phone.

'Can I have it?'

'I guess so.'

'Brilliant. I'll let Phoebe know.'

I return to the table to clear away half-empty glasses. Mark and Ellie are both staring at their phones. Ellie wanders out the room whilst Mark starts tapping at his screen. Is it a message from her, I wonder. Is she arranging their next session? Will he ever look up from his damn phone and see what's happening right before his eyes?

'I've got a few emails to sort out,' he says, getting up and walking towards the door without even glancing at me, without offering to help clear away, without asking me how my cancer-ridden, affair-clouded day has been. 'I'll do them in my office,' he adds, picking up his briefcase and wandering out.

The rest of the plates get chucked in the dishwasher then I pour myself a large glass of wine. I hesitate over the expensive stuff that Mark buys to take to dinner parties, never to be enjoyed at home with me. But I pass. Recently wine and I have not been the pals we used to be. Instead of the soothing calm before the shedding of inhibitions, I have experienced pain and cramps and general discomfort. The cancer again maybe. Ruining that little shred of joy as well.

★

I move to the lounge with an everyday glass of red. I sit in the dark until I can stand the gloom no longer. I put on a light and shut the curtains and sit down again.

All is quiet, all is calm, everything looks the same as it always has, and yet everything is different. Nothing looks the same from where I am sitting. Rather than reassuring me that our kids were young and cute once, the school photos lined up on the shelf make me want to howl and scream. The large black and white picture of trees lining a country road above the fireplace is a reminder that for maybe ten years we have been meaning to replace the cheap Ikea print with something more original but we've never got round to it and now probably never will. I casually stroke the corner sofa, which was bought after weeks of searching necessitated by the scale of the purchase and mine and Mark's disagreement over brown or black leather. I'd won that one and he'd admitted that it looked right when it finally arrived. We'd happily thrown popcorn at each other from either end as we watched *Gladiator* on DVD for the millionth time. Mark's favourite film. A happy memory with him. I grab hold of it and savour it.

We used to be happy. Our happiness seems to have eroded too slowly to notice until I woke up one morning and that became the day I discovered I'd lost him to another. I blame myself. Of course I do, I'm a woman. Clearly I've done something wrong. I nagged too much. I didn't sound interested enough when you droned on about tax-exemption clauses or year-end workload. I wasn't ready with a hot meal and a glass of red when you returned from that horrendous business trip to Hamburg. I didn't have enough sex with you. I put on weight after having the kids. I didn't put a ribbon in my hair or even try to make myself attractive for you. I put the kids first. It's all my fault, of course. I forced you to go elsewhere with my terrible behaviour. You complete and utter bastard.

Twenty years, I remind myself. We will have been together twenty years this year. In fact, of course, it was twenty years to the day on my birthday. I get down on my knees in front of the built-in cupboard in the alcove and pull open the doors. A clutch of DVDs fall out, clearly having been crammed in there by one of the kids… or more likely me. I reach to the back of the top shelf and start pulling out photo albums, all in different shapes and sizes. All recording experiences pre-2000 at a guess, at which point photographic opportunities were confined to digital cameras, destined never to see the light of day. That is until Facebook and Instagram appeared, allowing us to expose our finest moments to a raft of strangers out of the home whilst never taking the time to print them out and enjoy them in the home.

I love photo albums. Well, I used to when I had the time. I was the person who would keep tickets and invites and sweet wrappers, anything that recorded a significant event in my life. In that cupboard were albums from parties and holidays and Christmases gone by and of course endless photos of both Ellie and George's early years.

I seek out a slightly dog-eared black leather album and find my favourite photo of them. They are both grinning into the camera from a bubble bath with foam Mohicans on their heads. Ellie must have been about five and George three. Mark had taken the picture before George stood up and splatted a dollop of foam on his head. I styled it into two little horns, which George thought was the funniest thing ever. Mark sat on the bathroom floor in his suit with crackling bath foam in his hair, the kids laughing hysterically and pointing. What a moment. What a once-in-a-lifetime, bursting-with-joy moment.

I tuck the photo away quickly. It's too hard to see that this perfection once existed in our family. We got it so right. Where did it all go so wrong?

I pull out another album. A big thick cream one that has yellowed slightly but is still proudly labelled 'Summer 1996'.

I can practically hear Baddiel & Skinner and The Lightning Seeds singing 'Three Lions' as I flick through the early pages and catch sight of our Euro 96 celebrations in the clubs and bars of Corfu. There's a great picture of Karen and me somewhere, holding up an enormous England flag on the beach. A few pages later and I find it. I've always thought it was the best ever picture of me. I look frigging amazing! My hair is all blonde and halfway down my back. My legs, oh my legs, I would die for legs like that now. (Well, I don't actually have to now, I guess.) All tanned and slim but shapely. I actually have ankles, look at that. And I'm wearing shorts. I haven't worn shorts, since, well, probably 1996. Proper shorts, not mum shorts that finish barely above the knee. These were short shorts that you have to be brazen, an Olympian, unconscious or very young to wear. I look so happy. We'd just beat Holland 4–1, and I was totally in love with Teddy Sheringham who'd scored twice. I liked the small eyes with a side-parting look (which is slightly worrying as that is what my dad looks like in pictures of him in his twenties).

They were the easiest three weeks of my tour rep career, I remember. All we had to do was find a bar playing the footie, herd our charges in that direction at the appropriate time, then lead the singing of 'Three Lions', and all would agree that they'd had the best night of their entire lives.

I flick to the end of the album and quickly find the entries recording my epic birthday. A photocopied invite is inserted behind sticky back plastic.

COME TO JENNY'S
HUSH HUSH
DON'T TELL ANYONE
SECRET BIRTHDAY PARTY
1AM ON BATARIA BEACH, JUNE 26TH SEPTEMBER 1996
Come dressed for anything!!!

The invite preceded a plethora of out-of-focus, slightly faded photos that had been taken using a dozen or so disposable cameras.

You don't get photos like these any more. They'd be classed as rejects in this digital age. Drunkenly composed, a chaotic mix of arms and legs and squashed-up gurning faces. They capture a feeling of uninhibited joy where no one cared how the picture would turn out. Not like today's self-conscious selfies where the pout, the angle of the eyebrow, the positioning of the cleavage are all carefully posed and predictable. Selfies are not about how the moment feels but a record of how good one looks in that moment.

I reach for my phone and flick through the music until I find it. In my opinion one of the best songs ever written. It's another Oasis one but, you know, it was the nineties. You couldn't move for them. I listen to Liam Gallagher as he belts out the lyrics to 'Champagne Supernova'. We danced on that beach and sang this song to the sunrise.

There I am. I point at one of the last few shots as though I'm showing them to an imaginary friend. Riding high on the shoulders of my colleagues, arms raised high in the air, a glimpse of an early-morning sunrise on the horizon. It has the look of a festival, what with all the hands pumping the air, but it was my birthday. That was me in the middle of all that joy. That was me twenty years ago. What happened to that girl, I wonder. I'm not sure I'm recognisable from that girl who put all her efforts into having fun and enjoying life. Where did she go? I suspect she was slowly crushed out by responsibility and the slow creep of maturity. And now I am all that is left. I wish I had fought for her, stuck up for her, let her carry on her existence in this world. I think she may have lived this life so much better.

Chapter Fifteen

'How many do you reckon you'll get?' asks Maureen as soon as I enter her room the next day. I've arrived at work an hour early to see how my invalid friend is.

'Get for what?' I ask. 'This afternoon's armchair aerobics?'

'Your funeral.'

I gasp. I was all good with the practical, composed approach yesterday, but this?

'Jesus, Maureen, really! I can't worry about that.'

'Well, I do,' she replies. 'In fact your situation has made me think about it a lot so I've been writing a list of who might come to my own.'

'Really?'

'Yes. It's a good job I'm still writing to all the Pearson clan. They'll boost the numbers,' she says, looking thoughtfully at a piece of paper.

'You're only writing to them to make sure they come to your funeral?'

She thinks for a moment then nods.

'Pretty much,' she admits. 'Dorothy is a bit of a pain in the ass really but she still drives so I know she will be able to bring a few. And she's a nosy old cow so she won't be able to resist a good gawp at a funeral.'

The wind is totally out of what shred of sails I had left. I plump myself down on the edge of her bed.

'I reckon about fifty,' she continues. 'If Rod and Barbara don't pop their clogs before I do. If they go that knocks out the whole Bertram side of the family, which could be a crucial half-dozen.'

I really cannot think of any response to this.

'Fifty would be about right. Faye Wilton only got about twenty-five, it was terribly embarrassing. I must be able to get more than that.'

'Can we talk about something else?' I ask.

'Of course,' she says. 'Sorry, didn't mean to upset you. But these things do prey on your mind when…'

She stops mid-sentence, presumably when she sees the look on my face. We study each other for a moment. Funerals hadn't even entered my mind but they're well and truly there now.

Maureen puts down the piece of paper she has been staring at on the desk on wheels in front of her. 'Shall we leave funerals for another day?'

I nod.

'But you will have to—'

'Stop!'

I wanted Maureen's directness. I wanted her ability to help me pick my own path through this. It's mostly why I chose to tell her. But funerals, really?

'Have you told Mark?' she asks.

'About what?' I cough and draw myself up. I'll put funerals away somewhere for now to distress myself over when I have room.

'Everything,' she says, sounding slightly exasperated that I'm so complicated.

'No,' I reply firmly. 'And I'm not going to.'

'What?'

Now it's Maureen's turn to look taken aback.

'I'm not telling him I have cancer or that I know he's being unfaithful,' I declare.

She falls back in her chair, funeral popularity numbers forgotten.

'You have to tell him, Jenny.'

'Why?'

'Because he's your husband.'

'No, he's not, he's a two-timing little shit.'

'Well, he's that as well, but he is still your husband.'

'He gave up all rights to expect me to treat him like my husband the moment I caught him having sex with another woman.'

'You can't keep a secret like this from him. He has a right to know.'

'What, like I have a right to know if he's decided our marriage is over and he's gone elsewhere? He has no rights as far as I'm concerned.'

'But what if he finds out from someone else?'

'I'm not telling anyone apart from you.'

Maureen stares at me. It's not often she's speechless but I can tell she's struggling just at this minute.

'Parents? Friends? What about your children? You're being ridiculous, Jenny. Are you in denial? You did walk into this room and tell me you have cancer yesterday, didn't you? Because if you haven't then I have broken my arm for nothing.'

'I thought you'd just sprained it?'

'Broken, sprained, what's the difference when you're talking utter gibberish? You have to tell people, Jenny, if you really do have cancer. Or is that it?' she says, her eyes narrowing. 'Do you not have it at all and this is all a wicked plan to get me to hand over my savings for some bogus life-saving surgery and then you'll disappear off to Australia with all my money? Is that what you're up to? I have to say that's actually quite ingenious.'

'No!' I exclaim. 'Of course not. I really do have cancer.'

'Really?'

'Yes, I have cancer,' I shout at her. How dare she question my morals when I have a terminal disease?

'Well, you're not acting much like it,' she replies.

'What do you mean, not acting like I have cancer? What am I supposed to do? Roll around on the floor wailing? Attach a sign to my head with a skull and crossbones on? Dress in muted colours?'

'You don't look good in yellow actually,' interrupts Maureen, nodding at my lemon-yellow wool sweater. 'Makes you look awfully pale.'

'I have cancer, Maureen, which is probably why I look pale.'

'No.' She shakes her head. 'It's never suited you. You should steer clear of pastels.'

I blow my cheeks out. Maybe Maureen isn't the right person to be confiding in.

'Look,' I say. 'My mother, well, I've told you about my mother, haven't I? I know this sounds awful but me getting cancer would be just another way I have failed her. I'm not the daughter she wanted. I didn't turn into the professional like my brother did. In fact the only thing I think she has ever been proud of me for is marrying Mark and look how that's turning out. She wouldn't support me. She wouldn't be there for me like a mother should. All it would mean to her would be the inconvenience of losing her babysitter for Dad,' I add bitterly.

'And I can't tell Dad,' I say when Maureen doesn't speak. 'He can't process it. It would just add to his confusion.'

'That's very sad,' mutters Maureen. 'The poor man.'

'And as for my friends,' I continue, starting to get worked up. 'I've stupidly let the good ones slip through my fingers.' The photos from last night flash before my eyes, cluttered with friendships dropped purely because of geography and time. 'They're far away where they can't do anything and I don't want to talk to them over the phone. The ones who are left, well, let's just say I can't see any of them being the rock I need right now.

'But it's okay,' I continue. 'This is good. Really it is. I realised last night I don't want to tell anyone, not until I have to. I don't want to be that person. Why would I want to be the person with cancer? That's a terrible person to be. I can't bear the thought of the pity or the sympathy or, worse, people standing in front of me totally tongue-tied or saying something totally stupid that I have to somehow respond to.'

'You mean like some miserable cow telling you to be positive, it will all be okay?' offers Maureen.

'Yes, that's it exactly,' I cry. 'I can't stand the thought of someone telling me to be positive. I can't stand the idea of anyone trying to give me advice. Who do they think they are? You can't give someone advice when you have never felt how it feels to be told you are dying, can you?' I demand.

'No, absolutely,' agrees Maureen.

'I'm just not putting myself in that position, not yet. I've decided I want to be me, Maureen, until I have no choice and I have to become the cancer version of me.'

Maureen is nodding slowly. She's getting it, I think. I need her to get it. I need her to reassure me that I'm not a lunatic and this actually makes sense. Doesn't it? To be perfectly honest, when I was lying in bed at three o'clock in the morning wide awake, listening to the creaks and moans of the house, I was questioning my sanity. But when I woke up it was as clear as day to me. This is the only way I can deal with it.

'I understand,' she says softly.

'Brilliant.' I heave a sigh of relief. Making decisions makes me feel better. I feel back in control.

'And I have decided something else,' I say, trying to sound confident. 'I don't want to be this me,' I say, waving my hands disparagingly over my lemon-clad body.

'You want to be someone else?'

'Yes – well, no.'

Maureen looks confused now.

'I want to be the old me,' I clarify. 'The 1996 me, to be precise.'

'Right,' she says, although clearly she has no idea what I'm talking about.

'I figure actually that if I'm not going to be cancer me then I might as well choose to be the best me and the best me was 1996 me. I'm going back to 1996, Maureen, to be that person again. Because that's when I was happiest. That's when I was really living. It makes sense, doesn't it?'

I look at her expectantly.

Maureen's mouth is now hanging open. I've thrown too much at her this morning. She'll think she had too much sherry last night and this is all some bizarre dream. She has nothing in her to respond. What do you say to a woman who yesterday told you she has cancer and her husband is having an affair and today announces she wants to be twenty-five again?

'How utterly marvellous,' she eventually responds.

Chapter Sixteen

Surprisingly, it's a harder task to convince Doctor Death of my 'treatment plan'.

The hospital left a message on the answerphone yesterday to confirm a further appointment this afternoon. It feels like I've lived a whole lifetime since I was last in that soulless office only two days ago. I'm curiously proud of where I've got to in my head. I feel I'm in control, I feel I have a plan and that's soothing, comforting.

Until the doctor walks in with his dose of reality.

He sits down in front of me with a warm smile.

'Are we just waiting for your husband?' he enquires, flicking through papers in my file.

'No,' I reply. 'He's not coming.'

His eyes flick up to look at me, his warm smile gone.

'Oh dear,' he says. 'I thought he was coming with you this time.'

'Well, no,' I say, starting to feel uncomfortable. 'He's not.'

'Have you told him?'

I look away, for some reason feeling like a schoolgirl being told off by the headmaster.

'No.'

'I think you would find it really helpful to have someone to support you. To come with you when you see me so you both understand what is going on.'

'Well, I would find it helpful too.' My defiant schoolgirl side is kicking in. 'However, since I found out about his affair I'm not sure he's the kind of support I need. So it's not my fault,' I add, which is something I haven't felt compelled to add to any conversation since attending South Moor Comprehensive.

'Oh,' he says, putting the papers down and leaning back in his chair. 'Well, I'm very sorry to hear that. Is there someone else who you can call on?'

'I've told the people I need to,' I say sharply, not wanting to discuss this any longer.

'There are other people you can talk to,' he says, reaching into a drawer and pulling out a leaflet. 'You don't need to feel alone,' he adds, pushing it towards me.

I look down and read the title, 'WE NEED TO TALK ABOUT CANCER'. I stare at the word 'CANCER' and I'm felled. I'm down for a moment, unable to get up again. Suffocated by its meaning. I push the leaflet back towards him.

'I have people I can talk to,' I try to say with conviction. 'I am not alone.'

'Good, good,' he nods.

I pray for him to put the leaflet away. I can't look at that word throughout our consultation, it's blinding me. He doesn't, so I discreetly turn it over whilst he consults my notes again.

'So do you want me to repeat what I told you on Wednesday?' he asks. 'So you are absolutely clear.'

'I think I've got it,' I swallow. 'I have inoperable cancer of the cervix and bowel. I should have chemo to try and reduce it, which may prolong my life, but it is extremely unlikely I will be cured. A guess at my time left would be eighteen months to two years.'

He doesn't confirm my diagnosis, just studies me. He's trying to weigh me up. The woman with the cheating husband, who has cancer and who is speaking quite dispassionately about her prognosis. Is she for real, he is thinking. Suddenly he breaks out of his internal thoughts and leans forward again.

'That's about the long and short of it, yes. So today I wanted to take you through your different options on chemotherapy, of which there are a few so it might be an idea to take notes.'

'I don't want chemo,' I say.

He studies me again.

'That's a very big decision,' he says, taking his glasses off and rubbing his eyes.

'I know,' I say.

'May I ask why you have come to this conclusion?'

'I want to be me, at least for a bit longer,' I say.

I don't add that I don't actually want to be me, I want to be 1996 me, for fear he might rub his eyes out with confusion.

'The minute I start treatment I wave goodbye to me. My life is over. I've decided for the time being I'd like to keep living. Well, live even better in fact, knowing my time is limited. Until of course I have no choice.'

I feel as if I'm in a job interview. As if I'm trying to impress a prospective employer of my ability to make decisions about my own life. I rub my hands together nervously. I'm not sure what else I can say. Neither, apparently, is he. I suspect he's thinking he's not sure yet that I'm up to the task.

'Are you sure that this isn't a reaction to the situation with your husband?' he asks. 'I think you need to think very carefully about whether that is clouding your judgement here.'

I do actually consider what he is saying. Would I make a different decision if I was in a happy marriage, if I hadn't found Mark having sex in his office? The answer is, I don't know. Because that isn't my situation. The doc is right, if Mark was beside me now I could be saying something entirely different, but I would be making decisions based on the false premise that I had a faithful husband. I can't think about other possibilities because they would be lies. I can only make decisions based on what I know to be true.

'I have to factor my husband out of the decision-making process,' I say bluntly. 'What else can I do?'

'You have children?' the doc asks.

'Yes,' I nod and swallow hard. He's going to fell me again, I can feel it coming.

'Do you think this decision is the best for them?'

I start nodding vigorously because if I don't I might falter.

'I want to be their mum for a while longer. *Just* their mum.'

I've thought about nothing else to be honest. I ended up taking the picture of them in the bath to bed and tucking it under my pillow. Never have they needed a mother more. More than when they were five and three. And I don't mean a dying mother: they need a real mother. That's what I am going to be, whilst I still can. Whilst I still have the chance to have some influence.

The doctor nods. I'm getting to him. This could be within my grasp. What else can I tell him to convince him?

'I used to be a holiday tour rep,' I blurt out. Instant bewilderment crosses his face again. 'It was my job to make sure people had the time of their lives for however long they were with us.' Still bewilderment. 'That's all I want to do,' I plead. 'Have the time of my life however long I'm with us.'

He takes a long sigh. Easier to treat me than not to treat me. He's not trained to do nothing. This is a big ask.

'Okay,' he says slowly. I smile. 'But I'd feel much happier if you got some counselling. I need to know you are talking this through with at least someone.'

'Oh, I am,' I say.

'You have a counsellor?'

'Not exactly. A very old friend.' This makes me smile. Maureen would kill me if she heard me describe her as that – I must remember to tell her.

'I'd prefer it if you were also talking to a professional.'

I screw my nose up. The thought of sitting in an airless room every week talking about my death with a well-meaning stranger makes me want to vomit. Give me Maureen and her funeral guest list any day.

I reach out and take the leaflet still sitting between us.

'Perhaps I'll try someone in here,' I say and stuff it in my handbag, never to be seen again.

'Good,' he nods. 'That's good. And I think I'd better see you again in a couple of weeks, just to make sure you haven't changed your mind.'

'Okay,' I say. I suppose this is fair enough. He is casting what appears to him to be a lunatic with cancer out on to the streets. There is something, though, that I hope he can help me with in the meantime. 'I know I'm not having chemo but is there anything you can do to help with the pain?' I ask.

'Are you in pain?' he says.

'Sometimes, yes.'

I know I haven't mentioned pain before now. Not mentioned the physical impact of my illness apart from the stunning weight loss which has taken me back to my 1996 body. That's because I've been trying to ignore it. Not that I really can. Sometimes it's okay, sometimes it's just a dull ache, and then other times it's excruciating. It tears through me like labour pains and I hide myself away and weep into my pillow. I don't want pain reminding me that I have cancer. And of course my energy levels are down, but I'm going to bed early and taking it easy. I've not mentioned the pain before because it's tedious and I don't want it in my brain.

'Right,' he says, turning to his computer. 'Let's see if we can get you in with the pain specialist.'

'There are drugs for the pain then?'

'Oh yes,' he nods. 'You haven't a problem with those type of drugs then?' he asks.

'Absolutely not.'

He nods at me and says no more. I wonder what he's thinking. Am I just another person on death row to him or am I the one with the cheating husband who is refusing treatment? Is that how he'll discuss me with his colleagues later? I'm neither, I think. I'm Jenny. Jenny Sutton. Walking out of here as 1996 Jenny and, with any luck, a pocket full of pain-crushing drugs. Time to start living.

Chapter Seventeen

'I'm getting a divorce,' I eventually tell Dominic the hairdresser. I've sat there for two and a half hours and we've been through the usual subjects such as holidays, reality TV, music and the latest diet fads. There is nothing left in common to cover unless we start to get personal.

I guess I started it really. I asked him which pubs and bars he frequented in an effort to appear in the know about the local nightlife. He said that he and his boyfriend mainly went to restaurants or friends' houses, as the gay scene was pretty dire. And there we have it: we'd broken the seal. His sexual orientation was out (not that I'd ever been in doubt, given his over the top admiration of my suede skirt). So it was open season on personal questions as we faced the next hour together whilst he completed my hair extensions.

'I knew it,' he gasped, the minute I said the 'D' word. 'Women of your age, if you don't mind me saying, only come in here for a new look when divorce is on the cards. Are you a before or after?'

'A what?'

'A before or after? A *before* is contemplating an affair so is all out with the new hair and the new diet and the new clothes in the hope they can get in his knickers. An *after* is the one whose hubby has left them and they realise they need to start making an effort again or else they are on the scrap heap. Either way, new hair, new life. They always go together. Always.'

I nod at him in the mirror as he waves a comb enthusiastically at my reflection. I try not to dwell on the word 'life' in his conclusion.

'So I assume you are an *after* given that divorce is already on the cards? If you don't mind me asking, of course.'

'No,' I say, shaking my head. And I didn't. Actually, talking about my fictitious divorce was blessed relief. 'I don't mind. He had an affair with someone at work.'

'Classic,' says Dominic, delving into the back of my head. 'How long had you been together?'

'Since 1996,' I reply. His head pops round from behind me and looks at me in the mirror, then looks back down at the picture leaning against the hairdryer. There is Geri Halliwell from the Spice Girls in all her glory performing at the Brits in her Union Jack dress, blue knickers available for all to see.

'1996?' he asks.

'Yes.' I nod.

He stands up straight, his mouth slightly open, a strand of long auburn hair waving in mid-air.

'Wow,' he says eventually. 'So… er, did you meet at a Spice Girls concert or something?'

I laugh. The thought of Mark at a Spice Girls concert is laughable.

'No.'

'You were fans though, right?'

I can see Dominic trying to work out what's going on here. A middle-aged woman walking into a hairdressers to ask for a nineties Ginger-Spice-inspired haircut is odd to say the least, but roll a divorce into that, and something is definitely weird.

'I was a fan. He kind of was,' I explain. I lean forward and pick up the photo printed from the internet. 'This was the Spice Girls at the 1997 BRIT Awards.'

'I know,' says Dominic. 'I've seen it on YouTube, like, a million times.'

'We watched it live on the TV,' I tell him. 'Me and my husband. Well, he was just my boyfriend then. I thought she looked amazing. I had never seen anything like it, she had such balls.'

'Not in those pants she didn't,' says Dominic, returning to fiddle with the back of my head. 'You couldn't smuggle a peanut into them.'

'Geri made me proud to be ginger. I'd been born ginger but ever since my teens I'd dyed it blonde because, well, you would, wouldn't you?'

'Of course you would.'

'I figured I'd go back to my natural hair colour just like hers and then have that swish of blonde across the front,' I say, running my finger across the yellow streak in the picture. 'I didn't tell Mark – I thought he wouldn't like it. Gentlemen prefer blondes and all that. But he loved it. I mean, really loved it.'

I feel myself blushing at the memory of what happened when I got home with my new hair.

'Aaaaaah,' says Dominic, emerging from behind me again. 'I get it. This is a "Fuck you, cheating bastard husband, I'm going to remind you what you are missing" haircut.'

'Something like that,' I say.

Though it wasn't really. When Dominic put it like that it seemed petty and I didn't have time for petty any more. Petty was pointless. Petty was too small a word for my life now. I wanted to live in the big part of life, not the small, vague, quiet, safe sections I seemed to have frequented recently. A halfway-house attempt at an image change felt unsatisfying, weak, a waste of time. My actions needed to be big and bold and full of life and vigour. Hence there was no question of an inch off here and there and a change to a slightly different shade of blonde. Hence it was Spice Girls hair or nothing, 1996 hair or nothing. And it wasn't about some weird revenge on Mark, it was about living life in a bigger, bolder, brighter way than I had done for a very long time.

'He asked me to marry him,' I tell Dominic.

'I'm sorry,' he says, glancing sideways at me, hands poised an inch above my head.

'He asked me to marry him the night Geri Halliwell stood on the stage in a Union Jack at the BRIT Awards.'

'Had he planned it?'

'No. We'd had a bit to drink and when the show finished I was messing around, you know, pretending to be Geri. I even went and grabbed an England flag left over from the World Cup and tied it round me and started singing "Wannabe".'

Dominic instantly starts singing the lyrics into his comb.

'Mark pretended to be Posh Spice,' I told him after he'd done a couple of lines. 'You know, sticking his nose in the air and strutting.'

'How she bagged David Beckham I have no idea,' commented Dominic.

'We were crying with laughter.' I stop as the tears spring to my eyes. 'Then he just dropped to his knees in the middle of the living room, threw his arms open wide and said, "We have got to get married. Will you marry me, Jenny?"'

Dominic gasps, his hand flying to his mouth as though he's about to cry.

'What did you say?' he asks me.

'Yes, of course. A thousand times yes.' I can feel my face falling. I can feel my heart falling.

'Bloody hell!' says Dominic, appearing at the side of my face this time. 'Do you know what this reminds me of?'

'A troll?' I ask, looking at my reflection.

'No way! This is looking awesome,' he says, waving his hand over my head as though casting a spell. 'No, it reminds me of when I got a tattoo of David Beckham.'

'David Beckham?'

'Oh yeah, I'm obsessed with him and of course his hair.'

'But a *tattoo*?'

'Just a small one on my thigh. So very discreet.'

'Not sure you could ever class a tattoo of David Beckham as discreet.'

'It was a present to myself on my thirtieth birthday but I didn't tell Andrew. I thought it would be a nice surprise.'

'Was it?'

'No, he hated it. He said I had to have a tattoo of him to make up for it.'

'Did you?'

'Good God, no! He's bald. I told him it would look like I had a Weeble on my leg. We nearly broke up.'

'I'm not surprised if you told him he looked like a Weeble.'

'Oh, I'm always calling him a Weeble, especially when I'm cross with him. Like this morning, he deliberately took over half an hour in the bathroom when he knew I had to be in here early. Hence I look a shambles.'

He doesn't. He's neat as a pin in a tight-fitting T-shirt tucked into pristine jeans and box-fresh trainers peeping out at the floor.

'I said as he came out, "How long does it take to comb Weeble hair?"'

'I bet he didn't like that.'

'Oh, it's water off a duck's back with him. He'll come home tonight having forgotten all about it and wonder why I'm still in a strop. You have to be proper nasty to him or else it doesn't get through at all. It's exhausting. Makes him really hard to live with.'

'So why do you then?'

He stops and stares at my reflection, then shrugs and carries on weaving into the top of my hair.

'Because I love the flippin' Weeble head, that's why,' he says without making eye contact. As though he's admitting a failing and is embarrassed about it. Very different to the open way he grumped and complained about his partner's weaknesses moments earlier.

I wonder why we are often quick to explain to anyone who will listen the failings of our nearest and dearest. What mistakes they have made, how they have let us down in some small way, what they have done that has clashed with our world view and caused discord. And yet we rarely readily declare our warmth of feeling when we are reminded of the things that attracted us to them in the first place.

I look in the mirror and can see me and Mark messing around in that sitting room nearly two decades ago, laughing ourselves silly then agreeing to spend the rest of our lives together. Our life together fast-forwards to now as I see the petty disagreements and differences swallowing up and crushing the moments spent dancing and singing our way through life.

Killing them like cancer.

Chapter Eighteen

I can sense something is wrong before I've even entered the house. It's late Saturday afternoon. It's a warm sunny day. I can hear birds tweeting. The hanging basket I bought is still alive – a miracle, seeing as I have a knack of forgetting to water plants, forcing ourselves and our neighbours to watch the slow miserable death of many a pot plant decorating our garden. All should be well on the home front but the door is open. Unusual to say the least. As with all our neighbours, we tend to barricade ourselves in, suspicious of inviting casual callers, careful not to appear too welcoming. But not today. Today the shiny black painted door with the matt-silver door knocker is slung wide open, ready for any spontaneous passerby to pop in.

'Hello,' I shout as I step into the hall. It crosses my mind we might have been burgled. There might even be a hooded robber rifling through my cupboards as we speak.

'Mum,' shouts George from somewhere.

He sounds agitated but then he often sounds agitated.

I dash into the kitchen to check he's not tied to a chair but he is sitting on the table, head bent low. He looks up at me, tear stains down his face.

'What on earth has happened?' I say, rushing over and grabbing his shoulders.

'It's Betsy,' he moans. 'She's gone. Got out. She never stays out. N-n-n-n-never. I think she might have been r-r-r-run over.'

He starts proper crying now. Sobbing, his shoulders heaving up and down.

'Shhhhh,' I say, rubbing his back. 'Shhhhh. We'll find her. You just calm down and we'll find her.'

'We won't,' he sobs. 'She's dead, I know she's dead.'

My heart contracts. 'You don't know that,' I say desperately, putting my arms around him. We rock slowly together as I wait for the sobs to die down so I can get out of him exactly what has happened.

'Why's the front door wide open?' says Mark, bursting in through the kitchen door behind me.

'Betsy might be run over,' gasps George, his head flying up from my shoulder.

'What!' I hear Ellie exclaim. She must have followed Mark in. 'Are you serious? Oh my God, Mother, what have you done to your hair?' she cries as I turn to face her and she catches sight of my new look.

'Of course I'm serious,' says George, wiping his sleeve across his nose. He glances at my hair but my change in appearance is nothing compared to the disappearance of his beloved dog.

'She got out,' I add. 'And she's not come back. George is very worried she might have been run over.'

Both Mark and Ellie are now staring at me, Ellie in horror. I'm not sure if this is in response to my hair or the disappearance of Betsy. Mark is frowning, which is actually pretty much his normal face in regards to me.

'We don't know she's actually been run over yet,' I say. 'She might just have got lost, or stuck somewhere.' Inwardly I curse the fact that I never got round to microchipping her. That would have been some reassurance at least but somehow it never got to the top of the to-do list.

'Let's all go out and look for her,' I say.

'But I've looked everywhere,' wails George. 'I've been out for two hours, going up and down every road on the estate. I can't find her anywhere. I know she's been run over, I just know it, and it's all my fault.'

'It's not your fault, darling,' I tell him. 'How can it be your fault?'

'It *is* his fault if he let her out,' says Ellie.

'You can't say that,' I tell her, looking to Mark to get involved in this family trauma rather than me flailing around for the right words and actions on my own.

He's looking at his phone. Actually looking at his phone. We are dealing with the possible death of the family pet here and he is looking at his damn phone.

'Mark!' I cry.

'What?' he says, flipping his head up in surprise.

'Do something?' I ask, my eyes wide in wonder. I watch as he glances around and it finally triggers that there is a crisis going on right under his nose.

'Come on, guys,' he says, putting an arm around Ellie's shoulders. 'She'll be back,' he shrugs.

'But it's Betsy,' mutters Ellie as an actual tear falls down her face. This is Ellie, who normally reserves genuine feelings for ludicrously expensive brand names I have never heard of. This is a surprising reaction.

Mark wraps her in a bear hug.

'Look, if the worst comes to the worst, we could get a puppy,' he says into her neck.

'Really?' she exclaims, pulling away and staring at him, her eyes wide in delight.

'What!' I shriek.

George starts shaking his head.

'Like a Labrador or something,' Mark blunders on.

'Phoebe has a black Labrador,' Ellie says excitedly. 'Seriously cool, Dad, good choice.'

They high five. Yes, they actually high five.

'I was thinking more of a blonde one though,' says Mark, oblivious to the horrified stares from myself and George. 'Don't you think they look nicer?'

He looks at me. I have no idea how to arrange my face, never mind what to say, so shocking is the conversation between my husband and my daughter.

'I think you mean golden,' I eventually say through gritted teeth. 'Not blonde. You don't call them blonde Labradors.'

'Whatever,' he shrugs. 'I just prefer the blonde... I mean, golden ones, that's all.'

I literally cannot speak. I look over at George. His chin is down in his chest. I squeeze his hand.

'Betsy's not dead yet,' I say firmly. I try to control my breathing as the anger surges up inside me. 'What we are going to do is we are *all* going to go out and look for her.'

I glare at Mark and Ellie, daring them to protest. Daring them to utter another word about their way-too-hasty replacing of our beloved Betsy.

'And we'll put missing posters up,' I say to George. 'Someone will have seen her. We will find her. Betsy is still with us, I know she is. We won't give up on her yet.'

★

'Is everything all right?'

I hadn't heard Mark come into the bedroom. I am sitting on the bed with my back to the door, head in my hands. We'd all been out pounding the streets and putting pictures of Betsy on as many lamp posts as we thought we could get away with. There is still no sign but I am remaining optimistic. I have to. We can't lose Betsy. Not now. I can't cope with loss now. But I am shattered. My body was screaming at me that I wasn't fit for such exertion, which I had ignored until we arrived home, then crawled upstairs and collapsed on the bed.

But as soon as I hear Mark speak I rear up. And without warning a voice in my head shrieks, 'Tell him. Tell him now.'

Tell him what, I want to scream back. I know you're shagging someone and by the way, I have terminal cancer. I roll both facts around in my head. No, not ready, still not ready. We agreed, I tell my cancer self. We agreed not to let you out yet.

Instead I tell him about my feet.

'My feet are bloody killing me,' I say. 'I just needed to get these shoes off.'

'Right,' he nods.

He stands in the doorway just looking at me. He never stands still to look at me. Never. He's still not mentioned my hair. Is it conjuring up memories of happier times or can't he put into words how stupid I look? I watch as he casts his eyes awkwardly around the room as though building up to say something. He coughs politely, opens his mouth and then shuts it again. He walks around the bed and sits next to me.

Again, not normal. This is not normal bedroom behaviour in our household. We move about that room independently, coming and going at different speeds and times, rarely engaging, rarely interacting. I go to bed at ten; he rarely comes up before eleven thirty. He gets up and washes before seven, leaving me to wallow until after eight, rising to make sure the kids have left for school. If we had a speeded-up video cam record of our movements about that room it would look like we never touched or spoke to each other.

Mark reaches over and picks up my hand. Our thighs are touching on the side of the bed. I look at him. Has my transformation actually made a positive impact? Then it hits me like a ton of manure what is coming. He isn't holding my hand to tell me that now I look like Ginger Spice he is going to fall back in love with me. He is about to confess his affair. I can see it coming like a tidal wave. He is about to shatter our family, he is about to leave me. This is that moment when my life falls apart – though unbeknown to him it is already in tatters.

I can't bear it. I can't bear to give him his moment. This isn't his time to be the breaker of bad news. If anyone is breaking bad news around here it is damn well going to be me. I have to think fast.

'I've downloaded *Jerry Maguire* on Amazon,' I say quickly.

'What?'

'I've downloaded *Jerry Maguire* on Amazon. For us to watch tonight.'

'Jenny, really, I...'

'We have to watch it tonight,' I say, getting up, hoping distance will destroy his momentum. 'We *must* watch it tonight.'

'Why?'

'Because... because I already downloaded it and I think you only get twenty-four hours to watch it so if we don't watch it tonight it will be a waste of money.'

'I've told you about not downloading stuff until you're sure you're going to be able to watch it.'

'But I am sure. What's there to stop us?'

He stares back at me. If anyone can stop a husband leaving a wife it's Tom Cruise, surely. On second thoughts, I might have really screwed this up.

'The kids are going to watch it with us,' I lie.

'Really?'

'Yep,' I nod. 'They're both really looking forward to watching *Jerry Maguire* with us. And we really should spend time together tonight as everyone is so upset about Betsy being missing.'

He's looking totally confused now. Unsurprising really. He planned to share his infidelity and instead he's come home to find his wife has been replaced by a Spice Girl, the dog has run off and his teenage children allegedly want to spend Saturday night in with him, watching Tom Cruise get stressed. Things are certainly unusual around here.

'I'll go and get the popcorn on, shall I?' I head for the door.

'Jenny?' I hear him say.

I'm forced to turn. I can't pretend I haven't heard him. I feel like I'm about to open a door I had temporarily barricaded.

'I know what you're going to say,' I tell him, walking forward and putting my arms around him.

'You do?' he says, looking up at me, a very pained expression on his face.

'Yes,' I nod. 'You complete me too.'

I smile and squeeze him then turn around and stride for the door. Outside I breathe.

Chapter Nineteen

'Oh my lord,' gasps Maureen. 'Do you know who you remind me of?'

'Who?'

'Priscilla Presley.'

The images of Priscilla that pop up in my mind are not favourable. Plastic fixed features, pale face and big hair too dark for her complexion. A caricature, not a person. I dash towards Maureen's full-length mirror on the front of her wardrobe and look at myself. Am I a laughing stock?

'We got married on the same day, you know,' says Maureen.

'Really?' I say, turning to her in astonishment. This was a new fact.

She nods. 'It was good publicity.' She laughs and shakes her head. 'I wore a lot of heavy black eyeliner with my white dress because that's what you did in those days and that's what Priscilla did. And Ray wore a tuxedo, just like Elvis.'

'Wow, you must have been quite a sight.'

'We were in the paper. Ray rang them to say we were having an Elvis wedding.'

'So you were the first couple in history to have an Elvis-themed wedding. *You* set the trend.'

She grins. 'We did feel the bee's knees. We got loads of attention and Ray got loads more bookings. We went to America after that and were on the road until it all started to go quiet. It was looking like we were going to have to pack up and come home. Then Elvis died, of course. What a blessing that was! We were turning bookings down for years after that, Ray was so busy. If Elvis hadn't have died, well, we'd have been back here living in a bungalow, no doubt.'

She shudders at the thought, then looks me up and down again. I've teamed my flamboyant hair with a black shift dress and some red platform shoes. A confident update of the nineties was my thinking. A woman of a certain age who hasn't given in to plain knits and supermarket jeans. A woman who wants to be noticed for all the right reasons.

'You look like you could kick some ass, lady,' she adds. 'Perfect for where we're going.' She grabs her stick and starts to pull herself up from her chair. 'I wasn't going to ask you, given your circumstances, but seeing you like this – well, I think you're ready.'

'Ready for what? Where are you going?'

'A funeral.'

Chapter Twenty

'No!'

'Why not?'

'Do you seriously need me to answer that?'

'Come on, it'll give you some ideas.'

'On what?'

'How you want yours to be.'

I'm tempted to just walk out. She's clearly lost it and if she cannot understand why it's a bad idea then I'm not explaining it to her.

'Come on,' she says, still struggling out of her chair. 'You're all dressed up with nowhere to go.'

I am wearing black, I suppose.

'No. No way!'

'But I'll have to go on my own if you don't come.'

'You were going on your own anyway, weren't you?'

'But it will be more fun if you were coming too.'

'It's a funeral, not a party.'

Maureen stops short and looks at me.

'A funeral should be a party,' she says seriously. 'It's a celebration of Emily's life.'

'I don't even know who Emily is,' I argue, raising my arms in protest.

'Well, she's dead so that doesn't matter.'

'But what about her family?'

'She only had a son and he was a mean piece of work, which is why we need to go. Make the numbers up. I'll just get my coat.' She hobbles towards the hooks next to the door.

'But how do I explain who I am?'

What am I saying? I won't need to explain who I am because I won't be going.

'We'll say you're my… my… partner,' she says with a smile.

'Partner! As in…'

'Lesbian, yes.'

Now I'm speechless. This is not happening.

'But don't you think…'

'You would be out of my league. Possibly now you've spruced yourself up but I was always a bit of a goer in my youth. How do you think I managed to pull the East Midlands' pre-eminent Elvis impersonator?'

She reaches for her coat and busies herself buttoning it up.

'I'm not coming,' I say.

She looks up at me. 'Do you want Mark in charge of your funeral?'

I stare back at her as my mind is instantly filled with a classy but sombre affair. Everyone in black, tradition far outweighing any shred of personality whatsoever. Where would *she* sit, I find myself thinking with a shudder. Discreetly at the back, or at his side, as a 'friend' who's stepped up to support him in his hour of need?

'No,' I answer quietly.

'Well, you'd better come with me then. Come and see what you don't want, at a funeral you have no attachment to, so you can leave clear instructions. Get it over with then you don't have to think about it again, knowing it's all in hand.'

I stare back at her. I really don't know what to say.

'Oh, for goodness' sake, it's only at the crem, we'll be in and out in half an hour. They don't mess about at those dos, you know.'

And that's how I find myself going to a stranger's funeral in order to plan my own.

Chapter Twenty-One

We naturally fall into silence as we approach the crematorium. Maureen has been wittering on about some nonsense in the dining room last night over rhubarb but I've barely listened. I've been trying to convince myself that she's right and going to a funeral, when probably the next one I will be going to is mine, is a good idea.

The signs directing us to the car park are branded with the local council's colours of purple and yellow. Fine for sending you to the recycling centre but somehow unsuitable on arrival at a funeral. Perhaps they share the same cost centre, entitled 'Disposal', I think. Easier to brand everything the same so we know it's all about getting rid of stuff, whether it's human beings or a conked-out fridge-freezer.

I park discreetly as far away as possible from the crematorium building. After all, I'm not really supposed to be here so should save the convenient spaces for those who've actually met the person whose funeral they're attending.

'Might as well have walked from home,' grumbles Maureen, opening her door and starting to haul herself out.

I jump out and dash round to help. We don't need another accident today. Not here. What would Nurse Hagrid say if I had to call an ambulance to a crematorium car park?

'Why don't you just cut out the middle man?' she'd bellow. 'Shove her straight into the furnace, why don't you?'

We begin the slow amble across the tarmac, Maureen clutching my arm. The sling has gone but I'm glad of the need for concern for her wellbeing. It forces me to look at the ground to check for any potential trip hazards rather than having to look up at the tall chimney looming over our heads.

'It's the small chapel,' announces Maureen as we approach the edge of the car park and are faced with yet another garish purple and yellow sign.

'Is that the Oval Chapel?' I ask when all I can see are arrows to either a 'Main Chapel' or an 'Oval Chapel'.

'Yes,' she says, heading left without even glancing at the sign. She knows where she is going. A sad sign of someone her age: insider knowledge of the geography of every crematorium within a ten-mile radius.

I hold back, staring at the sign. You want to be in the Main Chapel really, don't you? You want to be the sort of person where your funeral guests are proud to turn right at this sign, not shuffling off down the left-hand side path to be with the less popular crowd. The thought turns my stomach.

I dash to catch up with Maureen as she turns the corner, bringing into full view the 'modern' sixties-style municipal toilet block that is the city's crematorium. The geometric, functional lines strip away any shred of grandeur or tradition that surely such an event should demand. I could be entering my kids' school for parents' evening (actually, not enough litter bins) or taking them for swimming lessons or on my way to borrow a book. It smacks of community building in the worst possible way. It's functional. Immaculately tidy but still functional and sterile. This is bad. Really bad.

A woman walks towards us with a clipboard and pen as I try to find something comforting to look at.

'We are here for Emily Stonehouse,' Maureen tells her. The woman checks something at the top of her pad then flips the paper over and looks back up.

'Maureen Merryweather,' Maureen tells her.

'And your name?' the woman asks me.

'Oh, I, er, I don't, I didn't…'

'Jenny Sutton,' interrupts Maureen. 'She's new at this,' she tells the lady and shuffles forward. 'Come on, let's make sure we get a decent seat,' she says over her shoulder.

'I'm so sorry for your loss,' the lady says to me with a fixed sympathetic smile.

'Thank you,' is all I can mutter before skirting around her to follow Maureen.

The chapel is small. I quickly count up the seats. There are four seats on either side of a short aisle and there are one, two, three, four, five rows. So how many is that? My brain freezes. How do I work that out? So it must be four times five, which is twenty, plus four times five, which is another twenty, so that's forty, right? I'm individually counting the seats to check my maths when I notice Maureen heading off to sit near the front.

'No,' I hiss, reaching forward and grabbing her hand. 'Let's sit at the back.'

'But there's plenty of room near the front, look.'

I glare at her, turn my back and sit myself down on the back row as far away as possible. For a moment I think she's going to ignore me and carry on, but she shakes her head then makes her way towards me.

'This is going to look terrible,' she declares, taking her gloves off.

'What is?'

'When the coffin arrives and we are sat here on our own at the back as if we don't want to be here.'

'For one, I really don't want to be here and two, no one will notice us once it starts filling up.'

Maureen says nothing, just purses her lips and folds her arms.

A couple walks in and takes the seats directly opposite us in the back row.

'See, now they've sat at the back,' hisses Maureen.

'So?'

'What if no one else comes? What if this is it and Emily's family arrive so the front two rows are filled, then two rows empty and then us at the back? How will that look?'

'More people must be coming,' I hiss back.

'I'm not so sure,' says Maureen, shaking her head. 'She hadn't kept up with her Christmas card list. I bet I haven't had one from her for a good five years. A lot of people will think she's already dead.'

'Really?' I gasp.

Maureen shrugs.

There is no one coming through the doors of the chapel. I keep looking behind us praying that somebody else will walk in. A coachload from her knitting group? Her second cousins twice removed? Any warm bodies would do.

I count how many are already here seated. Fourteen. That's it. That makes twenty-six gapingly empty seats.

'Perhaps everyone is waiting outside,' I whisper to Maureen.

She shakes her head in a knowing way. She knows this is it bar the close family, she's done this before.

I look at the empty seats in front of us. I think it is possibly the most miserable sight I have ever seen. Empty seats in the 'small' chapel.

And worse, a half-full back row planning a hasty get-away the minute it's over. No one wants to leave it at that.

'Let's move,' I say to Maureen. 'Come on, quick. Let's move forward.'

We move to sit behind a fat man in a too-tight suit.

'It's a very flattering photo,' says Maureen, indicating the picture of Emily Nancy Stonehouse 1948–2016 on the front of the Order of Service. 'Taken a good ten years ago, I reckon.'

She had a full rounded face, a slight double chin and eyes that disappeared when she smiled. Not overly flattering, I would say, so I dread to think what she might have looked like in real life.

A lone man in a jacket and shirt but no tie shuffles in and sits next to Maureen. We exchange sympathetic smiles. I wonder who he is to Emily. A cousin? A neighbour? An ex-colleague? An ex-lover or maybe even a current lover?

I look at the picture again of Emily smiling at me from the Order of Service. Unlikely, I think. The man is as skinny as a whip, his face flushed from years of excesses. They wouldn't look right together somehow. But who knows? Who will ever know? Secrets get buried with the dead, don't they? I glance over again and allow my mind to wonder at the secrets Emily might share with this man.

By the look of him I reckon he might have been her partner in crime. Literally. Did she plan a series of burglaries with him when her husband lost his job as a coal miner in the seventies and couldn't put food on the table? She knew they had to eat and she knew Jack could help her. Did her husband ever ask where the joint of beef came from or the endless supply of milk and eggs? Or was he too depressed? It was Jack who helped them survive. Jack and his skinny frame that could zip in and out of carelessly left-open windows like a ghost.

I look across at the man again and see that he has his head bent and his eyes closed in prayer. Unlikely for a petty criminal, I reflect, and begin to rethink Jack's story. As I'm staring at him, he opens his eyes and turns to look directly at me and winks. I look away in surprise. Who winks at a funeral? But then again, who comes to a funeral dressed as a Spice Girl? I smooth my skirt down over my knees and sit with my hands crossed primly on my lap.

The low-level hum of music steps up a gear and Maureen grabs hold of the chair in front and hauls herself up. Everyone is rising so I stand with my eyes fixed forward until I can sense it passing down the aisle to my right and I see it out the corner of my eye.

The coffin.

Chapter Twenty-Two

'You wouldn't have dark wood, would you?' whispers Maureen as we watch the pallbearers lower the box onto the plinth. 'It's too old-fashioned for you.'

I sit down before my legs give way.

'I do like the flowers on top of the coffin for a woman though,' she adds, lowering herself down to join me. 'Very pretty. But not pink, eh? You're not really a pink person.'

I look down at my hands. I can't look at the coffin – it burns my eyes. Suddenly the room is filled with everyone I know. There's Mark and Ellie and George on the front row. Mark is stony-faced, Ellie is wearing too much make-up and George's head has sunk to a new low. Mum is wearing her black fake-fur coat which she saves for special occasions, so that's something, and Dad is in his best suit and pristine black tie, the only sign of his illness the bewildered look on his face. Antony and his wife Mischa, along with their only son Lucas, sit themselves slightly apart from the others with chins held high, representing the sane, successful side of the family. I see glimpses of others: Zoe, Lisa, Heather, some childhood friends, Maureen, of course. Would I fill the main chapel, I wonder, or is it the 'small' chapel for me?

I can hear a man talking. I don't look up as I can't bear to catch sight of the coffin again. He's saying things about Emily. When I say 'saying', I mean he's reading a list of facts and figures. It's the Wikipedia version of her life. Where she was born, where she went to school, where she worked, who she married, what children she had, when and how she lost her husband, when and how she died.

Whilst important, it leaves no impression of who she really was. What made her happy, for example? Food by the looks of it. Maybe she baked the best Victoria sponge in the area or it was her favourite treat to go a hotel and partake in an all-you-can-eat buffet breakfast. She didn't need to stay over, that would have been wasted on her, it was just the breakfast she was after. Happiness to her was the ability to have four hash browns just for starters followed by full English then a bacon butty. On the side would be three mini croissants as well as as much white toast as she could fit in. Never brown toast. In Emily's opinion brown toast with English breakfast was just wrong, though she wasn't averse to slipping in a bit of continental with a few slices of cold ham and cheese as a cleansing course. A bit like sorbet.

This would give me an idea of the real Emily. She's jolly, she's down-to-earth, she's straightforward, she knows what she likes and doesn't care too much about what others think of her. If she did she'd be eating yoghurt at the all-you-can-eat breakfast buffet. Now that's a different kind of person entirely.

I manage to raise my eyes to look at the man still churning out Emily's statistics. He's in a suit, no dog collar. Clearly not a man of religion. I pick up the Order of Service and open it. Glancing down, I notice no hymns. In fact no audience participation whatsoever. I look down the page for evidence that someone else will speak of Emily apart from this stranger who has no idea about her or her obsession with breakfast buffets. No one else is mentioned.

I look towards the middle-aged man on the front row who must be her son. He's staring up at the ceiling. He could be anywhere. I hope he's here somewhere. No one is going to talk about the real Emily Stonehouse. I wish I could. I think I would if I could. Everyone deserves to be explained at their funeral. Their stories told. Their foibles discussed. That is what makes us human, not the list of dry facts and figures that are merely signposts to our lives.

I look down at the Order of Service again. It will be over too soon. It's going too quickly and I know what that means: the end is nigh. I've never been to a cremation before. All the other, thankfully few, funerals I have attended have been in a church, followed either by a burial or a family cremation. Neither of which I have ever been witness to. I know I don't want to see what happens at the end. I don't need to see it. I don't think I will be able to hold it together and somehow it's too personal. That moment is for people who at least knew Emily, not an interloper like me.

I have to get out. I have to make an escape but I've boxed myself in. I'm against the wall. Maureen and Jack, the burglar-cum-Spice-Girl-fancier, are in my way. Disturbing the proceedings, however, is still preferable to having to witness Emily's last moment – I just can't do it.

The man at the front is currently reading a poem. I wonder if it was of Emily's choosing or someone just picked out of a book entitled *Good Poems for Funerals*. I suspect the latter.

I bend my head low and get up, squeezing past Maureen and Jack, muttering quiet apologies. There's rustling as people turn round to try and work out why Geri Halliwell is bailing, but all I can feel is relief as I reach the aisle and turn my back on the poetry and the coffin and the flowers. I walk as quickly as decently possible in my high-heeled shoes to the door.

Outside, I gulp in the fresh air and fall against a brick pillar. It's started drizzling with rain and I can feel it flattening my beautiful blow-dried ginger hair with a blonde streak. I hold the backs of my hands out at my sides and feel the drops prickling my skin. Tiny sparks of feeling. I walk away from the pillar and feel the sparks on my face. It's never felt so good to feel the rain, it makes me feel alive.

Chapter Twenty-Three

I wait in the car for Maureen. I soon see her appear next to the purple and yellow sign. She looks at me from across the car park then raises her hand as if hailing a cab. I get the message.

'Well, I've given him something to think about,' she says as she drops herself down in the passenger seat. I wait as she faffs around with the seatbelt.

'Who?' I ask.

'Simon, Emily's son. I told him that Emily might have lasted a bit longer if she hadn't had him to worry about.'

'Very thoughtful of you.'

'Well, he's such a waste of space. Always has been. It's about time he felt some responsibility.'

'For his mother's death?'

'Yes, why not? She worried about him day and night. I reckon he took ten years off her. So, are you glad you came?'

'No.'

'So what are you going to do about yours?'

'My what?'

'Your funeral.'

'Jesus, Maureen! Who are you?' I say, turning to face her. 'The ghost of funerals yet to come or something?'

'Would you rather I sat here and told you to be positive, everything is going to be fine? Is that who you want me to be? Or do you want me to help you tackle it head-on and make sure you do this thing properly?'

This is not a version of 'Would you rather' I can say I'm particularly enjoying.

'You choose,' she demands. 'I can do the pathetic holding-hands stuff if you want me to. *Oh dear, poor, poor Jenny. How are you feeling, dear? Is there anything I can do, dear? It must be so awful for you. You are so brave. You just stay positive, dear, and everything will be fine.*'

'Stop!' I shout, holding my hands over my ears. Bloody hell. Maureen can be so annoying.

We sit there for a few moments not speaking. A hearse glides slowly past us.

'I don't want to go like this,' I mutter.

'That's the spirit.'

'What?'

'I said, that's the spirit. You're right, you don't want to go like this. It's rubbish. Fine if you're old and there's no one left to really care. But you. No, this isn't you.'

'That's the point, isn't it, though? This isn't for me, is it?' I say, pointing out the window.

'The car park?'

'No, all of this. All of this funeral palaver, it's not for me. It's for the people you leave behind, that's who it's for. I won't bloody be here, will I?'

Maureen leans back in her seat, blinking.

'I hadn't thought of it like that,' she says.

Honestly she takes my breath away sometimes.

'Fuck it then,' she tells me. 'Let's not worry about the funeral. Shall we go?'

No, she *really* takes my breath away.

'Seriously?' I say. 'You drag me to a funeral for no reason!'

'I thought it might help but you are exactly right. The last person who needs to worry about their funeral is the person whose funeral it is. And do you know what?'

'What?'

'I'm not writing to Dorothy any more. Why should I care if she's at my funeral or not? I'm crossing her off the Christmas card list as soon as we get back. All those years I've wasted keeping in touch. What was I thinking?'

I shake my head and start up the car.

'People should really have their funerals before they die,' mutters Maureen. 'They're wasted on the dead. What you need is a going-away party rather than a funeral.'

The words 'going-away party' float through my brain.

Somewhere from deep in my conscious I hear a crowd shouting, 'Jen-ny, Jen-ny, Jen-ny.'

I slam the brakes on.

'That's it!' I say, staring at Maureen.

'What's it?'

'You are a genius. That's it! A going-away party, I'll have a going-away party.'

'A what?'

'A going-away party,' I declare. 'A going-away party, 1996 style. You've nailed it. That's how I want to do it.'

I grip Maureen's hand excitedly whilst she stares back at me in shock.

For the first time in days I finally feel like I have something to look forward to... whilst I die.

Chapter Twenty-Four

Being at a funeral has sparked a peculiar desire to see my mother. There's a first. I drop Maureen off, thankfully now buzzing with thoughts of helping plan my party/wake rather than my funeral, then I drive over to my parents' house, unannounced and without reason. I wonder what my mother will make of that. It will either send her into a complete spin or she will think of the first thing she can as a reason for escape.

'What are you doing here?' she asks when she opens the door. 'And… and…'

She's looking me up and down, trying to sum up her review of my new look. I wince even before the words come out.

'Why?' is all she can say with a look of astonishment and disdain.

'Do you like it?' I ask defiantly. I can't really answer the why question. She shakes her head.

'You look like something from… I don't know… Essex,' she says.

'Great,' I reply. 'Just great. You going to invite me in then?'

'Er, well, yes, I suppose I could go and do some shopping. That would be handy. I'm low on teabags,' she says, stepping to one side.

'Oh, I can't stop long,' I say as soon as I'm safely in the hallway. 'It's just a flying visit.'

I can see the look of utter confusion on her face. You don't call in on my mother, you book an appointment or you respond to an urgent demand, in my case. Promptly or prepare for hell.

'You have lost weight finally so I suppose you can carry off that kind of look,' she mutters as I take my shoes off. 'But maybe tone it down a little bit, hey? You don't want people saying you look like mutton dressed as lamb, do you?'

'Do *you* think I look like mutton dressed as lamb?' I ask her when I straighten up. I'm feeling a bit dizzy, as the blood has rushed to my head.

She nods. 'A little,' she says but she means a lot.

'Cup of tea?' I ask brightly.

She stares at me. The confused look is back. I cannot remember the last time my mother and I sat down and shared a cup of tea and a natter. If ever. She turns without a word to the kitchen, her mid-height court shoes clacking on the wooden hall floor.

I sit myself down at the kitchen table and watch as she flicks the switch on the kettle in silence and reaches up into an overhead cupboard for the teabags. I'm not sure why I'm here. It might be because, amongst the other revelations outside the crematorium, I also realised that, whilst everyone else will experience my death, actually the effect on me is that I will experience everyone else's death in one fell swoop.

Come my passing, everyone is dead to me.

All my relationships come to dust, gone. I must mourn everyone as I make some kind of attempt to prepare for the end. Including my mother.

I think in the back of my mind I always thought that one day I would do something that she would be proud of, show warmth towards. We might even achieve a glimmer of a mother–daughter relationship. I thought we still had time to get there, that I would connect with her, but time is running out. That is what going to a funeral does to you.

'I've been to a funeral this morning,' I announce.

She spins round, teaspoon in mid-air.

'Dressed like that!' she exclaims.

I bite my lip. She could have asked whose it was. She could have expressed concern for my loss. She could have said a simple, 'Oh dear'. But no, her instinct is to leap to me showing myself up as usual. I can feel tears prickle my eyes. I bite my lip harder.

'Was it one of your gay friends from Greece?' she asks, curling her lip and putting a mug down in front of me.

'No,' I gasp. 'Whatever made you say that?'

'Well, I can imagine one of them having, you know, a *themed* funeral.'

I think my mouth must be on the floor. I don't know what to say, I'm utterly flummoxed.

'Yeah, that's right,' I eventually say sarcastically. 'He wanted the Spice Girls to be his pallbearers.'

My mother sits down in front of me. She's not listening to me now, I can tell. It's not even registered what I just said.

'The coffin arrived in the back of a pink stretch limousine. It was amazing,' I continue.

'Mmmm,' she nods, looking into the distance. 'Very classy.'

Silence.

'Do you know what kind of funeral you want?' I ask her.

She blinks several times. I suspect the subject of her own funeral has never crossed her mind and if it has she has skipped past it. She's a healthy fit woman who prides herself on her healthy eating habits. She doesn't intend to go anywhere any time soon and in any case my dad will go first, without question. That is the next family funeral everyone is expecting, not hers; there is no way she is going anywhere before she has been released by my dad's death. It would be exceptionally rude of him to hang on much longer.

'I prefer not to think about it,' she says eventually. 'But Antony has a copy of our wills. There's guidance in there.'

'Oh, he will be coming to your funeral then, will he?'

I think she might slap me.

'And what's that supposed to mean?'

'Well, it's just that he doesn't bother to turn up to any other family stuff.'

'He's a surgeon, Jenny. He puts his patients first.'

'Yep,' I agree. 'Particularly when he's on his annual Caribbean Christmas holiday.'

She falters. I watch every year as my mother asks my brother earlier and earlier if he will come and spend Christmas with them and every year he's always just booked a holiday, but of course is gutted that he won't get to share dry turkey and useless Christmas presents with his family.

'He has to have a holiday some time,' she says, staring down into her tea. 'He always calls though, doesn't he?' she adds, looking up again. 'As soon as he gets up, he's on the phone to wish us all a merry Christmas.'

He most certainly is. The worst part of Christmas Day for me is about three o'clock in the afternoon when Antony puts his duty call in. Mum comes off the phone flush with excited chatter about what the temperature is in the Bahamas, what's on the five-course Christmas lunch menu and what's in their Christmas cocktail that they are currently sipping on the beach, being waited on hand and foot. The call always seems to coincide with the moment I contemplate the mammoth pile of washing-up, Ellie and George wanting to kill each other and Mark and his mum falling asleep on the sofa. Despite the fact I'm the one who has cooked Christmas dinner for her every year since I've been married, my mother still insists on declaring that she wishes she could be with my brother on Christmas Day.

'Yes, it really is terribly good of him to call us,' I say. 'It wouldn't be Christmas without Antony ringing it in from the sunshine.'

Christmas suddenly rears its head as a future event to dread or possibly one to not even be around for. Either way is depressing. Can you believe that? Christmas will not be an event high on my list to mourn. What happened there? How have I inhabited a life that doesn't enjoy Christmas? I stare back at my mum. I want to tell her that she ruined Christmas.

'I'm not cooking Christmas dinner this year,' I blurt out.

I might as well tell her. Either way I will not be living the Christmas hell I usually experience. If I'm alive, I'm going to make damn sure it's a good one, and if I'm dead… well, they'll have to sort themselves out, won't they?

'What do you mean, you're not cooking?' Mum asks me.

'I'm just not.'

'Why?'

'Because I don't enjoy it.'

She blinks.

'And you say every year I overcook the turkey.'

'Well, you do.'

'So what's the point? I hate cooking it and you don't like eating it. So let's drop the pretence, shall we?'

'But your dad likes it.'

'He'd prefer sausages.'

'You can't have sausages for Christmas lunch.'

'Antony has a barbeque every Christmas.'

'That's because he's not here, he's on a beach.'

'I know!' I say, slamming my fist on the table. 'He's never here.'

She blinks again and looks away.

'He visits when he can,' she says quietly.

'When did he last visit?'

She looks up sharply.

'I saw him in April,' she replies.

'You went to his house in April, I looked after Dad. When did he last come here?'

She tries to hold my gaze.

'August,' she mutters.

'Last August?'

She nods.

'Nearly a year ago. He hasn't seen Dad in a year?'

The truth is, I know exactly when Antony last came because Mum had me painting the spare room and then he said he couldn't stay over. But I want to hear her say it.

'He's very busy,' she says again.

'Too busy to see his own dad in nearly a year?'

She says nothing but her shoulders sag. I'm getting through to her, I can tell, but whereas I thought I'd get some joy out of my mother admitting my brother wasn't the hero she bills him as, actually all I feel is sad for her.

I realise her image of her surgeon hero son is her pride and joy despite its falsehood. It makes her happy, it's her badge of honour that she has succeeded in life and I'm trying to rip it from her. I suddenly see her for what she is: a woman trapped in a marriage to someone she no longer knows. Her status as a bank manager's wife has faded to nothing and she is desperately trying to grasp hold of the threads in her life that elevate her to something meaningful. Her only remaining status symbol, the most important thing in my mother's life, is being the mother of a surgeon.

She says nothing. She's looking down into her tea, her mind fighting hard to work out the defence for her beloved son.

'Why don't you go to the Caribbean this year with Antony?' I say.

She looks up sharply.

'Don't be ridiculous,' she replies. I'm actually relieved to see her 'my daughter is an idiot' face return. 'Your father can't travel all that way.'

'He can stay with us,' I reply. 'Or I'll get him into Shady Grove for a couple of weeks – they do respite care there. He can go for some day visits beforehand, get him used to it.'

My mum's mouth is hanging open. She wants to tell me I'm being ridiculous – her default mode with me. She wants to tell me I've come up with another stupid plan that yet again shows the enormous intelligence gap between my brother and me. She is trying to think of a rebuke, but there is none to hand. This ridiculous idea of mine makes her want to cry with happiness, but because I've come up with it, something does not compute.

'Antony *is* going to the Caribbean this year, isn't he?' I ask.

'Yes,' she nods. 'He's booked where they went last year – you know, the one with five pools and the swim-up bar.'

'What's it called, can you remember?'

'Oh yes, I have the address because I sent Lucas a present last year. So hard for Antony to fit the presents in his suitcase so I post them so he doesn't have to worry about it.'

'Right, you go and find the address and we'll get it up online, shall we?' I say, taking out my phone. 'Let's just check they have availability before we call Antony.'

★

Five minutes later and the glorious blue sea of the Bahamas is filling my phone screen. I try not to feel sick with envy at the images of pure white sand and palm trees. I plug in dates for availability for two weeks over Christmas and heave a sigh of relief that there appears to be no issue, other than needing a second mortgage to secure a room. The money will not be a problem, I know, as Dad is a careful man who planned to be very comfortable in his old age, though sadly he didn't get to enjoy it. It's about time somebody did.

'Ring Antony,' I say to Mum.

'What, now?'

'Yes, now.'

'He'll be at work.'

'He might not be. Come on and then you can get it booked.'

She looks at me in nervous anticipation then gets up to fetch the phone.

'Hello dear. I'm not disturbing you, am I?… No, everything's fine, I just wanted to tell you something, that's all. You know you're going to the Grand Hyatt for Christmas again… Yes, well, your sister has come up with the most brilliant idea.'

She smiles at me. I cross my fingers. We are not quite there yet.

'I'm coming with you.' Her hand flies up to her mouth in amazement at what she has just said.

'Oh no, it's fine,' she says. 'Jenny will take care of him or she can get him into the care home she works at. To be honest, I think he might quite enjoy that,' she giggles.

She goes quiet for few moments as my brother presumably flounders around for other excuses as to why she can't join them.

'Antony, Antony,' she interrupts after a while. 'It's fine, we've already checked. I can book a room now if I like, there are lots available. I think I'm going to really treat myself and go with a sea view actually. Waking up to that every morning, well, I can't believe it. It will be like a dream come true. No, actually, it *will* be a dream come true…

'Okay, darling, you go if you need to, but I thought I'd let you know. Yes, yes, okay. I'll wait until you call me tonight and then I'll book it. Bye, darling.'

She puts the phone down. She's grinning from ear to ear. I look down and my phone instantly starts to ring: it's Antony. I cut him off and shove the phone in my pocket.

'Well, I'd better go,' I say, standing up. 'Things to do, you know.'

'I'll need you to come and look after Dad so I can go and buy new clothes for my holiday,' she says. 'I might need two days,' she adds thoughtfully. 'I bet you have to dress for dinner – you know, in a hotel like that.'

'I bet you do, Mum,' I say, turning to leave. She follows me to the door.

'I'll give Roy a ring as soon as you've gone. Let him know. Gosh, they'll need to reorganise the bridge night whilst I'm away. Yes, I'd better ring him straight away so they've got plenty of notice.'

'Bye, Mum.'

'Bye, Jenny. At least you don't have to cook Christmas dinner now after all,' she says and gives me a little hug.

Yes, a hug.

Chapter Twenty-Five

I drive around the corner, park on the side of the road then get my phone out and call my brother back.

'Did you get my message?' he barks.

'No, I thought I'd just ring and actually talk to the real you.'

'Mum just rang and says she's coming on holiday with us at Christmas.'

'I know. I gave her the idea.'

'What the bloody hell did you do that for?'

'Because she'd much rather spend Christmas with you than me.'

'Oh, thanks a bunch! That's great. You've just done it to get her out of your hair. How *very* generous of you!'

'No. Generous is me hosting Mum and Dad for Christmas every single bloody year whilst you swan off to get pissed on cocktails and congratulate yourself on what an amazing man you are because you cut people up for a living. Generous is me visiting at least twice a week so Mum can get out and do stuff, despite the fact she doesn't appreciate it and treats me like a dogsbody and an utter failure, whilst you remain on her pedestal even though you do absolutely fuck all to help her out. And generous is me sitting with my sick dad and talking to him and holding his hand, despite the fact he mostly doesn't remember who

I am, when you haven't seen him for nearly a year. *That* is what I call generous.'

There is silence on the end of the phone.

'We live three hours' drive away and my job—'

'I know about your bloody job. I get it rammed down my throat every single time I see Mum. You becoming a surgeon is the best thing that ever happened to her. You may be a brilliant surgeon but you are an utterly shit son.'

'I don't have to take that from you.'

'Yes, you do. You really do. Because I'm not doing it any more. I can't do it any more. You have to be involved with Mum and Dad, you can't just swan in and out on your state visits and expect that to suffice as your family duty. I've got stuff going on, you know. I'm not a surgeon but I still have a life. They're your responsibility too. What if something happened to me?'

There, I said it.

'But you are on their doorstep, Jenny. I can't be doing a six-hour round trip every five minutes.'

'But what if something happened to me?'

'You're just being ridiculous now. Don't talk like that.'

'I'm just saying that you can't take this situation for granted any more. We need you back in the family. *I* need you back in the family.'

There's a long silence before he speaks.

'Fine. I'll take her on holiday.'

It's a start, I guess. I look forward to it all being Antony's idea and hearing from my mother that he's the best, most considerate, most caring son a mother could wish for.

Chapter Twenty-Six

It's very strange. Your thoughts can run along on a fairly positive thread for quite some time and then something happens or is said and you are winded by the starkness of what it means. It could be as simple as someone telling you they can't wait to see the next series of *The Great British Bake Off* and that they're thinking of applying to be on it next year. Next year? Will I be here next year? It hits you physically in the gut and you have to choose whether to let it fell you and stop you in your tracks, or to fight back and bat it away with everything you've got.

Of course, you don't always have a choice. You will be felled and there is absolutely nothing you can do about it. And then you will find yourself crying over cake. Well, pretending you are crying over cake rather than something that's really worth shedding tears over.

1996 is my defence. My weapon against death. 1996 will keep me up above the depths of gloom. I dig out the *Trainspotting* soundtrack on CD and post it into the battered stereo in the kitchen, praying it will work. It does and the next minute I'm dancing around the kitchen to 'Born Slippy' alone, apart from a flood of memories making me feel warm and happy and alive. 1996 will barricade me against the grim reality of now.

I've decided to hold back on mentioning the 'party' at home until I have some of the details nailed down. I can see Mark throwing ice-cold water all over my secret wake that I have every intention of attending and enjoying. Clearly I wouldn't tell him the motivation behind the event but that would only make his pooh-poohing even harder to bear. His casual dismissiveness of one of the most significant moments in my life would hurt, even if he had no idea of its importance.

Instead I decide to lead him in gently to my rekindling of the nineties. I get in the car and drive to his office. I park outside then send him a text suggesting we revisit an old tradition we have long since neglected.

IT'S A LOVELY EVENING!

I wait for him to reply to this well-used signal. Back in the day, if it had been a particularly sunny day, we would call each other at work and one of us would inevitably end up saying, 'It's a lovely evening' – basically code for 'I'll meet you in the beer garden of The Bridge at 5.30pm'.

I sit with my phone in my hand, willing him to reply. Praying he remembers those long warm nights spent eating scampi and chips and drinking warm white wine.

?

This was his reply.

I SAID – IT'S A LOVELY EVENING

I HAVE TO WORK LATE

I'M OUTSIDE – I'LL DRIVE

?

*I'M OUTSIDE. COME ON – YOU CAN GO IN EARLY IN
THE MORNING.*

I'M REALLY BUSY.

*RIGHT – I'LL GO AND GET FISH AND CHIPS AND A
COUPLE OF TINNIES AND I'LL BRING IT UP TO YOU
IN HALF AN HOUR. YOU NEED TO EAT.*

NO – STAY THERE. I'M ON MY WAY.

Next minute he's hurtling through the door not looking remotely
like he's looking forward to a lovely evening.

'What are you doing here?' he demands.

'Come on, Mark. It's such a lovely night, you can't waste it here.
Let's go sit in a beer garden.'

'Are you insane, woman?'

'Insane? Insane? Insanity is to sit in a glass house on a night like
this staring at a computer screen.'

'But you know I'm busy.'

'I know you are but everyone deserves a break, Mark. Come on,
what have you got up there in that office of yours that could be more
exciting than spending the evening with your wife?'

I hold his stare. I watch him recoil ever so slightly at my remark.
There have been no further attempts to end our marriage since the
weekend, largely because I have ensured we have not been in the
same room alone together. I'm hoping he's bottled it for now and
told 'her' that it's just not the right time yet. And you never know,

taking him down memory lane might also make him think twice about what he's doing.

'Anyone would think you have a hot new secretary or something. Is that what's keeping you at work so late?' I plough on.

I keep the tone light and jovial. I'm teasing him. Fear flashes over his eyes.

'Of course not,' he says sternly. 'I've still got Jean.'

Oh, so he wasn't shagging his secretary then. Jean is at least sixty and a bit of a bulldog, to be quite frank.

'Well, you'd better get in then, hadn't you?' I say, nodding at the passenger seat. 'Or else it will be last orders by the time we get there.'

He stares at me for a moment longer then sighs and walks around the front of the car to the passenger seat in the lolloping style of a teenager having been picked up too early from a party. He gets in and puts his seatbelt on then instantly gets out his phone as I put the car into gear.

'I'll just need to tie up a few loose ends,' he mutters.

Let her know that he won't be out to play tonight, I think.

'Okay. Then shall we leave our phones in the car?' I say. 'I sometimes feel there are three of us in this marriage.'

He turns to look at me sharply as I nod down towards his phone.

'Oh, okay,' he says. 'Or I could just put it on silent?'

'No,' I say firmly. 'No way! Even worse. You'll be looking at it every two minutes if you do that. It stays in the car. She'll have to cope without you for a couple of hours.'

'Who?' he says, turning to look at me sharply again, the fear back in his eyes. A part of me is enjoying this.

'Who what?'

'Who's she? You said, "She'll have to cope." Who do you mean?'

'Oh, I meant your phone, silly. You're so attached to it, I assumed it had a personality and everything.'

Mark shakes his head in bewilderment and returns to tapping frantic messages for the entire duration of the short drive to the pub. We pull into an already busy car park despite the fact it's still before six.

'See, lots of other people have worked out it's a lovely evening,' I say, leaning forward to open the glove box, indicating he should deposit his phone in it.

'But what if one of the kids needs us?'

He has a point. George is still reeling over the disappearance of Betsy and it's my mobile number on the missing posters.

'I'll keep mine in my bag,' I say. 'Just in case someone rings about Betsy. And at least I'm capable of having it on my person and not checking it every two minutes,' I conclude, giving him a knowing look.

He throws his phone in with a sigh and jumps as I slam the door shut. That's her out of the picture for the evening.

★

'I haven't had scampi for… I don't know how long,' says Mark, leaning back in his bench seat overlooking the river and taking a swig of rosé wine.

'The nineties probably,' I murmur.

'You're probably right. It was surprisingly good.'

'Mmm,' I nod. 'So simple.'

'That's it,' he said. 'You're right. Just simple. Easy.'

I smile to myself. It's been a remarkable evening. Truly. A few days ago and this scene would have seemed improbable at best. To me, never mind anyone else. Sitting with my husband having a pleasant meal on the banks of the river enjoying the late-evening sunshine. No way, so many things were going on that would prevent that happening. He has a mistress, I have cancer and it's a school night. Oh, and the minor detail of the fact that we haven't been out together like this alone in goodness knows how long.

We did try to keep having date nights after the kids came along but at some point they dwindled to nothing. We stopped going out together as a couple. I don't know why. Who knows? Babysitters were too hard to find, we were too tired, we had too much good stuff backed up on the TV to watch. We were too busy socialising with other couples. Whatever it was, we stopped doing it: we stopped dating. Maybe that's the key to a good marriage. You must never stop dating. Never stop putting yourself through the sheer exposure of being out and about and being solely responsible for the other one having a good time. Perhaps if Mark and I had carried on dating there wouldn't have been room for someone else.

'Shall we see if they still do the New York cheesecake?' asks Mark.

'Only if it's part of a meal deal,' I say, grinning.

He grins back and my insides light up.

'I wasn't that bad, was I?'

'You were. The times I asked if we could share the chocolate fudge cake and you wouldn't let me because chocolate fudge cake wasn't in the Monday night offer so it would have cost us a whole fifty pence extra.'

'We were saving for our wedding.'

'Fifty pence at a time?'

'If we'd have put all those fifty pences in a jar I bet it would have bought us—'

'Three boxes of confetti,' I interrupt. 'Seems odd sat here at the end of a meal and you not getting the wedding spreadsheet out,' I add.

It was all coming back to me now. I'd forgotten how we'd planned our wedding in this very beer garden. I say *plan*. What I actually mean is that Mark would cross-examine me on any decisions I had made over the weekend that might have a cost implication on the big day. He would scribble notes on his spreadsheet then screw his nose up for a while and ask me questions like, 'If you really want another bridesmaid then we really have to decide if we want to take a couple of guests off the daytime list or reduce the honeymoon by a day because there will of course be another outfit to pay for.'

The funny thing was, my dad was actually paying for the majority of the wedding, but in his wisdom he had taken Mark to one side and jokingly said he needed to keep an eye on my extravagant tastes. Mark had taken this to heart and in order to impress my father had constructed a spreadsheet to control the expenditure on our romantic day. It was worthy of an entire government department. The only spreadsheet to rival it may have been the separate file set up purely to establish the best-value napkins for the reception. (A search that went global once Mark found out that one of his company's suppliers in China had a sister factory producing paper goods. The columns and rows required to establish the best-value white paper napkins were shockingly numerous once shipping costs from Taipei had to be factored in.)

'But didn't you enjoy the wedding so much more knowing that it hadn't got out of control and cost your father a small fortune?'

Did I? Yes, I did, but only because I loved the fact Mark cared about how much my dad was spending. He didn't take it for granted. I even enjoyed the close scrutiny on the day of the stiff white thick paper napkins that cost the same as the cheap two-ply you could get from Wilkinson's. We took several home with us and they were proudly stored in a memory box as a key symbol of a successful day.

It was getting chilly now but I didn't want to suggest going inside. That would break the spell. Inside was all fake rustic charm with manufactured vintage screaming from every corner. Outside was still stuck in the nineties with rickety wooden picnic benches set on islands of concrete, cigarette butts floating in little puddles of water on the nearby grass. Not attractive, not comfortable, but real.

I'd take real nostalgia over the fake kind indoors any day. I'd take sitting there waiting for a massive plate of fried food and a basket full of plastic wrappers containing non-brand ketchup that tastes like vinegar and vinegar that tastes like acid. I'd take being surrounded by tables still waiting to be cleared from lunchtime excesses, tomato-stained napkins stuffed into pint pots and dregs of wine attracting half the local flying insect population. I'd take it because I'd take the buzz of people slowly winding down from a hard day at work. Kicking back, letting go, being a happy contented version of themselves. No longer trying to be anything other than just someone sitting in a beer garden having a drink and a laugh. I'd rather be that person there than the one indoors trying to fit into the hipster vintage decor. Where the surroundings lead me to a version of myself I don't want to be. Trying to act cool despite the fact I don't have a beard. No, all I want to be is sitting in a beer garden, having a drink and a laugh, just like I used to in 1996.

Mark is scrutinising the laminated dessert menu. I realise he's not mentioned Sebastian's once. He's not once said that he'd rather be in the stiff, perfectly creased surroundings of the city's premier fine dining establishment. He's having a good time. I knew he would.

'Yes,' he says, pumping his fist ever so slightly. 'Want to share a cheesecake?'

I shake my head. I wish I could but my insides are doing somersaults already from having eaten too much scampi.

'All right then, I'll let you have a chocolate fudge cake. As long as you let me have a bit.'

That's it, I'm winded. Tears spring to my eyes like blood seeping out of a freshly cut wound. I'm going to cry over cake, I think. Bloody cake. How can I cry over cake? I rub my eyes quickly, hoping I can get away with some comment about the cigarette smoke sweeping over us from the next table.

'Shall we move inside?' asks Mark, seeing me glance over at the smokers.

'No,' I say quickly. 'I'm fine. No pudding for me though.'

'Not even share mine?'

I shake my head, trying not to let the tears break through again. I've never wanted to share a pudding more in my life. Sharing a pudding now would mean everything. It's ours, it's what we did. We shared warm chocolate fudge cake with cream in that beer garden from 1996 to 1998. I'd watch as Mark would carefully divide it down the middle to make sure it was fair. He'd always ask which half I wanted. I loved him for that. I loved that he cared that I got a fair portion and he didn't just assume because he was the man that he should have more. I'd give anything to watch him do that now. A symbol of love and care and affection if ever I saw one. You don't share chocolate fudge cake like that with a casual mistress, I was certain of it.

But my insides can no more ingest another morsel than I can pole vault over the width of the river.

'I've eaten too much already,' I tell him sadly.

'You're not still on a diet, are you?' he asks.

I don't quite know how to take this. His voice hints at criticism. Like that would be a bad thing. Implying I was either too thin or that my diets never worked anyway so why was I bothering. But as far as he was concerned this diet had magically worked. I'd lost twenty pounds and it was visible surely. Though he'd never acknowledged it.

'What makes you say that?' I ask.

'Well, it's just, well, you're starting to look a bit too thin, that's all.'

I nod. How many times have I dreamed of someone saying that to me? Being accused of being too thin is like being told you've won too many Oscars in my book. Magical, magical words if ever they come your way. If only I didn't have to get cancer to hear them.

And if only they had been preceded by a compliment. It would have been nice to hear Mark tell me at some point in the last few weeks, when I hit the sweet spot, that I looked fabulous, instead of waiting until I was in the too-thin phase to remark on my weight loss.

'I'll take that as a compliment,' I say sarcastically.

'No, no,' he flaps. 'You look great. You just don't need to lose any more, that's all.'

Again, music to my ears in different circumstances. The battle is over. I am at one with the size of my body for the first... and the very last time.

'Do you like my hair?' I pluck up the courage to ask him. He's not mentioned it once and I suspect it's because he hates it.

'Of course,' he nods.

'Remind you of someone?' I ask.

He nods, smiling.

'Ginger Spice?' I say.

'No,' he replies. 'It reminds me of you,' he says quietly.

He holds my gaze for a fraction of a second too long, as though he's about to say something else. But then he changes his mind and picks up his glass to take a large swig.

I take a deep breath and look around me. Most people have now retreated inside. There's just two other tables aside from ours left. A group of five lads in their twenties, on the way to getting hammered, sit to our right. The conversation ebbs and flows and bursts into raucous laughter every minute or so. There'll be much texting about sore heads and paracetamol tomorrow as they battle through a work day with a hangover in the way only someone in their twenties can get away with.

Then there's a couple with a baby in a pushchair fast asleep. They're enjoying grown-up conversation perhaps for the first time in weeks. The man reaches over and tucks the blanket closer around the baby, then smiles in relief at the woman as he pours her another glass of wine. Happiness and contentment surrounds us.

I look back at Mark.

'Go on then,' I say. 'I'll share a fudge cake with you.'

I smile. He hesitates – he'd wanted cheesecake.

'Good call,' he nods and gets up to go to the bar and order one portion and two spoons.

Chapter Twenty-Seven

Somewhere around three o'clock in the morning I decide I'd better have this going-away party soon.

Two reasons.

As I'd looked at my husband as he carefully divided the chocolate fudge cake, I realised I couldn't hold off not telling him about my illness much longer. You see, going back to 1996 just might be making me fall in love with him all over again.

Despite everything.

Despite the affair.

Sharing cake with him has reignited nostalgia for our early passion I had not anticipated. I know he's sleeping with someone else, I know he's an utter bastard, but in 1996 he rocked my world. He *was* my world. I loved him with all my heart. Time and tiredness have eroded it to virtually nothing until tonight, as we'd sat like the courting couple we once were, sharing cake.

He felt it too, I think. There was a flicker of recognition in his eyes of times gone by as the plate had arrived, along with two spoons nestled together in a single napkin. We'd eaten and then left as I began to shiver in the fading light.

We'd hardly spoken on the way home. No need. Both lost in our own thoughts as to why the evening felt significant. I'd felt an enormous desire at that very point to share with him what was really going on. To come clean. Suddenly it felt like he *could* be the one I would lean on. Suddenly it seemed possible. I only stopped myself because of the simple selfish desire to carry on feeling like this. Warm and loved. I hadn't felt like this in a very long time and couldn't bear to give it up for just mere pity. The declaration of my illness would poison these feelings soon enough. It felt good, so good. Just a little bit longer.

The second reason is because I'm finding it harder to hide my pain, despite the best efforts of the handful of tablets I'm taking daily. I'm rolling around on the floor in agony in the middle of the night, my stomach protesting and waves of nausea washing over me. I know I won't be able to hide how much pain I'm in much longer. Soon the cancer will demand I show my hand and so it's time to act fast and get on with the things I need to do before my life changes forever.

I stuff an A4 printed sheet into Maureen's hand the following afternoon. I'd spent an hour trying to blow-dry my hair back into Geri style but it wasn't having any of it. I wasn't looking my best.

'Nice of you to make the effort,' says Maureen, reaching for her glasses then peering down at the piece of paper I'd given her.

'Turns out this look is quite high-maintenance,' I reply. 'I've booked in to have a blow-dry with Dominic tomorrow.'

'Mmm,' she nods, still looking down. 'Twenty-first of July?' she exclaims, her head flicking up.

'I think I need to get on with it,' I reply.

She nods her agreement, seeming to understand. 'But to organise a party in two weeks?'

'I know,' I say. 'But seize the day, eh?' I smile weakly. 'Pointless hanging around.'

She looks me up and down then turns back to the draft invite I've given her.

'There's one problem,' I declare. 'Well, two actually.'

'I think you mean several.'

'Actually I do.'

'Venue.'

'First problem,' I nod.

Lying on the bathroom floor at three in the morning, the revelation that I needed to have my going-away party soon had both soothed and then terrified me. I so wanted and needed to do this and yet I had no idea how.

'Here, you have it here,' says Maureen, glancing around her room.

'Are you out of your mind?'

'Not in here exactly. Not in my room. I mean, out there in the grounds – it's perfect.'

'You must be insane.'

'Any better ideas?'

I'd wracked my brains. I wanted to be outside. I wanted everyone to feel the sunshine on their backs. It had to be outside but our garden, well, it wasn't big enough. It had been our compromise when we bought the house. For some reason five bedrooms seemed more important than a garden you could swing a cat in. Most brand new estate developers clearly thought so too, given the paltry postage stamps most new-builds were offered with these days.

'Sandra will never allow it,' I say. 'Why would she?'

'So don't tell her. She's no idea what's going on in here at the best of times. We could build a crack den on the back lawn and she wouldn't notice.'

'You been watching *Breaking Bad* again?'

'Don't tell me what happens,' she says, covering her ears with her hands. 'I'm only on episode twelve, series two.'

'I can't have a party here without permission. I'd get the sack,' I say.

As soon as I say this we exchange a look. A look that says getting the sack is the least of your problems when you know you're dying anyway.

'Why don't we say it's my party then?' says Maureen. 'She'll have to agree to that. And it will be a Saturday so she won't be here anyway – she never shows her face on a Saturday. About time the grounds got used for some fun rather than for us crocks hobbling round and talking to the damn roses.'

I sit down heavily on Maureen's bed.

'A party at an old people's home,' I say, screwing my nose up. 'It's not really what I had in mind, to be honest.'

'Well, come on then. Where were you thinking of?'

I look at her blankly and shrug.

'That's settled then. Shady Grove it is. Think of it as one of those mob flash things.'

'Flash mob?'

'That's what I said. Only it will be a flash party, a really flash party.' She collapses in peals of laughter at her own wit. 'So who are you thinking of inviting?'

'Second problem.' I sigh.

'Well, you will need to invite everyone here of course.'

'What?'

'You can't have a party here and not invite the residents. What you going to do with them, lock them in their rooms?'

'Ideally,' I mutter under my breath.

'Come on, they won't be any trouble. Well, Sheila might, but as long as you keep her off the booze she'll be fine. We'll just sit them round tables at the back. You won't know they're there. So who else?'

I cough. This is where I decide that this whole going-away party might be a terrible idea. A non-starter if ever there was one.

'I want to see my old friends again. All my old tour rep mates from Greece. That's who I really want to be there. I want that party. I want the people who came to my birthday party on the beach in 1996.'

'The ones you've lost touch with.'

I nod.

'And you mock my Christmas card list.'

I nod. Who knew that as I watched my life flash before my eyes that the one thing I would regret would be not having a Christmas card list? Maureen holds my gaze in a look that says she totally believes that her generation is far superior to mine by mere fact of its ability to keep an up-to-date Christmas card list. I bow my head in shame.

'Well, surely we can track them down on the internet,' she says when she has made me squirm long enough. 'You must be able to find at least some of them.'

Indeed, I've already looked. Four in the morning saw me at the kitchen table typing names and locations that might somehow narrow down the billions of people now caught up in cyberspace. I'd found a few. The men were easier than the women. Marriage can wipe a woman's previous identity out, making it virtually impossible to track anyone down unless you were around at the time of the nuptials.

But Dave Brownsord, the epic DJ at my party, popped up soon enough, and by scrolling through his Facebook friends I eventually found Kev and Ian and of course their big mate Sean. I of course knew that if I found Sean I'd probably find my old mate Karen. She had the biggest crush on him when we were in Greece. So much so that Sean walked all over her. Got her to do all his dirty work. She was the one who sat up every Sunday night and went through his expenses for him, counted up how many receipts he'd written for trips and called the coach company to confirm his transport. She even went to meet the planes he was meant to on a Sunday morning if he was too hungover. She was like his personal PA, taking all the pain of being a rep out of his hands and smoothing it over.

Sean was the only reason why we ever fell out. Like the time when I found her in the all-night launderette doing his washing whilst he was out on the town showing some female holidaymakers how to have a good time. She never knew where she was with him. He dangled her on a piece of string and would occasionally rein her in and feed her a morsel of how being his girlfriend would feel like. He'd take her out for a flash meal or hire a boat for an afternoon's sailing and a picnic on some remote beach. He'd feed her just enough to keep her slaving away whilst I would try and convince her that a picnic once a month wasn't enough to reward her for the hours she spent playing nursemaid.

I totally blame Sean for why Karen and I lost touch. When I called our apartment a couple of weeks after I'd fled for England it was Sean who picked up the phone and not Karen. When I enquired he'd said she was out buying them dinner. Then he'd informed me he'd moved into the apartment that Karen and I had previously shared. How convenient, I thought, for him to be actually living with his maid rather than two blocks away. I said I looked forward to receiving a cheque for the advance rent I'd paid at the beginning of the season. He put the phone down.

I'd tried a couple more times and eventually got through to Karen, at which point I lambasted her about allowing Sean to move in and take advantage of her and my pre-paid rent. She told me she was very happy. I put the phone down this time. We never spoke again.

And there she is nestled amongst Sean's two hundred and twenty-two Facebook friends. Karen Smith, as she is now called, beaming out at me. How was I ever going to find a Karen Smith? Thank goodness for Sean Hounslow is all I can say.

The assessment of how the last twenty years had gone according to Facebook for Karen looked pretty good at first glance. She was clearly married, hence the new surname, and there was a daughter who seemed to be at university. But, on closer scrutiny of the very few photos hobnobbing about her page, there was also another child. A much younger one. Maybe seven or eight? What was that all about? Two marriages perhaps? But Karen didn't strike me as the sort. She was always so very loyal. Two marriages and kids by two different fathers was not her style. I struggled to find any pictures of men who looked like husband material, and then I spotted it. My heart sank for her because it was as clear as day what had happened. So clear I bet I could have predicted it way back in 1996.

The older girl was called Sienna Hounslow. So she'd married him. She'd married Sean and then clearly he'd done the dirty on her as he was always going to, leaving her to be a single mother until she presumably met Mr Smith, the father of Evie, the younger child. Of course that's what had happened. Sean followed the easy life for so long and then skedaddled the minute he found a fresh bit of skirt willing to do his bidding. Utterly fucking predictable. I felt sad. I felt bad. I wished I'd been there for her. Maybe I could have stopped her marrying him. At the very least maybe I could have held her hand when he walked away whilst I bit my lip and stopped myself saying, 'I told you so.'

'I've tracked some of them down,' I tell Maureen.

'So have you been in touch?'

'I've sent them all messages. But that was only a few hours ago and I've heard nothing since. They won't be able to come, will they? Not with this short notice and me contacting them out of the blue. I haven't seen them all for twenty years.'

The message to Karen had been the hardest. What do you say to someone who has turned out to be your best friend of all time? The person you shared everything with at a time in your life when you absolutely needed to share everything. When you were facing the baffling arena of trying to find your future through the medium of work and men. When you were constantly trying to navigate your way through opportunity after opportunity, trying so desperately hard to make the right choices. Well, that was your constant challenge anyway, until every so often you could say, fuck it, fuck it all, it's time for play, and you would let go and hang the consequences. That's your twenties, a desperate attempt to grow into your future whilst every so often getting childishly drunk on your youth.

In twenty years I'd never managed to replace Karen, despite a constant search for someone to step into her shoes. Maybe it's not possible. Maybe the person you share that growing-up time with can never be replaced. The person who held your hand as you faced your first foray into the adult world. The person who held your hand as you pogoed around the kitchen at two in the morning, high on gin and your discovery you were both totally into the same boy-band. The person who held your hand when she got her first promotion and you didn't and said it wouldn't change anything. The person who held your hand and laughed until she cried at the state of the one-night stand you'd brought home and made you realise you were worth so much more than that. The person you were silly and serious with during the time in your life when you can get away with both. Before any real responsibility, whilst you were working out what kind of responsibility you wanted.

Maybe you cannot replace the person you live through that part of your life with. There's an understanding of the real you. The you without the husband or the kids or the career that's either taken off or not. The you that you have defined before your choices of husband and family start to define you. Before success or failure, smugness or resentment has managed to weave its way into your personality. The you before the passing of time got hold of you and shook you until maybe you don't even recognise yourself.

I'd sent Karen my phone number. Said I'd love to catch up. Said I was trying to organise a get-together and would love it if she could come. Said I was trying to get hold of some sumo suits for old times' sake. I thought that might make her smile. Give her a happy memory to banish the achingly long silence that has existed between us. All I could do was wait and see if she could put the passage of time behind her and pick up the phone.

'They'll come,' says Maureen.

'I wouldn't,' I shrug.

'You would,' she replies.

I think about it. She's right. Of course I would. If anyone from that time contacted me and said they were planning a reunion I would be in there like a shot. A chance to relive the memories from those days? It would feel like being offered a fizzing sparkling cocktail on a cold wet foggy winter's afternoon. A chance to be uplifted and transported away from the gloominess of now to a happier, brighter past where the everyday monotony has been airbrushed away, leaving only the good times for us to fawn all over like they were our greatest achievement. Maybe they were.

'But what if the others are still drinking cocktails every day?' I say half to myself.

'You what?' says Maureen.

I look up at her. 'What if they're all happy and leading great lives and don't need the shot in the arm of their twenties to cheer them up?'

'They'll come,' she says, with either the certainty of age and wisdom or sheer bloody-mindedness. 'So who else?'

'I guess I should invite some of the other school mums,' I say without enthusiasm.

'You should,' agrees Maureen. 'Don't shut them out now. You need them and they might surprise you. Give them a chance at least.'

I nod. I'll have to somehow make up for my outburst last week but strangely I've missed the messed-up bunch.

'Oh, and I'd like to ask Mark's friends,' I add. 'Well, his old mates. You know, from way back. Not that he sees much of them now but they were good to me back then when I moved here with him. We had some good times – I couldn't have a nineties party without them.'

The gang Mark had arrived on the plane with in Greece all those years ago had proved to be good genuine lads, who were just out for a laugh, but when push came to shove, would do anything for you. I'd become really fond of them all until one by one they seemed to slip through the net of people's lives moving in different directions. Mark had aggressively continued to climb the career ladder whilst the rest settled into more mundane roles, choosing to work to live whilst he planted himself firmly in the live-to-work camp.

His long hours led to missed lads' nights out, which led to them eventually not asking him until they only gathered for special occasions. Mark's social life became more wrapped up in dinner with colleagues, where talk inevitably strayed to work whilst I was left to make small talk with wives about local shop openings or where to get a decent haircut. Dull, dull, dull. I longed for long nights down the pub with Mark's proper mates that would inevitably end up in a visit to a kebab shop and a bottle of whisky in front of a recording of *Eurotrash*. That was fun, not the laboured three-course meals with matching crockery and napkins that wouldn't iron. That was hard work. Give me a kebab in front of the telly any day.

'So, food then?' enquires Maureen.

'Do we need food?'

'Yes, you do.'

That makes me feel old. When did I reach the age that food at a party became a requirement rather than an afterthought?

'I have an idea!' announces Maureen.

'We are not using Barbara,' I say. Barbara is the cook at Shady Grove and knows only one texture, slop.

'George,' says Maureen. 'You keep telling me how much he likes to cook.'

'He couldn't cater for a party!'

'Why not?'

'He's fifteen and he can barely say boo to a goose. I couldn't put him under that kind of pressure, it would destroy him.'

'Poppycock,' says Maureen, bending over and ticking something on a list in front of her. 'Bring him with you tomorrow, I'll talk to him.'

'You don't know him, Maureen. You don't know what he's like. He'd never cope.'

She looks up at me but says nothing.

'What?' I say.

'You do realise why he can't cope?' she says eventually.

'Oh, do please tell, because we've spent hours in therapy waiting for someone to tell us why our son can't cope.'

'Because you don't let him,' she states simply. 'The slightest problem and you cope for him. You dive in to solve it. He doesn't cope because he never has to. It's your generation all over. What do they call it – chopper parenting?'

'I think you mean helicopter parenting.'

'Yeah, that's it.'

'I'm not a helicopter parent.'

'Yes, you are.'

'No, I'm not. Who do you think you are, Dear Deirdre all of a sudden?'

'She's a waste of space if ever I saw one! Anyway, I like to model myself more on Judge Judy. She talks a lot of sense.'

'You need to get out more.'

Maureen looks offended. 'I don't need to get out more to be able to tell that you are compensating for Mark with George,' she states.

'What?'

'George is a big disappointment to Mark and *you* are trying to compensate,' she continues. 'You're overly protective; you're smothering him, doing everything for him, trying to make it all right when all you're doing is magnifying the problem.'

I am beyond startled at Maureen's outburst. Yeah, she's blunt with her advice but I've never known her to stray into parenting territory – she hasn't even got any kids of her own.

'Why have you never said this before?' I demand.

'Don't shoot the messenger, will you!'

'I'm not.'

'You are.'

I feel sick – I think Maureen might have a point.

I should walk out. I came here to organise a party, not discuss what a terrible mother I have apparently been. I stare back at her defiantly.

'Bring him tomorrow after school,' she says. 'We need to agree the menu.'

I nod, although I want to cry. I want to cry over all the times I've put my arms around George to comfort him, rather than telling Mark to acknowledge his existence as his son instead of the ball of issues we have nurtured within him.

'Is it too late?' I murmur.

'I don't know,' Maureen says flatly. 'Just bring him with you tomorrow and let's see what we can do with him.'

'What shall I tell him?'

'The truth,' she shrugs. 'We're having a party and he's being commissioned as chef.'

'He sees his therapist on a Wednesday.'

Maureen raises her eyebrows.

'I'll bring him,' I nod.

Chapter Twenty-Eight

It's five thirty when my mobile rings. I pick it up. It's not anyone on my contacts list but I know straight away who it is.

'Hello,' I say.

'Oh hello, is that Jenny?'

'Karen?'

'Yes, yes, it's me.'

I want to cry.

'Oh, I'm so glad you've called me,' I gush.

'Well, how could I not? A party, you know I'm always up for a party,' she laughs. And I laugh too. And twenty years melt away.

'So how are you?' I ask.

'Good, really good, and you?'

'Fine.' My voice cracks. I'm not ready to answer this question truthfully yet. I wonder if I will ever be ready. There's an awkward silence.

'So what's brought this on?' she asks cheerily. 'It's a bit out of the blue, isn't it? Especially after all this time. How long is it?'

'Twenty years.'

'Is it really?'

'Yeah, 1996. You remember, it was Euro 96 year.'

'Oh yeah, three lions on a shirt. I remember.'

'We spent half the season with a St George's flag painted on our faces.'

'And Kev got one tattooed on his arse, do you remember? He said he would if we got to the semi-finals.'

'Oh God, I'd forgotten that! He didn't sit down for a week.'

'Yeah, that's right. He's added a few more since then.'

'You still see him then?'

'Yeah, we've kept in touch. We meet up every so often.'

A pang of regret ripples through my entire body. I have to ask.

'And any of the others? Do you still see them?'

She pauses.

'Yeah, actually. We all get together about every couple of years or so.'

The silence hangs heavy. Images of missed raucous happy times go racing through my head. Images of people reminiscing time and again about the good times. The sparkling cocktail on a dreary winter's afternoon. Oh, how I would have drunk it all in. How many reunions have I missed – maybe ten? What was I thinking?

'We would have invited you but Dave has sort of been the one who's organised it each time. I guess as you weren't there at the end you kind of got missed.'

'It's all right,' I say quickly, trying not to mind. 'I was the one who left. I was the one who needed to make the effort to stay in touch, not you.'

'Well, I've already had a load of messages from some of the others you've tracked down. Wondering if I knew what was going on. I said I was going to call you. See how are you are, see what the crack is.'

'Oh, I'm fine, I'm fine. I just wanted to… I just thought I'd like to see you all, that's all.'

'It's very short notice.'

'Oh, I know. I'm sorry but… er, an opportunity came up at a venue and I thought I'd just go for it. The more you think about and plan these things the more unlikely they are to happen. So I thought I'd just do it and cross my fingers. And it's just been my birthday so it's sort of a belated birthday party.'

'Well, it's funny because we were due a gathering this summer and Dave hadn't got round to organising it so you've given him a free pass. He's delighted. I think quite a few can make it by the sounds of it.'

'And you? Can you come?'

'Yes, of course, I'd love to come. I'd love to see you, I really would. It's been far too long.'

I let out a breath.

'It'll just be me. Julian will stop at home with Evie and Sienna – they're my daughters.'

'Oh yes, of course,' I say. 'Well, I saw that you had children on Facebook. That's great. And you're married then?' I ask tentatively.

'Oh yes, second marriage actually.'

'Really?' I feign surprise. I get ready to roll out the sympathy over the demise of her marriage to shit-bag Sean.

'Yes, well, life hasn't exactly been straightforward since I last saw you.'

'Oh, I'm so sorry to hear that.'

'So, do you remember Sean?'

Do I remember Sean? Of course I bloody remember him! He still owes me rent. He still owes me the friendship I should have had with you for the last twenty years.

'Yes, I remember Sean,' I say.

'Well, we ended up having a baby together.'

'Wow, congratulations.'

'A girl, Sienna, and he did the decent thing, he asked me to marry him. And so we did, by which time we were back in the UK and I was working in sales for a confectionery company full-time because Sean was struggling to get a job... And anyway, to cut a very long story short, Jules was my area manager. And, well, I'm not proud, Jenny, but we ended up having an affair and I ended up leaving Sean and eventually Jules and I married and had Evie.'

'You left Sean?'

'I still feel guilty,' she says.

'You left Sean,' I say again.

'I thought you of all people would be pleased. You never liked him, did you?'

'I'm over the moon,' I say, laughing, unable to help myself. 'I knew you were not meant to be but I always assumed he'd do the dirty on you and leave you devastated. But you having an affair and leaving him is the best news I've had all year. Brilliant, just brilliant! Sorry, am I meant to say that?'

'It's fine,' laughs Karen. 'I didn't realise you hated him that much.'

'I didn't hate him, I just hated the way he treated you.'

There's a silence on the other end of the phone.

'I'm sorry I never called,' she says quietly.

'No, no,' I say. 'It's not your fault. Like I said, I was the one who left. It was down to me to make the effort. I guess I was so wrapped up in trying to make a new life and forget what I'd left behind, I didn't want to hear what you were up to. I'd have been so jealous.'

'So what's happened with you then? You still with Mark?' she asks.

'Oh yeah,' I say. 'We got married, two kids, nice house, a dog...' I pause, hopefully we still have a dog, I think. 'All good.'

'Well, it was all worth it then,' she says.

'Oh totally. Living the dream, Karen.'

'And are you working?'

I laugh.

'Yeah, kind of. I'm a tour rep for geriatrics.'

'What?'

'I run activities at an old people's home. I use everything I learnt in Greece. Still spend half my time in toilets and half my time sorting out petty arguments.'

'Sounds like a riot.'

'It has its moments.'

There's a silence neither of us knows how to fill. A strangeness descends as we both weigh up how much of the last twenty years we want to rake up right at this moment. Blind. Without the aid of sitting in front of each other with the lubrication of wine.

'You look well on your photos,' I say eventually. It feels too soon to sign off just yet.

'You mean I've put on weight,' scoffs Karen.

'No, I don't. I mean you look well. You look happy. You look like you are having a good life.'

'Mostly I am,' she replies. 'I can't complain. But it's all edited highlights on Facebook, isn't it? Even Victor Meldrew would be having a whale of a time on there. I tend not to post pictures when I'm screaming at the girls because they are driving me demented, or of the third time I've fed them pizza that week because work has kept me out late again and I've not got round to doing a food shop, or my face when Jules tells me he's going away with work the following day, like I should have read his mind and organised a babysitter because I want to go to book group because for the first time this year I've actually read the flippin' book. I don't post *those* pictures.'

'We eat a lot of pizza,' I reassure her.

'Thank God for that! If I see another picture of a green salad I might throw the iPad away.'

'I'll put up pictures of our pizza if you want.'

'Will you? Every time you have pizza?'

'Sure.'

'That would make my day. So how's time treated your body?'

'Excuse me?' I panic.

'Don't tell me, you haven't put on a pound since I last saw you, you lucky bitch! Mind you, can you imagine if we ate and drank now what we used to, how enormous we would be. I only have to look at a bottle of wine now and I can feel it clinging to my thighs. So go on then, tell me. You've not gained any weight, have you?'

I shouldn't be surprised that talk has drifted to our bodies. Our weight and the way we looked was something we obsessed over and had many a late-night conversation about.

'Well, I did,' I admit. 'Back to the land of pastry and cream cakes didn't do me any favours and then of course two kids. I was enormous. Truly. But I have to admit that it's more under control now.'

'Don't tell me. You've done Weight Watchers, haven't you? I've tried it but I just can't get on with it. Does my head in.'

'No, it wasn't a specific diet. Just a change of lifestyle, I guess.'

'Bloody hell! You got into Pilates, didn't you? A lot of women swear by it.'

I'm about to deny any addiction to any form of exercise but I realise it might be easier to agree with Karen at this stage.

'Yeah,' I say. 'I do a lot of Pilates. It's changed my life.'

'Wow. And we couldn't even get you down to do aqua-aerobics. Who'd have thought it?'

'I know,' I mutter. 'Who'd have thought it? I guess it can't help, working in confectionery,' I say, trying to be sympathetic.

'Oh, I don't do that any more. Jacked that in years ago. I run my own events company now. We're doing really well actually.'

I'm afraid to say this hurts. I know my congratulations should be spewing out of my mouth at a rate of knots but they're not. It hurts to hear this because I am jealous. Jealous as hell. She's doing the thing she loves, she's successful and she's healthy. Everything I am not.

'Wow, that's brilliant,' I manage to utter. I must sound positive then cry about it later. 'Congratulations.'

'We can give you a hand if you like. With your party. Did I hear someone mention sumo suits?' She giggles. 'You got hold of any yet?'

'No.'

'I can get one of my girls on to it if you like. No problem. Anything else you need?'

Girls! She's got girls who work for her.

'A foam gun, maybe a few gazebos, oh, and a bouncy castle would be good,' I say.

There is silence on the other end of the phone then a roar of laughter.

'I'll sort it,' she says. 'Send me a list. Just like the old days, hey?'

'Yeah,' I agree. 'Just like the old days. Thanks, Karen.'

'Look, I gotta go,' she says abruptly. 'I need to pick Evie up from her dance class.'

'Well, thanks for ringing and for your help.'

'It's so good to hear from you. Seriously. We'll speak soon, yeah? Twenty years, eh?'

'Twenty years. How did we let that slip through our fingers?'

'I don't know,' she replies. 'Let's make sure we don't let the next twenty pass us by. Promise?'

'Of course. Promise.'

Chapter Twenty-Nine

I smell burnt toast the minute I walk through the door the following day. I figure it must be George as, according to Ellie, white carbs are so not what anyone is eating right now. Apparently, these days, what you eat is as much a part of your identity as what you wear and white carbs are the equivalent of Gola trainers to this generation whereas wholegrains and seeds are the new Benetton sweater. I suppose I should be glad that Ellie is careful about what she eats, but rejecting toast for fashion purposes doesn't seem like a healthy decision somehow.

A light haze of smoke is lingering in the kitchen and a chair is still standing under the smoke alarm where emergency action was clearly required to quell its warning. I spot the square battery discarded on the counter top. George has his back to me, hunched over the cooker. I remember now he mentioned he was going to cook dinner. He wanted me to buy artichokes whilst I was out but I've forgotten. I curse myself. I'd got too carried away looking at new clothes to match my new hair in shops frequented only by teenagers or women with no taste. It had been so enjoyable considering clothes for fun rather than clothes that were appropriate. Eventually I'd settled on a new pair of knee-high leather boots with stiletto heels and matching soft leather miniskirt. I'd also been into MAC Cosmetics and let them make me over. I had a smoky eye that was just to die for; I felt like a million dollars.

'Toaster's broken,' says Ellie, who is sitting at the table with her back to me, staring into a laptop. Phoebe lounges opposite her, a can of Diet Fanta poised at her lips. 'Phoebe put a five-grain bagel in and it didn't pop up then it stunk the place out and set the alarm off,' continues Ellie. 'I thought you said you were going to buy a new one?'

Throughout this Phoebe and I are engaged in a stare-off. She has looked me up and down, literally, and then curled her lip in disdain at my makeover. I'm now awaiting her verdict, refusing to be stared down by a seventeen-year-old.

'Jennifer,' she says eventually. 'I love what you have done with yourself. Is that a wig?'

Ellie whizzes round, eager to support Phoebe's opinion.

'Extensions, actually,' I say just as Ellie's jaw drops.

'What the fuck, Mother,' she exclaims, eyeing my dramatic make-up as well as my skirt and my boots.

'Ellie!' I cry, putting my bag down and grabbing the battery off the side. I step onto the chair, which is difficult given my too-high heels.

'Ooh, nice boots!' says Phoebe. 'You didn't get them from the charity shop, did you? My mum had a clear-out the other week and they look like a pair she used to wear a long time ago. She'd be delighted to know they have gone to a good home.'

She says all this as my arms strain to reach up to reattach the battery. I glance down and see that Ellie and Phoebe are mouthing something at each other. No doubt communicating the horror that is my appearance. Ellie will be enthusiastically agreeing with whatever Phoebe thinks because that's what she does. Agrees with Phoebe. Agrees with the Beastie, whichever crooked path she chooses to drag her down.

I can't stand it. What am I doing up here watching this happen right in front of my eyes? I step down and stand in front of my daughter.

'What do you think?' I ask her.

Her mouth hangs open and she glances uncomfortably at Phoebe.

'I want to know what *you* think, not what she thinks,' I say, throwing a cursory thumb in Phoebe's direction. Ellie's eyes flare in indignation but still she looks to Phoebe for permission to give it to me with both barrels. I catch the tiniest of nods from her friend and so it comes.

'You look ridiculous,' she says with a sneer. 'Why are you doing this?'

Phoebe snorts, trying to suppress her giggles. Ellie casts her a triumphant smile.

'Because I wanted to feel better about myself,' I tell her calmly.

Phoebe erupts. Ellie, to her credit, fights to stop herself from laughing in my face.

'Do you know what?' I continue. 'I decided I should look how I want to, not how other people think I should look. Listening to others' opinion on how you should look is for losers.' I turn to Phoebe and address this last point straight at her. 'I think I look fucking brilliant,' I say.

'Mum!' exclaims Ellie.

'And even if no one else thinks I look fucking brilliant, I *feel* fucking brilliant, so I really don't give a damn what anyone else thinks, especially you.'

I stab my finger towards the Beastie. Out of the corner of my eye I see George hunch up his shoulders further to shield him from the confrontation going on behind him.

Phoebe stares back at me, her eyes wide, a slight smile still playing on her lips.

'What *she* thinks matters,' I say, moving my stabbing finger to point at Ellie. 'What she thinks matters, except I have no idea what she thinks because it's too buried under the vile poison you spread all over it before it even surfaces.'

'Mum, stop it!' shouts Ellie.

'I don't have to listen to this,' says Phoebe, rising slowly from her chair.

'No!' cries Ellie. 'Don't go.'

But Phoebe doesn't even look at Ellie, just continues to stare me down.

'I'm out of here,' she declares and turns to leave.

'Don't go,' shouts Ellie. 'Just ignore her.'

'Bye,' says Phoebe, holding two fingers up over her shoulder.

Nothing is said until we all hear the front door slam.

'What the hell did you do that for?' exclaims Ellie, tears streaming down her face. 'She's my best friend!'

She's not, I want to tell her. You can do better than that. You'll leave school and meet new people and you will realise Phoebe wasn't a friend and you will assign her to the friendship graveyard where all friendships that were formed through proximity or convenience inevitably end up. Especially school friends. School friends are a lottery. Who you sit next to in Physics or who you end up in detention with on your first week because you forgot your homework. You rarely are selective; you haven't the guts at that age. Some get lucky. Some hit the jackpot and find their BFF, but most just grin and bear it until they suddenly find they haven't talked in years to the person they spent every waking hour with in school. And they realise they haven't even missed them.

'You can do better,' I tell Ellie. 'You're so much better than her. She's mean. She's mean to everyone. She's mean to me, she's mean to George—'

'She's not mean to me,' shouts Ellie, pushing past me to get out of the room.

I look at the back of the door she has just slammed. The sad truth of my daughter's closest friendship finally dawns on me: being friends with Phoebe keeps her out of the firing line. Ellie is keeping her enemy closest.

I sigh. 'I'm so sorry, George, I forgot to get your artichokes,' I tell the back of his head. He turns.

'It doesn't matter,' he says. He blushes then adds, 'You were great.'

'Was I?'

'Yeah, what you said, brilliant.'

'Thanks,' I reply.

We stare at each other awkwardly. He looks like he is waiting for me to say something.

'Has anyone called you about Betsy yet?' he finally asks, desperation flooding his face.

'No,' I say. 'Sorry. Shall we go out and look again later?'

He nods. 'Someone will call,' he tells me as he turns back to tend his food. 'They have to.'

He's right, I think. Artichokes don't matter.

★

A few minutes later Mark bursts in from wherever he's been hiding, closely followed by Ellie.

'What on earth has been going on?' he demands.

'Mum was horrible to Phoebe, just horrible,' sobs Ellie from behind him, tears streaming down her cheeks.

Mark is staring at me and I brace myself for attack. I watch him do a double-take at my make-up and new clothes. He opens his mouth and then closes it again.

'I can't believe it,' continues Ellie. 'What kind of mother does that? Phoebe's not speaking to me. No texts, no Messenger, no Snapchat, no nothing. I've tried everything. She's ruined my life,' she gasps, waving her finger in my direction.

'Phoebe only left the house two minutes ago,' I point out. Mark hasn't taken his eyes off me. I'm not sure if this is good or bad.

'Mum's right,' says George, turning round and staring at Ellie. 'Phoebe's a bitch.'

Ellie gasps. I'm not sure if it's at the content of what George has just said or the confidence in his delivery.

He walks up to me and holds his hand up to offer me a high five. I'm so dumbstruck by his clear, concise, un-stuttering summary of events that I leave him hanging. He nods solemnly at his hand and I raise mine to slap his and he smiles. Another smile from George. A head held high, chin-up, open smile. I beam back.

'You stay out of it,' roars Ellie. 'No one cares what you think.'

'*I* care what he thinks,' I say.

'I think you look beautiful by the way, Mum,' says George.

I look at him. I fall on him, enveloping him in my arms. I want to cry. I want to hold him there forever. I can feel the tears slipping out my clamped-shut eyes. The world stops for a moment as reality hits me hard. Harder than ever before. I don't think I can breathe. I want to scream in anguish as thoughts of loss engulf me.

But I don't.

I gulp. I wipe the tears swiftly away and open my eyes when I think I can bear to see again.

'You look so… young!' says Mark, his arm now over his daughter's shoulder but his eyes still on me.

'Like when we first met?'

He nods.

He looks confused. Confused at the memories it drags up. Happy memories of happier times. Memories that can have no place in his state of extra-marital-affair mind.

'What am I going to do, Dad?' whines Ellie, looking up at him.

He's still staring at me.

'Let her stew for a bit,' he says eventually. 'She'll come round.'

'No, she won't! Mum has to apologise. Tell her she didn't mean it.'

'But I *did* mean it,' I say.

'Phoebe is sooo mean,' adds George.

'But she's my *friend*,' squeals Ellie.

'Maybe if she wasn't so mean she would have more friends and wouldn't be thinking right now that she has to come crawling back because if she doesn't, she has no one to hang out with.'

'Do you think so?' asks Ellie.

I shake my head in despair.

'Yes,' I sigh. 'She only has you. She'll be in touch.'

'And then you'll apologise?'

'No!'

'Dad, tell her she has to apologise.'

Mark says nothing. I wish he would say something. But he won't. I know he won't, it's down to me. I gather my thoughts. This needs to count.

'I will not apologise and when she phones, you will not pick up the phone,' I say.

'What!'

'You will ignore her. You will call someone else. Someone you can be yourself with, someone you are not constantly trying to hide your weaknesses from. Someone you can laugh with and cry with and be silly with and not worry about whether you're going to be sniggered at because you're wearing the wrong brand of mascara. The next time you touch your phone it will *not* be to talk to Phoebe, it will be to call someone who treats you as a friend, *not* as a minion.'

Someone like Karen, I want to add.

Wow, where did that come from? It so doesn't sound like something I would normally say. It sounds like the speech of a woman who has nothing to lose, who knows she has only a limited amount of time left to speak her mind. A woman who needs to make sure she passes some vital lessons in life on to her daughter.

Mark is staring at me now with his mouth open.

A faint melody fills the air and Ellie reaches into her jeans pocket faster than Quick Draw McGraw. A quick glance at the screen and I can see Phoebe's name glaring out at me. Ellie's finger flies up to accept the call but never gets there as Mark grabs the phone from her hand. He looks at it in amazement as though he cannot believe what he has done.

Phoebe's name continues to throb as Mark holds the phone out of reach.

'Let me have it,' cries Ellie.

'Your mum is right,' he says, slipping it into his back pocket.

Ellie looks between her parents in disbelief. I look at Mark in utter amazement. This must be the first time in years he has backed me up against Ellie. If ever.

'Are you serious?' Ellie asks her dad.

'Yes.' He nods.

She screams in frustration and stalks out of the kitchen for the second time that afternoon.

'Thank you,' I say to Mark.

He nods.

'What you said,' he says, 'well, you were absolutely right.'

'She needs more of a firm hand,' I say, 'to help her make the right choices.'

He keeps nodding. He's listening.

'I said I'd go out and look for Betsy again with George later. You coming?' I ask.

I can tell he's about to say he's too busy but then he appears to change his mind.

'Okay.' He nods. He's still looking at me.

'You look great, by the way,' he eventually says then turns to leave the room.

Chapter Thirty

I'm lying in bed reading a book when Mark comes up that night. Yes, a book, a *real* book. The iPad has recently been banished to reside downstairs. I can't stand the temptation to surf the internet waves for information about my cancer. It sits there innocently charading as a gateway to knowledge that might change things. I don't need that right now. My mind needs to be focused, not distracted by a million other opinions on my illness. Mine is the only opinion that matters so I have buried my head in a book to escape. Escape into a fictional world of nonsense that neither expects me to assess how factual it is nor asks me to draw any conclusions.

My book-buying pretty much halted at the time our first tablet entered the house. Anything published after 2012 I reckon didn't stand a chance against the barrage of portable content that flooded our home. Our bookcase is a museum, a relic of times past. Although a shelf has been cleared to accommodate the various gadgetry that needs charging every night. Long white curly wires connected to extension cables make an untidy mess against the geometric uniformity of novels standing to attention.

After we'd spent another two hours pounding the streets in the fruitless search for Betsy that afternoon, I'd run my eye along the spines, looking for something to read during a much-needed bath. A raggedy, clearly much-loved book, to the extent I could not read the title, sparked my curiosity. Of course, it had to be. The nineties bible for a new generation of women that got passed from pillar to post after its 1996 release. Next to it rested another sure-fire hit I remember Mark devouring by the pool during his holiday. He was reading it for the fifth time, I recall him claiming – he didn't want to risk buying something different in case he didn't enjoy it as much.

I'd taken both books upstairs, ran the bath and read until my fingers were too wrinkly and dampness was starting to curl up the already curled-up pages.

I'd moved to the bed and I am already a quarter of the way through when Mark strides in at ten thirty. He's been out for a meal with one of the new investors.

'Good dinner?' I ask, not looking up.

'Fine,' he replies. I can hear wardrobe doors being opened and the swish of clothes being discarded.

'Food nice?'

'It was fine. Didn't really notice. A lot to discuss, you know.'

'Sebastian's?'

'Yeah.'

Wow, I think. Over sixty quid a head is a lot to spend on food you didn't really notice. I want to ask if he enjoyed our night in the pub garden more but I don't – I don't need to ask really.

I lie there and listen to him in the en suite. If he's taken his iPad in he'll be a while but if not, he'll be in and out in no time. I glance over to see his tablet still charging on the bedside table. Sure enough, moments later the gentle whir of his electric toothbrush sparks up, followed by a gargle of mouthwash.

'What's this?' he says when he emerges, pausing over his side of the bed.

'It caught my eye on the bookshelves this afternoon,' I reply. 'I remembered how much you loved it. Thought I'd just bring it up, see if you fancied reading it again.'

He picks it up and gets into bed.

'I've got some stuff to organise on *Clash of Clans*,' he says absent-mindedly, turning the book over to read the blurb of *The Firm* by John Grisham.

'Look what I found for me,' I say, pushing the cover of *Bridget Jones's Diary* under his nose.

'Haven't you grown out of that by now?' he asks. 'I thought it was all about single women in their thirties trying to get laid.'

'Actually no, it would seem,' I say. 'It's really about just being a woman and it strikes me reading it again that not a lot has changed. Apart from technology, of course. She talks about VCRs and in-trays and waiting for men to phone rather than text. All that's different but fundamentally nothing has changed in twenty years.'

'Mmmm,' he nods. He's opened the Grisham book. He's reading the first page.

I go back to Bridget and her knickers. It's quiet, it's calm. There's no niggling movement of elbows as Mark knocks down fruit on *Candy Crush* or navigates his way through the day's news. There's no blue light nudging us awake, demanding a level of alertness. Just a soft orange glow from two bedside lamps as stories lull our eyes shut. As our minds escape to other lives, relieved of the stresses and strains of our own.

I can hear his breathing slow and steady, then slower and steadier, until I hear a faint plod of the book hitting his chest. I turn over and carefully lift it out of his hands then place it on his bedside table, clicking his light off as I lean back. I stare at him up close. I study every wrinkle, every line, every eyelash, then I kiss his forehead. He snuffles and twitches then turns towards me onto his side, his arm reaching over my waist. I turn away from him as slowly as I can, then reverse into his body as we lie like two spoons in a napkin, waiting for a couple to share a dessert. Sleep comes quickly.

Chapter Thirty-One

'I'm having a party,' I announce the next morning.

Mark has overslept. His reading an actual book distracted him from setting his alarm and now he's dashing around the bedroom like a whirling dervish, swearing under his breath about a presentation he needs to finish before nine.

'On the twenty-first,' I add. 'It's on the calendar.'

'Since when?' he asks, ramming the fat end of his tie through the knot.

'Yesterday.'

'You decided to have a party yesterday?'

'No, I put it on the calendar yesterday.'

'But when did you decide to have a party? You never mentioned it.'

'Oh, a while ago. Well, actually, to be perfectly honest, after I went to that funeral. Made me realise we haven't had a party in too long.'

'What funeral?'

'Oh, erm…' I'm already struggling to remember her name. 'Emily Stonehouse.'

'Someone from the home?'

'No, a friend of Maureen's, actually.'

'Oh,' he says, turning away to pick up his watch and cufflinks from the top of the chest of drawers.

'And well, my birthday was a bit rubbish, wasn't it? Decided I needed to put that right.'

'The only thing that was wrong with your birthday was your choice of restaurant,' he says, turning back to face me.

Not the fact you left me high and dry to go back to work to shag what's her face, I thought.

'Well, whatever, I thought it was time we had a party.'

'I don't have time for a party just now,' he says.

The temptation to shout at him that if he gave up shagging his mistress he might have time is almost too much to bear.

Despite falling asleep quickly it had been a bad night. Nights are the worst thing about having cancer. Reliving 1996 doesn't shield me well at three in the morning when I'm positively shaking with fear at the blackness, not of the night but of death.

The middle of the night is when it looms and engulfs and swallows me up and I have no defence, no distraction, nothing. No radio tinkling away in the background, constantly keeping me out of the depths of my mind. No TV throwing me lives and stories separate to my own to mull and chew over in the blessed relief of not having to dwell on my own. No friends or enemies or family to occupy my thoughts as I deflect requests and phone calls and texts and demands, putting out fires then reigniting them. In the middle of the night I long for the drone of daytime television to keep the wolf from the door.

But if I wake as I did last night, still in the arms of my husband, the wolf makes his attack and savages my brain with thoughts and feelings so black and vile that I could be physically sick. The party, the vision of the party, weakly tries to fend off the wolf as I explore food options, cocktails and where I might find foil dishes for custard pies. These thoughts struggle against the force to confront what it will feel like to die. The terror of what there will or will not be after I am gone. What is contained in the blackness of death.

It's a battle but eventually the image of me on the shoulders of my friends singing Oasis at the top of my voice sends a tear down my cheek but seems to quell the ferocity of the attack. 'Champagne Supernova' weaves its way through my mind and the next thing I know, Mark is charging round the room like a bull in a china shop, cursing the fact he's slept like a baby.

'You don't have to do anything,' I tell him. 'Just turn up. It's on the calendar,' I re-confirm.

I was sure to do this before mentioning the party. The calendar is sacrosanct. If it's not on the calendar it ain't happening, and if it's on the calendar and you have neglected to previously note something you have already arranged, well, that ain't happening either. First to the calendar wins every time.

He looks at me and sighs, then looks at his watch. He wants to argue. He wants to tell me it's a waste of time and money but he doesn't have time. If I'd planned it, telling him now would have been a genius move. I pat myself on the back.

'We'll talk about it later,' he says, grabbing his jacket from a coat hanger.

'Of course,' I say, knowing that by the end of today I will have hopefully put everything in motion, committed money, invited more people, so a conversation about not having the party will be immaterial. This party is happening. The wolf whimpers away into the corner for another day.

Chapter Thirty-Two

All four of them look at me blankly.

'Did you say 1996?' asks Zoe.

'Oh yes, brilliant, hey?' I say, nodding enthusiastically. 'It's going to be such a laugh.'

I grin back at her and watch the colour drain from her face. She'd been very gracious in accepting my apology over the phone earlier. I'd told her I'd had time to think about what I said that day in the café and I explained that everything I'd said was untrue. I'd just had a terrible birthday. Mark hadn't performed like the loving husband that Geoff clearly is.

There had been a pause on the other end of the phone. I could practically hear her brain whirring.

'Well, I appreciate that you are being very honest with me, Jenny,' she eventually declared. 'I know that I'm a very lucky woman.'

'Exactly,' I agreed. 'I'm just jealous, that's all, but it's no excuse for that rubbish I said about you buying wine in the Co-op. I just hope you are a big enough person to be able to forgive me.'

'Of course I'm a big enough person,' she said. 'I'm sorry that you were jealous, I really am, but what am I supposed to do, not talk about what me and Geoff get up to or the lovely things we go and do and see?'

'Of course not, Zoe. It's not your problem, it's mine.'

'Okay, well, apology accepted. Let's put it behind us, shall we?'

'Zoe, you are a true lady.'

'Well, I try.'

'Lunch at Nourish?'

'That would be lovely. I'll tell the others, shall I?'

'Oh, I've already invited them.'

'Oh, and they said yes?'

'Yes. See you at twelve then.'

The other three do have the decency to look a bit sheepish when Zoe walks in, for not consulting her on whether they were permitted to accept an invitation from me. Emma hides behind a menu, Lisa pretends to send a text and Heather makes a big play of getting Zoe a chair from another table so we can make up five.

I proceed to pour my heart out to them about what a disaster my birthday was, which was why I'd been in such a bad mood last week. I apologise profusely whilst they all nod kindly and Lisa presents me with a gift bag containing two sets of cactus lights.

'You were weird that day,' she says as she hands them over. 'I was going to bring these over after they got delivered but I wondered if it was the cactus lights that had upset you.'

'No, these are brilliant,' I say, pulling out the two strands. And they are. Even without being lit up they make me smile.

'They need batteries,' points out Lisa. 'I would have put some in but I'd already taken everyone's money and it seemed too complicated to ask for more.'

'It's okay, I've got some at home.' I stuff them back in the bag and put it under my chair.

'I would have been upset if my husband had taken me to The Purple Burrito for my birthday,' says Zoe. 'Geoff's managed to book Le Manoir aux Quat'Saisons in Oxford for our wedding anniversary by the way. We're staying over.'

'How lovely,' I beam at Zoe.

'Thank you,' she replies with a nod of acknowledgement.

'Well, Mark's trying to make up for it,' I announce.

'Oh, good for Mark,' says Emma. The relief is written all over her face. She's not comfortable if any of us are bitching about our husbands.

'I can put him in the right direction for a light-up palm tree,' says Lisa. 'Direct import from China. They're so cheap, they're insane.'

'Do you think that's because they've been made in a factory employing children as slave labour?' asks Heather, peering over her glasses at Lisa. 'Do you really think you should be buying from such people?'

'They supply Smith & Jones on the high street,' says Lisa. 'Says so on their website.'

'Of course it does,' says Heather. 'I always buy my light-up palm trees from Smith & Jones.'

'Actually he's organising a party for me,' I interject.

'Who is, Mark?' gasps Zoe. 'For you?'

'Yes,' I confirm. 'Isn't that brilliant?'

Zoe looks confused. A party might trump a night away at a fancy restaurant.

'That sounds lovely,' she says. She doesn't pat my hand this time.

'That's wonderful,' says Emma, practically bursting with happiness that we are going to live happily ever after because Mark is organising a party for me, even though he isn't.

'You will all come, won't you? It's the weekend after next. Thought we'd do it quick to get it in before the summer holidays and everyone takes off to faraway places.'

'That reminds me,' says Zoe. 'I must book my fake tan in before we leave for St Barts.'

'Is that the twenty-first then?' asks Lisa, looking at her phone.

'Yes,' I say. She starts tapping.

'It's in the diary,' she confirms.

'Brilliant,' I reply.

Emma fishes out a diary from her bag. 'Yep, we can do that,' she confirms.

'I know we're free,' adds Heather, without referring to anything. I don't think she gets out much.

'And you, Zoe?' I ask. She's scrolling through her phone, wrinkling her forehead.

'It appears so,' she says. 'We must have had a cancellation.'

'Oh, that's so brilliant. I'm so pleased you can all come, I can't tell you.'

'So is it at your house?' asks Emma.

'Oh no, it's at Shady Grove actually. On their lawn – more space.'

'Oh,' says Emma, looking slightly surprised.

'Oh, and it's fancy dress,' I add.

'Seriously,' says Zoe. 'Fancy dress?'

'Yes,' I say. 'I love fancy dress.'

'Any particular theme?' asks Zoe. 'I do still have a Marie Antoinette gown in the loft from an eighteenth-century ball we went to a few years ago.'

'The theme is 1996,' I announce.

All four of them look at me blankly. I smile inside.

'Are you serious?' Zoe eventually says. 'What on earth do we wear for that?'

Lisa immediately dives in to Google '1996' on her phone.

'Oh yeah,' she nods, 'I get it now. There's some great stuff here. We can so do this, girls,' she says, looking up. She grins at me, genuinely excited, and I'm so grateful to her. 'What are you going as?' she asks.

'Ginger Spice, of course,' I say, pointing to my hair, which everyone has been too polite to mention.

'What a riot!' she exclaims. 'Right, you leave it with me. I'll get this lot sorted,' she says, casting her thumb at the other ladies. 'We won't let you down. I've got this, you just wait and see.'

Chapter Thirty-Three

Okay, so I have to tell you something: I've become a stalker.

I know, I'm not proud, but sometimes I'm so filled with the absolute need to see them, to watch them live, that I get in the car and drive to their school and park outside at lunchtime when I know I might see them drifting out.

I watched Ellie today. Phoebe has not been mentioned so far this week. Then again, no one has been mentioned, as she's not talking to me. I watched as she wandered out of the gate, running her hand through her hair before looking back to check on her accomplice. I braced myself to see her best friend but instead a boy appeared with floppy hair and a slouch. I gasped. This is new. A boy? Is a boy better than Phoebe? All the pitfalls of a potential boyfriend flash through my brain. Kissing, groping, sex, teenage pregnancy! Despite all that, I was still relieved not to see Phoebe.

I'd watched as he smiled warmly at my daughter and draped his arm protectively around her shoulders. For some reason an image of Ellie standing at the altar in a wedding dress blundered into my mind. A cruel reminder of an image I will never see. I'd screwed my eyes tight shut, trying to blot out the picture and prevent the tears spilling out. I turned on the engine and drove to work.

Later that day I return and watch George amble through the gate looking nervously around, head bent low. What am I to do with him? The times I have been tempted to come clean with Mark for the sole reason of talking about George and how we might suit him to life more. Make him at ease with the world. I know I need to somehow see a brighter future for him. See him on his way in a positive direction rather than gazing into a motherless black hole. I know I cannot leave him like this.

I flash my headlights at him and he wanders over.

'Has someone called about Betsy?' he asks hopefully, getting into the car.

'No,' I say. 'Sorry.'

His face falls. He reaches to put his seatbelt on. My heart might break. At this very moment it might break.

'So why are you here?' he asks.

'I wanted to see you,' I say, looking at him. He looks up at me and frowns.

'Are you okay?' he asks.

'Fine,' I try to say brightly. 'Why do you ask?'

'You look ill,' he says.

I gasp at the shock of it. The last thing I was expecting him to say. No one has said it to me. Not one person, so I thought I was getting away with it. My fictional 'Lean in 15' diet regime ready as back-up in case anyone mentioned my weight loss. Nobody had. I couldn't work out whether that made me happy or sad.

'Do I?' I say, hurriedly putting the car into gear and looking behind me over my shoulder to hide my face from him. 'I feel fine,' I add. 'Bit tired, that's all.'

'You need to eat more,' he says, looking straight ahead now. I gasp again. 'You wouldn't share the stroganoff with me I made last week – you love stroganoff.'

Who is this boy? He's a teenager. He isn't supposed to notice these things. Isn't he supposed to be a self-obsessed moron by now? Why couldn't I have a normal teenage son like everyone else? Life would be so much simpler right now.

'I've been trying to be good,' I say. 'You know, lose a bit of weight.'

He doesn't say anything for a moment.

'You can stop now,' he says.

'Right, okay. If you say so.'

I look over and he's staring out of the passenger window. I can't help it – I reach over and touch his hand resting on his knee. He grasps my fingers then pulls his hand away. What am I doing? What exactly is the benefit of pretending I don't have cancer? The gloom descends like a blanket being dropped over my head. And I remember. Pretending you haven't got it is a lot easier than being suffocated by it, day in day out.

'I need you to come to Shady Grove with me,' I say.

'Why?'

'I need your help with something.'

'What?'

'I'll tell you when we get there.'

He looks over at me. He sinks down into his seat and dips his head deep into his jacket. We talk no more.

George follows me wordlessly into the reception area and I hear him shuffling behind me as I sign him in. I wonder if he has noticed the smell: detergent, polish and old. I'm sure he has. Has he spotted the noticeboard full of rules and regulations all designed to make the staff's lives easier rather than the residents' lives better? There are three fire extinguishers, the two smoke alarms and four panic buttons in reception alone. You only have to walk in here to feel on the edge of some kind of fatal catastrophe. Maybe that's what happens when you put a load of people close to death in one house together: you are always prepared for the worst.

'This way,' I say, striding off down a beige corridor in search of Maureen. She said she'd be in her room but on a nice day like today she's more likely to be out on a bench in the grounds. He follows me, occasionally having to jog a few steps to catch up.

When there is no answer at door number twenty-two, I suggest we head out to the gardens. George says nothing. I hope Maureen is right about all this. She's only met him once when I invited her round for dinner and yet she claims she is going to cure his anxiety by putting him in a high-pressure situation. Only someone of her age would think you could cure a mental disorder by sheer hard work and cooking!

I find her in the plum spot: sitting on Alice. Or rather a bench dedicated to Alice by her husband in 1985. They don't let you do that any more. Dedicate a bench, that is – Sandra said the grounds were starting to look like a bus station as there was a new bench arriving practically every week.

'And who wants to be reminded that a lot of people die here?' she famously said in a staff meeting.

So Alice's husband was lucky. He got his bench to remind us all of his wife's last resting place in the spot with the best view of the enormous lawn at the back of the main house where many an oldie would look out at the beautifully manicured lawns and no doubt pass wind.

'Hello,' she says as we approach. 'Just as I thought,' she adds. She holds out her hand and George takes it to shake, not raising his gaze from the floor.

'Now you sit down here,' she tells him. 'We've got work to do. Shall we say an hour?' she says to me.

'What do you mean, an hour?'

'Come back and get him in an hour,' says Maureen. 'We should be done by then.'

'But don't you need me?' I ask, acutely aware of George looking at me as though I have delivered him into the hands of Satan against his will.

'Ooh no,' says Maureen. 'We'll be fine, won't we, George? In any case he'll have much better ideas than you. Now go away, you've got bingo to set up.'

'Well, if you're all right…' I start to ask George.

'Of course he's all right,' dismisses Maureen. 'After he's taken his coat off. You must be sweating in that, lad.'

I turn away as George begins to remove his coat ever so slowly as though if he does it slowly enough this ordeal won't be happening to him. I take a breath. It'll be okay, I tell myself. How much damage can an elderly lady do to a fifteen-year-old boy?

I peer through the window a few times but all I can see is the backs of their heads. Every time I look, their heads seem to have got closer, which I take as a good sign, but this time I can't see George at all. It's as though he's disappeared – until I realise he's bent down as if he has his head in his hands.

After fifty-eight minutes I walk out the patio doors and cough loudly as I approach the bench. Both their heads turn instantly to face me.

Maureen offers me a smile. George looks like I've caught him doing something he shouldn't. His cheeks are rosy red – I'm not sure if it's embarrassment or he's caught the sun. I really should have made him put some sunscreen on.

'So do you want to go and get that book from my room, George?' says Maureen before I can ask how it's gone. She reaches in her pocket for her key and waves it at him. He glances at me then grabs it and takes off at speed. I watch him head towards the patio doors, stumble slightly, struggle with the handle, then disappear.

'Sit down, won't you,' says Maureen. 'He'll be a while. I've hidden the book I've sent him for right at the back of the shelf. And given he's a bit drunk, it might take him some time to find it.'

'What?' I say, staring at her.

'I've hidden the book. He won't find it quickly.'

'Did you say he was drunk?'

'A bit, I think. Not legless or anything.'

I'm speechless.

'I couldn't decide if ouzo was going to be appropriate to serve as an arrival drink so I asked around to see if anyone had any and sure enough, Mabel's daughter brought her some back from Greece last year. Thought I'd try it with George to see if he thought it would go with his food. I had this brilliant idea that we would have a Greek theme, you see.'

I'm still speechless.

'Sorry, didn't I tell you about the theme? Must have come to me after you left yesterday.'

'He's drunk!'

'No, just a bit tipsy, that's all.'

'He's fifteen!'

'Is he? I thought he was the seventeen-year-old?'

'No, that's Ellie. Even if he was seventeen I wasn't expecting to leave him with you so you could get him pissed!'

'I keep telling you, he's not drunk, just loosened up a bit.'

I stand up. What am I to do with her? She's out of control.

'He's got some great ideas for mini kebabs,' says Maureen. 'You know, fancy ones. Not with onion or anything. Heritage tomatoes, he mentioned at one point. Whatever they might be. But his idea is that we do fancy kebabs. All finger food, you see. Less washing-up. He's a very clever lad, your boy.'

'You got him drunk. What will Mark say?' I'm pacing up and down now, trying to work out how we sober him up before Mark gets home.

'Mark won't notice,' shrugs Maureen.

'He will. He's got a real thing about kids and alcohol.'

'George says Mark never notices what he does. Apart from when he's being rubbish at Maths. He said he could run around naked all day and his dad wouldn't give a fuck.'

'Maureen!' I exclaim – about something, I'm not exactly sure what. So many options are available.

'That's what he said and before you ask, yes, he did use the word "fuck".'

'Please stop swearing,' I beg.

'Just trying to be accurate. Just trying to convey George's depth of feeling. You really need to sort that out.'

'His swearing?'

'No! Mark ignoring him. I told you, didn't I, that it was a problem? George confirmed it to me. He thinks his dad's ashamed of him.'

I sit down. Months of therapy haven't got us this far. Months of trying to wheedle out of him some inner feelings that might allow us to help him. It's cost us a fortune. If only I'd known all I needed was a batty old lady and some alcohol.

'Is that what he said?' I ask. 'He thinks his dad is ashamed of him?'

'Not in so many words. But that's what he's trying to say. He said he feels like he is letting his dad down because he likes cooking rather than Maths.'

'He actually told you that?'

'Yes.'

'How?'

'I just asked him a few questions, you know, in between talking about kebabs and drinking ouzo.'

I lean back on the bench. It's going to take me a while to process all of this.

'Oh, and he thinks you might be having an affair.'

'What!'

'Don't worry, I told him that I definitely knew you weren't. I mean, look at the state of you! Why are you wearing pastels again? I keep telling you they wash you out.'

'But what on earth makes him think that I'm having an affair?'

'The new look, the weight loss and the fact that you and his dad never talk to each other.'

'Seriously? And his conclusion is that *I'm* the one having the affair? I've a good mind to just tell him. Tell him about his dad.'

'Calm down,' she says, laying a hand on my arm. 'It's probably not what George needs to hear right now, is it? And, anyway, that's the least of your worries.'

'What! Do you mean there's more?'

'Well, yes, there is actually.'

'Who are you, Jeremy Kyle? What was going on out here?'

'No, don't worry, he hasn't got anyone pregnant yet. Quite the opposite in fact.'

'What!' I leap up again. 'What do you mean, he hasn't got anyone pregnant yet. What are you talking about?'

Maureen is smiling. Smirking, to be exact. I don't see that there's anything to smirk about. She starts giggling. Why is she giggling? How can she be giggling when she has just mentioned my teenage son and pregnancy in the same sentence?

'Why are you laughing?' I demand, bending forward so my face is close to hers.

'Ooh, I couldn't say,' she says, laughing even harder.

'Tell me,' I demand. I'm getting cross now.

She coughs and attempts to compose herself, then collapses in giggles once again. I grab her shoulders and shake her.

'Tell me!'

'He's just, you know…'

'No, I don't know, so please tell me.'

'He just thinks he's wanking too much,' she manages to spit out before she hides her face behind her hands, the colour having risen to her cheeks.

I sit down again, staring at Maureen. Did she really just say what I thought she said? Her pink cheeks and near hysterics would suggest she did.

A sense of relief floods over me. The relief of talking about my teenage son's wanking habit rather than anything else.

'Did… did he say how often?' I find myself asking before I start to feel the giggles rising in my throat.

'No,' replies Maureen. 'And I didn't ask. That's between him and his, you know, thingy.'

She just said 'wanking' and now she's too embarrassed to call a penis a penis.

'So what did you say?' I ask.

'I said we have all been through it and it will pass,' she replies.

I look at her. What do you say to that?

'Thank you,' I say eventually.

'You're welcome.'

We sit in silence for a moment as I try to recall and categorise the revelations that have passed between us over the last five minutes. I'd expected to leave here with George a gibbering wreck and the prospect of an evening on the phone to catering companies. Now I have no idea what I'm leaving with.

'I was just telling your mum about the heritage tomato thingies,' pipes up Maureen as George suddenly appears in front of us. 'Can you explain them to her?' she adds. 'She's never heard of them either.' She turns to me – 'They sound amazing.'

'They're just old breeds,' says George, the very slightest of slurs perceptible. 'From the old days. I thought the people who live here might enjoy them alongside the kebabs.'

He sits down with a thump on the floor in front of us. As if he was worried that, if he didn't, he might fall over.

'You see,' says Maureen. 'Such a clever idea, such a clever boy. You should be very proud of him,' she tells me.

'I am,' I say, smiling at George. 'We both are.'

George says nothing.

'Oh, I did have one idea,' I tell him as I suddenly remember something I'd seen in a photo in one of my old albums. 'Something we had a lot of in the nineties.'

'What's that?'

'Vodka melon. Do you think you could have a go at that?'
He smiles back and nods before he falls over.

Chapter Thirty-Four

'I really don't have time for this,' says Mark as we pull up outside a row of terraced houses. 'I thought you said it was an emergency. Why are we here?'

'Look,' I say, pointing upwards. 'It's for sale.'

'So?'

'Our old house, our first house.'

'I know what it is, I just don't know why we're here.'

'Don't you want to see it?'

'No.'

'Oh look, that must be the estate agent coming.'

I get out of the car before Mark can make any other comment and walk quickly towards a shifty-looking man in his twenties wearing a suit that doesn't fit. Without a shadow of a doubt the man I booked the appointment with on the phone this afternoon.

'Mrs Sutton?' he says in a way that makes me feel a hundred and seven. 'And you must be Mr Sutton,' he says, diving forward to shake Mark's hand whilst failing to even offer to shake mine. A black mark, I think. Good job we aren't actually interested in buying the property or else I'd have some serious issues with dealing with this young man.

'We'll get you inside, shall we?' he says, fishing keys out of his pocket. 'You're actually the first ones to view the property,' he adds over his shoulder as he struggles with the sticky lock. 'It only went on the market yesterday.'

Mark flashes me angry glances behind his back. He's no idea what he's doing here. Neither have I really but when the alert came through I couldn't resist. I knew I couldn't not go and see the house I moved into with Mark in 1996. It was fate, surely.

I follow the estate agent boy down the hall and turn right into the open-plan downstairs space. Except it isn't. Someone in the last fifteen years has put a wall up to cordon off the living room. Who does that? Who puts up walls when everyone else is knocking them down? I cast my eyes around the very small-looking dark room. What have they done to our house? Our 1996? Perhaps we shouldn't have come. It looks weird with other people's stuff in it and a bloody great big wall.

Estate agent boy leads us through a newly created doorway into what is now a kitchen dining space. I heave a sigh of relief. It's much more like I remember. The kitchen that Mark and I put in – in 1999 – is still there, complete with its black and white tiled floor and exposed floorboards in the dining area. The memories come flooding back. The noisy, drunken dinner parties, the dancing round the table to Kylie and the Spice Girls and Oasis. The early-morning clearing-up, gagging as beer and wine dregs were cast down the plughole and glass after glass lined up on the counter ready to be washed and dried by whoever had ended up kipping overnight on the sofa or in the spare room. The smell of bacon and sausages as Mark presided over a massive fry-up to set people on their way out into Sunday, to the next sofa they could find to sleep off their hangovers. The early-morning dashes to get out of the house to work and the late-night suppers in front of the telly when

Big Brother actually had nice people on it and the *Cold Feet* crew were just extra members of our gang.

This is why I wanted to come. This is why I wanted Mark to come. To feel it again; feel what it was like in the early days.

Estate agent boy is droning on about something to do with energy efficiency and power-saving light bulbs but I haven't really been listening to him since we walked through the door.

'Let's go upstairs,' I say, talking over estate agent boy and grabbing Mark's hand. I lead him up the open staircase.

'What are we doing here?' he hisses in my ear.

'Shhhhh,' I say sharply.

'The master bedroom is right at the top of the stairs,' says estate agent boy, after I have already taken the turn.

'They've varnished the floor,' I say as we walk in. I'd spent a whole weekend sanding down the floor but had never quite got round to varnishing it. I wish I had – it looked gorgeous.

'Do you want to wait downstairs?' I turn round and say to estate agent boy.

'Would you like me to show you the other bedrooms first?'

'No need,' I chant back.

'Erm, okay then,' he says. 'I'll be just downstairs.'

He glances at Mark as though expecting him to explain this odd behaviour, then turns and leaves the room. I wait until I can hear the plod of his footsteps going down the stairs.

'Are you going to tell me what on earth is going on now?' hisses Mark.

'The estate agent said they were in the same position as us when we left,' I tell him. 'They've got a second child on the way, they need more room.'

I look around the bedroom and catch sight of the trademark technology owned by all young families: a baby monitor. It looks different to how I remember ours, more like a *Star Wars* robot. I look up at Mark. His hands are on his hips in frustration. I walk towards the big bay window overlooking the green. They'd play football there on a Sunday morning, loads of them. Their shouts and hollers and whistle-blowing were the soundtrack to our coffee-drinking, croissant-eating, newspaper-reading Sunday mornings.

Utter bliss.

'We made our babies here,' I say, turning round. 'In this room.'

His face drops.

'Do you remember?'

He doesn't say anything, he just shrugs. He has no idea what is going on.

'Do you remember the night we made Ellie?'

He still doesn't know what to say; he looks more bewildered by the minute.

'How on earth do you know exactly what night it was?'

'We'd walked across the green into town,' I say, pointing out of the window. 'I bet we had a race down the track. Do you remember how we used to do that?'

In the summer there would be an oval of faint white lines drawn on the grass, presumably for the nearby school. Often we would leave the house on a Friday night at the end of a hard week, hand in hand to head to the city's pubs. As we approached the white lines there would be a pause in conversation until one of us wouldn't be able to resist breaking free and making a sprint up one of the lanes. Mark would always win, mostly because he had more suitable footwear, and would shout over his shoulder just before the finish line, 'Loser buys the first round.'

'I always won,' he conceded.

'And I always bought the first round.'

He shrugs again, as if to say it was my own fault for wearing high heels.

'It was Tim's birthday that night,' I say.

Tim, aka Stubby, was the guy who had first come on to me when I had greeted Mark and his mates at Corfu airport all those years ago. Turned out he was actually Mark's best mate and a really great bloke. He just got a bit leery when he was drunk, that's all. He had been the one who had come round and put up some extra shelves when I moved in with Mark, as well as offering me a four-pack of Stella as a moving-in present. Like I said, he was a great guy.

'We went to meet him and his new girlfriend in that tapas place, do you remember?' I continue. 'We were a bit naïve as to how to order tapas so we didn't order enough. We weren't naïve when it came to ordering carafes of the house red though, were we?'

'Was that the night of the hangover from hell?'

'Yeah. Julie threw up outside the restaurant, she was in such a state. She said it was the nerves caused by meeting Tim's friends but I think it really was the entire carafe that she had to herself. Tim was legless too. They went home at nine, do you remember?'

'Yeah, didn't we carry on?'

'We did, like a pair of idiots. Thought we were all right. We went for one in Soda Bar and that tipped us over the edge.'

'Didn't we go to McTurks for a kebab?'

'We were starving. Turned out a couple of chorizo sausages and a cube of potato weren't filling enough. We brought them back here. It was like there had been a kebab massacre in the kitchen the next day.

There was cabbage, garlic mayonnaise and pitta bread everywhere. Still, the sex was good.'

'We had sex?'

'Yeah! The smell of chilli sauce turns me on to this day. You stank of it.'

'I'm starting to get flashbacks. Was there cabbage in your bra?'

'There was,' I say excitedly. 'You slipped your hand inside my bra and next minute you're pulling half my kebab out.'

He smiles. Thank God for that smile.

'We were like animals that night. It was like the kebab had released something in us.'

'Are you sure it wasn't the dodgy red wine?'

'Possibly,' I nod. 'But I woke up the next morning feeling very content.' I smile.

'And with the hangover from hell.'

'I have never known a headache like it. I think we lay in bed all day. I might have sent you for a reviving McDonald's at some point but I think that was all we managed.'

'It's the wine, you know. We drink much better quality wine these days,' says Mark. 'Means we don't feel like that any more.'

I seem to remember quite enjoying it. We lay in bed all day in each other's arms. Sleeping, moaning, whispering. It was actually a really lovely day. One of the best.

'I changed the bedding about a week later,' I tell him. 'I found a condom screwed up down the bottom corner of the sheet. I realised it must have fallen off. Four weeks later, I realised I was pregnant.'

'You never said.'

'What? That I'd found a condom?'

'Yeah.'

'Probably because I really wanted to be pregnant but I was worried that you weren't ready. But I was ready. Finding out I was pregnant with Ellie was one of the happiest days of my life.'

I'd taken the test in the middle of the night. I'd bought a kit but hadn't dared use it, then I woke up at three in the morning and couldn't stand it any longer. I sneaked into the bathroom and found my prayers had been answered.

'I've slept with someone.'

For a moment I think I have misheard but it only takes a look at his face to know he just said it. His mouth is slightly open as though shocked at his confession. He's white as a sheet, searching my face for a response.

'I know,' I manage to whisper.

He reels in shock.

'How? When?' he asks, his face stricken.

'I came to see you at work one night. You were in your office with… with her.'

He sways a little. I'm frozen to the spot. I don't know what to do. I'd always thought I would be in control of this situation when it happened – I hadn't expected it to be thrust upon me. Especially not here in this familiar/unfamiliar room. In this room where our lives began. Where our children's lives began. Mark drops down onto the edge of the bed and puts his head in his hands. It's a vintage-style floral-patterned quilt cover. We never had one of those. It was Mark's house when I moved in and it took a long time to filter in signs of femininity and it never quite reached the choice of duvet cover.

'How long has it been going on?' I ask. My heart is pounding. I don't know where we're going. I've tried so hard to be in control of things recently that being out of control of what might come out of this conversation is terrifying.

Mark lifts his head from his hands and stares hard at the fitted wardrobe door in front of him.

'A few months.'

'How long?' I ask again more urgently. He looks up sharply.

'Since I went on the New York trip.'

I remember that trip. It was last December. I'd always wanted to go to New York in December. See the Christmas lights and go ice-skating in Central Park. It sounded so romantic. Clearly it was.

'She went with you?'

'Yes,' he whispers.

'Did you go ice-skating?'

'No,' he says, shaking his head. 'No,' he says again.

This gives me a curious relief. Him taking her ice-skating would have felt like a betrayal. He knows I would have loved to do that.

'You just shagged her,' I say. 'That's all right then.'

'No, no, it isn't,' he says.

'Too bloody right it isn't,' I say, raising my voice and fighting the urge to hit him, batter him with everything I've got. Hurt him really bad. Hurt him until he can feel how much he is hurting me.

We're staring at each other, my breathing heavy as a result of my heart pounding, when we hear the tapping of estate agent boy's leather soles across the wooden floor down below.

'Everything okay?' he shouts from the bottom of the stairs.

I say nothing.

'We're fine,' shouts Mark, his voice cracking. 'Just doing some measurements. Won't be long.'

We both hold our breath as we listen to his footsteps tap again across the floor and fall silent, presumably as he returns to the carpeted lounge.

'I'm so sorry,' says Mark. 'Really I am.'

I almost laugh at the inadequacy of it. I walk over and sit on the large sill of the bay window. She's made a cushion for it – I always wanted to do that but never got round to it. She's clearly a better woman than I'll ever be.

I sigh and look over to him. I should tell him. I should tell him the only reason I found him fucking over the filing cabinet was because I have cancer. I was on my way to tell you this horrendous news but you were too busy screwing around to listen. You think you feel guilty now about having affair. Well, you throw cancer into that and see how it feels.

'Why didn't you say anything?' he asks. 'When you found out?'

I want to laugh again. This situation is absurd. Ridiculous. I brace my hands on the edge of the sill and look up. I don't want to tell him. Not like this. I don't want his affair to tarnish my cancer. I tell him now and his response, everything, will be sullied by the fact he's just admitted adultery. That's not fair. My cancer deserves more: it's an only child, not a twin.

'How could you not say anything?' he asks.

'I wanted you to have the decency to tell me,' I say.

He looks down in shame. He says 'Sorry' to the floor.

'It's over,' he adds. 'I ended it.' He puts his head in his hands again then looks up to study the built-in wardrobe door. It's pine, it's not very interesting.

He swallows. His face has an expression I have never seen before on him: confusion and fear. I wonder what particular aspect of this mess he is confused and fearful of.

'When did you end it?' I ask.

'Last week,' he says. 'It was weak and stupid,' he continues, shaking his head. 'I don't know why I did it, I really don't. She meant absolutely nothing to me. It's the stupidest thing I have ever done.'

I'm not sure he's saying this to convince me. I think he's saying it to voice his complete confusion as to how or why this has happened.

'So what happens next?' I ask quietly.

'I don't know,' he cries. I can see that this is the truth.

'I don't know,' he repeats with a pleading tone in his voice. Like he wants me to tell him what to do with this sordid mess. Like he wants me to tell him it's all okay and give him all the reasons why we should just stay together and ignore what has happened so that he doesn't have to think of them.

Of course I could give him one big fat enormous reason: I'm dying of cancer, that's why we should get past this. Maybe he should know all the facts. Maybe he should know that he could be facing two years of torture ahead of him as he watches me die if he sticks around. Or he could leave, then forever have to live with the guilt of deserting his wife virtually on her deathbed. If he knew that, what would he do? Would it be different?

I stand up and pull down my brown suede skirt.

'Well, I think you'd better make your mind up, hadn't you?' I tell him. I walk past him, leaving him to contemplate our future together in the very spot where so much of our lives began.

★

'So what's the verdict?' estate agent boy asks me, rubbing his hands together as I descend the stairs. He must be well excited we've spent so long up there – he probably thinks we're a sure thing on this one.

'I think it's more suitable for a young couple,' I tell him. 'It feels like a great place to start something and I don't think that's where we're at any more.'

Chapter Thirty-Five

I get in the car. I can see Mark standing at the door of number forty-four talking to estate agent boy. The temptation to drive away and leave him stranded is almost too much to bear. He's raking his hand through his hair and casting me occasional nervous glances. What is he talking to him about? Anything perhaps to avoid getting in the car with me. Eventually I switch the engine on, prompting estate agent boy to shake Mark's hand for the second time and bid his farewells. Mark walks towards the car without once making eye contact.

I'm in gear and releasing the handbrake before he even gets his seatbelt on. His safety is not my priority right now. We're on the ring road before he caves and breaks the silence.

'Perhaps I should move out for a while,' he says. 'Give us some space.'

'Space to shag her until you get her out of your system?'

'I *said* it was over,' he reiterates. 'I was thinking of going to stay with Mum and Dad for a bit.'

'Oh.'

'I want you to know that I didn't plan this, you know. I didn't go looking for it.'

'Oh, it just fell into your lap over a cosmopolitan and a hotdog, did it?'

It was tearing me apart that it started in New York. Their 1996 in Corfu was 2015 in New York City. It was breaking my heart to think of it having such an epic beginning. Mark's and mine was an epic beginning, not theirs. But suddenly Corfu didn't sound so fancy.

'I just need to get my head straight,' he says. 'The deal should finalise next week too and I just can't think. It's all too much.'

'My heart bleeds for you,' I say. 'An affair and the deal of the century. No wonder you're stressed.'

'That was red by the way.'

'What?'

'You just went through a red light.'

'I don't need you to tell me how to drive!' I shout in frustration. 'I need you to tell me what my future is. That's what I need you to do, since you've decided to play fast and loose with it.'

I stop. I know I'm not being entirely fair. I know my future – the big bad wolf comes and reminds me most nights now. The truth is I have no future for Mark to play fast and loose with. Still, that doesn't mean he can tell me how to fucking drive, does it?

Mark is hanging onto the handle in the roof, leaning as far away from me as possible. He's rubbing his eyes with his free hand. Playing for time. Trying to make a decision.

'I'll go to my parents' tonight,' he says eventually. 'Just for a few days, then we'll talk.'

Talk! What does that mean, talk?

'What will you tell the kids?' I ask.

That's a great question. I almost pat myself on the back. I've been storing it up for a few minutes. Waiting for the right moment. Here is the reality, Mark. You've got kids you might have to confess an affair to. Add that to your stressful, overloaded week.

'I'll tell them I'm going on a trip for now,' he says. 'They probably won't notice I'm gone anyway.'

'I was going to ask you to spend some time with George this week.'

'Why?'

'Because you never do and because he needs you and because, well, because he's wanking a lot apparently.'

'What! How do you know that?' he says, looking at me sharply.

'Maureen told me.'

'Maureen?'

'Maureen from Shady Grove.'

'How on earth does she know?'

'She's planning the food for my party with George – he's in charge of catering.'

'You're kidding me. He can't manage that.'

I'm tempted to stop the car but we're on the dual carriageway now so I'll just have to do my best to continue.

'I think he can,' I say. 'And so does Maureen.'

'And who the hell does Maureen think she is to be the expert on our son all of a sudden?'

'The woman who got him to say more in an hour than me, you or the damn therapist have managed put together.' I decide not to mention the fact she got him drunk. 'Now will you talk to him about this wanking thing or not? He needs to know he's normal. Perhaps don't use yourself as an example of how to gain control over your urges though, eh?'

Mark slumps back in his seat.

'Do you really think it's necessary?' he asks.

'Yes!' I say. 'It's called being a dad. It might be something you want to think about whilst you're on your "trip".'

He turns away from me and looks out of the window.

'I just need a bit of time, Jenny, that's all. Please.'

'Time,' I say, nodding. 'Yeah, don't we all?'

I sit in the lounge whilst I listen to Mark parading upstairs across our bedroom as he packs his suitcase. There's no other sound. George and Ellie are both in their rooms, either ignoring the arrival of their parents or protected from every move by headphones pumping out tuneless noise.

My phone beeps next to me on the arm of the chair: it's Karen, she's left me a message. She's found two sumo suits going begging and a foam machine. Oh my God, how I have missed her! She says she's driving back from a meeting in Nottingham, something to do with a new wine-tasting venue. She wants to call in as she says she'll be virtually passing our front door.

Her timing's not great, to be honest. The day your husband walks out is possibly not the greatest day to deal with a reunion with your best friend you lost touch with twenty years ago. But, I figure, what's the worst that can happen? I break down and tell her my life is a disaster whilst she shares with me her gloriously happy, post-affair marriage and wildly successful event-planning career? I can deal with that, can't I? Piece of cake.

I hear Mark knock on a door upstairs and then open it, closing it behind him. He's not in there long. Then there's a second knock: George's room this time, I think. He goes in. He's longer than with Ellie. I hope that's a good sign. Normally he wouldn't even bother to tell either of them he won't be around for a few days. He'd just leave me to fill in the gaps when they eventually realised they hadn't seen him in a while. So I don't know how long it should take to tell your son you are going on a 'trip' for a few days – and by the way let's talk about what you've been getting up to in this room all alone.

Ten minutes later there's a thud in the hall as the medium suitcase hits the floorboards. Hopeful, I think. It's not the large suitcase.

Mark walks into the living room. 'Possibly the worst moment of my life,' he says.

'Packing for your trip?'

'No, talking to George.'

'How did he take it?'

'Actually all right. I told him I could manage it in the time it took my mum to turn off her alarm, get out of bed, go to the bathroom and knock on my door to get up.'

'Boys are disgusting,' I say.

'You asked me to talk to him about it,' he shrugs.

'Did you make him feel better?'

'I think so,' he says. 'Who knows?'

'He needs you, you know.'

He looks at me with a pained expression.

'And that's not meant to be emotional blackmail. Irrelevant to all of this going on,' I say, pointing to the suitcase in the hall, 'he really needs you. He's growing up, you need to try harder with him.'

'For goodness' sake, Jenny, I've just talked to him about having a wank, what more do you want?'

I doubt very much we will have a sensible conversation at this precise moment about Mark's lack of interest in his son. My attack on his parenting skills would just be used against me, rather than propelling him to do anything about their fractured relationship. I will have to bide my time on that one. Squeeze it in at a less rocky moment. Whenever that might be. There is one last thing I have to mention, however, before he departs for his childhood bedroom to get some 'space'.

'I've invited Tim and Julie over for dinner on Friday night,' I announce.

Mark is speechless. He raises his arms in wonder. He may have expected me to have lain down in front of the door to stop him leaving, but he wasn't expecting me to throw in a conversation about wanking with his son followed by a random dinner invite to his best mate who he hasn't seen in far too long.

'When did you do that?' he eventually asks when his mouth has stopped opening and closing in a struggle to comprehend anything that is going on.

'This morning,' I say. 'Looking at pictures of Chester Green online reminded me what a great time we used to have. We've not seen them for ages. Thought it would be good to catch up – you were such good mates.'

He's shaking his head now in wonder.

'What the hell is going on here, Jenny? It's like you're trying to send us back in time. What with the ridiculous visit to Chester Green and now inviting Tim round? We've moved on, Jenny. That was the past. Look, big fancy detached house,' he says, waving his arms around the room. 'And as for me and Tim, well, we live in completely different worlds now. He's not interested in my negotiations on supply chain protection any more than I'm interested in how many bathrooms he managed to fit this week. We were always destined to drift apart. No big deal. I just don't get why you are suddenly obsessed with the past.'

I look up at him in his smart suit and tie, all still perfectly in place despite the epic journey we seem to have been on over the last few hours.

'Maybe because I liked you better then,' I say.

I can't help myself. One thing that thinking about 1996 all the time has achieved is to make me realise that maybe Mark isn't the person now that he was then.

'What on earth is that supposed to mean?'

'You've changed,' I say.

'I haven't!'

'Yes you have.'

'Well, if growing up and making a success of my life is change then maybe I have, but how can that be a bad thing?'

I sigh.

'You used to be fun,' I say.

He turns away.

When he turns back, he's red in the face.

'Well, I'm very sorry if I haven't been "Fun Time Frankie" whilst I've been working my arse off to keep this family in the manner to which it is accustomed.'

'We never asked you to do that.'

'Do what?'

'Sacrifice fun for work.'

'Someone in this family had to earn a decent living.'

'You can earn a decent living without turning into a...'

'A what?'

'Well, a bit of a twat actually.'

His eyebrows flare up until I can't see them. The gasp is audible. I feel bad. I know the man I love is somewhere in there. He hasn't gone. I just wish I could find him.

'You just seemed to forget how to laugh somewhere along the way,' I say, hoping it will cause the 'twat' accusation to be quickly forgotten.

'Maybe you didn't give me anything to laugh about,' he spits out in fury. 'Come on, Jenny, it's not been good for a while, has it?'

'Is this where you blame me? Blame me for you not being able to keep it in your pants?'

'I'm not blaming you, I'm just admitting that it's felt like we've been struggling.'

'Of course we've been bloody struggling! You're never here, Mark. Not in mind or in body. Obsessed with bloody work, obsessed with this bloody deal. You've no idea what's going on right under your own nose,' I say bitterly.

I bite my lip quickly. Tears are poised and tears would be bad right now. Tears would just confuse matters.

'And you pass everything off as a joke,' he spits back. 'You take nothing seriously. You won't talk to me seriously about anything. This deal… this deal… is huge, Jenny. Enormous, and all you can say about it is that it's turned me into a twat. This is the biggest thing that has ever happened to me and you think I'm a twat. What do I do with that, Jenny? I want you to be proud of me, just a bit. But nothing, you couldn't give a toss.'

My heart is beating like a train right now. I don't know how to respond. He's right, I do think this deal has turned him into a twat, but I married him partly because he cared about this stuff, because he was focused, because he had a plan. I admired it then and somehow I have come to despise the fact that it distracts him so, because it has consumed him. Maybe it's not him I despise but the fact that I wasn't good enough to distract him back. That ultimately work was more appealing than me.

'We used to laugh,' I sob. 'We used to laugh all the time. I miss that Jenny and Mark, I wish I could find them again. I wish I could know them again – they were fun to be around. What happened to them, Mark? What happened to us?'

He's still standing by the door, braced to leave, but my final words stop him in his tracks. He looks at me with sadness for the first time in his eyes.

'I don't know.' He swallows hard and turns to head into the hall. I hear the rustle as he puts his coat on and the jangle of keys as he takes them out of his pocket to let himself out. I get up and rush out into the hall – I can't let him leave like this.

'They'll be here at seven on Friday,' I tell him.

'Who will?'

'Tim and Julie. He was really chuffed I'd rung. Said he's looking forward to seeing you. He said he misses talking crap with you.'

He turns to look at me mid key turn.

'I told him it was your idea,' I say.

He sighs and momentarily closes his eyes.

'I'll speak to you tomorrow,' he says.

Chapter Thirty-Six

I'm sitting there in the dark in the lounge. I've heard George leave his room and go to the bathroom twice – whether this is to relieve himself or perhaps destroy the evidence of another type of relief, I have no idea. However, I know my head will explode if I include that on the carousel of worries currently whirring around in it.

I hear my mobile ring and leap up to search for it in the kitchen, hoping it's Mark. Why, I have no idea. No good could possibly come of a conversation with him just now, but still I hope it's him. But when I discover my phone glowing from the bottom of my handbag it shows the name of the last person I want to speak to. In fact the last person I *ever* want to speak to. My finger hovers over the end call button but I conclude this is too risky. Who knows what evil deeds this person could get up to if armed with the excuse of 'But you didn't answer my call?'

I mentally prepare then press the pick-up button.

'Hello Antony. Unlike you to call me. Has there been a bush fire on the Bahamas and the Hyatt's been razed to the ground so your holiday with Mum has had to be cancelled?'

'No.'

'Oh. Then let me see. Lucas is taking his GCSEs in three years' time and must stay home and revise so your holiday with Mum has had to be cancelled?'

'Don't be ridiculous, Jenny.'

'Well then, I can see there is only one other reason why you would ever choose to phone your only sister.'

'Oh yes, and what do you suppose that is?'

'In a bid to avoid spending Christmas with your mother you have taken the extreme step of getting Mischa pregnant with triplets and so your holiday has had to be cancelled?'

'No, Jenny!'

'Is it Brexit then? Are you worried about leaving the country in case all the silly people vote to do something you don't agree with whilst you are gone? Oh, I know! The Bahamas have cancelled Christmas because Christmas in a hot country is a bloody stupid idea so you're not going. You're staying here and coming to ours for Christmas lunch.'

'Now you're just being ridiculous.'

'I know. I wasn't serious about the last one. It's a complete fantasy to think that you would step foot in a house with only three toilets on Christmas Day.'

'Have you finished?'

'I think so.'

'I'm calling because Lucas has just had a text message from George inviting us all to some kind of party you're having.'

'Really?' This is the last thing I'm expecting him to say.

'Yes. What's going on, Jenny?'

'Oh well, erm…'

Which way do I fall on this one? I need to think really fast.

'Well, I didn't invite you because I didn't think you'd come. You never come to family parties.'

'Well, Lucas has told George we are free now and he wants to come. He says George has told him there will be sumo wrestling suits and a foam gun and it's at an old people's home where they let children drink alcohol?'

I think for a minute.

'That about sums it up,' I say.

There's silence at the other end of the phone.

'What kind of party is this, Jenny?'

'Does it matter?' I say. 'It's sort of a belated birthday party, not that you would know that, of course, because you never remember. Really it's just an excuse to have a laugh. Celebrate being alive.'

I stop myself. Tears rise up in my throat like a tidal wave. I cough to try and dispel the urge to break down.

'Please come,' I manage to sputter out.

'What did you say?'

'I said I'd really like you to come. I'd like to see you.'

'Is everything all right, Jenny?'

'Of course it is. I can say that I would like to see my only brother just once in my life, can't I?'

'Well, it sounds like we've got no bloody choice anyway! Lucas has already said if we don't let him come he'll refuse to go to the Bahamas.'

'Seriously? What kind of mental damage are you doing to that child if he would rather come to a party in a geriatric home than go to the Caribbean?'

'He's perfectly fine,' Antony snaps back. 'Just acting like a normal teenager.'

'Normal teenagers don't have Caribbean Christmases to use as emotional blackmail.'

'How is George's counselling going?'

Touché, I think.

'So you're coming then?'

'Well, it sounds like Lucas is going to need a chaperone, given your track record with parties and alcohol.'

'Well, good, good. By the way, it is fancy dress, you know.'

'What? Jenny, when are you ever going to grow up?'

'Never,' I say. 'Probably never,' I add more quietly.

'Do we have to?'

'Yes.'

'Is there a theme?'

'Of course,' I say. 'The theme is *The Muppets*. Can't wait to see you in a Kermit outfit!'

Ah well, I think after he's rung off, at least they'll boost the numbers and, actually, I would like to see my brother. I should see him – he might be useful in the coming months, what with handling my situation and our parents.

I think about going upstairs and getting changed ready for Karen's arrival. I should go and put my suede skirt on – I look good in it. But I can't be bothered. Besides, it's just Karen. I know I haven't slapped eyes on her in twenty years but it's still just Karen.

Odd how much more relaxed I feel about catching up with my friend from two decades ago, much more so than when I'm off to see my current friends. There's no hiding with Karen. She's seen me warts and all. She's seen me with my head stuck down a toilet bowl, retching at three in the morning, and with tears streaming down my face when *he* didn't call. I've no idea who he was but I remember he didn't call. She's seen me fooled and dazzled by a charming man, then bewildered and distraught when he disappeared off the face of the earth. She's seen me hurt and lost and vulnerable and ecstatic, and playful and joyful and young. She's seen all of those things. But she has never seen the mask of fake togetherness and maturity that we tend to compose in middle age, rarely letting our guard down even to our closest friends. When do we stop doing that? When do we stop wearing our hearts and minds on our sleeves? Is it maturity that does that to us, that teaches us not to expose ourselves for who we truly are?

Fuck maturity, I think. I won't wear the suede skirt. Karen won't mind seeing me in my black leggings, a baggy top and scruffy nineties hair. I won't have to explain it to her.

'Check you out,' she cries as she bursts through the front door some time later. 'Bloody hell, you're sooo skinny,' she continues, engulfing me in a massive hug. 'You never said you were this skinny.'

I bury my face in her neck. She smells good. Expensive. Now the mature thing to do would be to tell Karen why I'm so skinny. Put her out of her misery about why I have managed so successfully to ward off middle-age spread. Fuck maturity, I think.

'Thanks,' I grin shyly when we pull apart. 'Sorry I look a bit scruffy, I didn't dress up.'

I take in Karen's gorgeous designer dress skilfully hiding some additional curves, and handbag to die for. She not only smells expensive, she *looks* expensive. I wasn't expecting that. What I was expecting, however, was the massive open smile on the hugely recognisable face, albeit slightly more lined and under a highlighted bob coiffed to within an inch of its life. I fall forward again to hug her, tears threatening my eyes.

'It's so good to see you,' I mumble.

'You too,' she murmurs back. 'You too.'

★

Half an hour later and we're crying in the kitchen. Tears of laughter, rendering us nearly speechless.

Karen has reminded me of the time we'd informed a group of particularly troublesome male holidaymakers who were celebrating the end of A-levels that their mums had rung to see how they were and ask if they were eating enough. We told them this during a booze cruise in front of a gaggle of twenty-something girls they were desperately trying to pull.

'Do you remember we heard them telling one poor girl that they'd all just graduated from university? It was so obvious they hadn't. They all had acne and they couldn't take their drink. I've never seen a group vomit so much.'

'I bet there's a crowd out in Corfu right now doing exactly the same thing. Pretending they're older, throwing up all the time and asking where they can buy Clearasil.'

'Did you watch *The Inbetweeners Movie* in Greece?'

'OMG, utter genius and so true!'

'Do you remember when we told a coachload of tourists that a lump of concrete was actually a sacred statue and if you rubbed it, it would make you more virile?'

'All because we'd got lost and couldn't find the way to that weird temple and so we had to make up a few alternative historic monuments to hide our lack of having a clue what we were doing.'

We collapse again in laughter, clutching each other's arms. The warm glow of rose-tinted memories has engulfed me and I absolutely love it. The fact that my husband has just walked out is temporarily banished from my mind.

'Oh hello?' says Karen, suddenly looking up as she wipes a tear from her eye with a tissue.

Ellie has slouched in. She barely acknowledges us with a nod, then walks over to the fridge, opens the door and stares in it.

'This is Karen,' I say to her back. 'We used to work together in Greece. She's helping me with the party.'

Ellie takes out a can of Coke, shuts the fridge door and turns round.

'Hi,' she says.

'We were just reminiscing,' Karen tells her, 'about crazy things me and your mum used to get up to.'

Ellie doesn't raise a smile, just her eyebrows.

Me and Karen glance at each other, sharing instantly the pain of raising teenage daughters.

'So I guess you must be about nineteen?' asks Karen.

Ellie looks up sharply.

'Seventeen,' she mutters. She's flattered, I can tell. Oh, to be still of the age when being mistaken for being older is a compliment.

'I love your hair,' says Karen.

I am in awe. How does she know exactly the right things to say to my daughter?

'Thanks,' she says, giving her tresses a little shake. 'I really want to dye it but Mum won't let me,' she adds.

'Of course she won't,' cries Karen, throwing her hands in the air. 'She's jealous as hell of that hair you've got. Why would she let you change it?'

'Jealous?'

'Of course she is. Compared to that way-too-colourful cacophony she's currently sporting there's no way she's going to let you do that to yours.'

'Thanks,' I say.

'Why is your hair like that, by the way?' she adds, turning to me.

'I fancied a Ginger Spice look,' I reply.

'Oh, I see,' she says, screwing her face up.

Admittedly it's not at its best. I haven't washed it in days but I didn't think it looked that bad.

'Your mother doesn't want you to end up like her, that's why she won't let you dye it,' Karen tells Ellie. 'It's why we stop our daughters doing most things, you know. Stop them screwing up like we have.'

'Right,' nods Ellie as though this actually makes sense to her. 'I'm going to take this upstairs,' she says, indicating the can. 'Bye,' she tells Karen.

'She hates me at the moment,' I blurt out as soon as the door is shut.

'No, she doesn't,' replies Karen.

'She does. Her best friend won't speak to her because I told her what an evil bitch she is. She's demanding an apology before she will have anything to do with Ellie again. I'm being blackmailed by a seventeen-year-old!'

'Wow,' says Karen, 'what a cow!'

'She's vile, utterly vile. She's one of those cool girls who thinks having fun and being silly is beneath them. She's mean, *really* mean, Karen.'

Karen puts a hand on my arm. 'I meant you,' she says.

I laugh. We both laugh.

'I want her to grow up with a friend like you,' I splutter. 'And then have the intelligence to hold onto them.'

I think the sad tears are about to wash away the happy ones.

'She'll find her true friends,' says Karen. 'They're not always where you expect them to be. You just have to let her get on with it.'

'And she's got a boyfriend she won't tell me about,' I sniff.

'She will,' says Karen. 'When she's ready.'

'I just… I just want her to be happy,' I say.

'You can't do that for her,' answers Karen. 'It's what I've learnt with Sienna, that you just have to step away and let them make their own mistakes. We did, didn't we?'

'Didn't we just!' I reply. Big fat massive enormous mistakes it feels like. Or maybe that's only with the hindsight of a death sentence hanging over you.

'But do you know what I think the most important thing to do with raising daughters is?' states Karen, leaning towards me. 'Listen to this, because it's golden advice, really it is. You will not hear a better piece of advice than I'm about to give you.'

'Right,' I say, all ears. I need all the advice I can get at the moment.

'Have fun with them. Have a laugh. Be stupid. Teach them that. Teach them to be silly and stupid and ridiculous so they don't fall down the utterly hideous trap of taking life too seriously. That's my advice.'

'Genius,' I mutter.

Chapter Thirty-Seven

I hadn't meant to come here. I don't know why I'm here. All I know is that just driving into the entrance of the hospital has made me want to run away to the nearest rock and crawl under it. I park in the car park furthest away from the cancer clinic, trying to tell myself that I'm visiting for another reason entirely unconnected to the dreaded C-word.

Maybe it was the conversation I've just had with my mother that's propelled me here. It had dawned on me as I dragged myself into bed the night before that if Antony were coming up to my party then I would have no choice but to invite my mother along too. There would be war if my brother was in the county and she wasn't involved. So this morning I'd dragged myself to see her and shared with her the amazing news that I was having a party.

'What do you want to have a party for?' she'd asked.

'I just felt like it,' I shrugged. I was beyond trying to explain it to her. She wouldn't understand, however I put it, even if I came out with the truth.

'When did you say?'

'Next Saturday.'

'It's terribly short notice.'

'I know.'

'What should I do with your father?'

'Bring him. He might enjoy it. And it will give you both a chance to look around Shady Grove. See if he's comfortable there, ready for his stay over Christmas.'

'There is that, I suppose. Shall we see how he is? See if we are both up to it on the day? You don't mind, do you, if we decide it's just too much for us?'

'No, that's fine,' I'd sighed.

We'd stared at each other over cooling cups of tea. An awkward silence descended. We were actually getting quite good at sitting in silence at the kitchen table. It almost felt comfortable. Almost, but not quite.

'Margaret is going to take me to Meadowhall to buy clothes for my holiday,' she finally said. 'As she quite rightly says, we need to go soon whilst it's still warm because there won't be any summer clothes in the shops before Christmas, will there?'

'No,' I replied and counted to ten.

'Will you come and look after your father whilst we go next Tuesday?'

'Yes,' I said.

Silence again.

'Can you tell me about when I was born?' I asked.

'What?'

'When I was born. What happened?'

'What do you mean, what happened?'

'You know, when you had me. Was Dad there? Did I come quickly? Was it an easy birth?'

'What on earth do you want to know about all that for?'

'Because you've never told me. Because I'd like to know how I arrived on this planet.'

'Well, erm…' She nervously sipped her tea. 'Well, it's a very long time ago now.'

'I know it is but there must be some things you can remember.'

'I remember your dad was at work and I rang and they said he was on the counter, you know, serving customers in the bank. They said his break wasn't until eleven and could I ring back then.'

'Did you tell them you were in labour?'

'No. I thought I could last another half hour so I put the phone down.'

'Seriously?'

'Well, yes. I didn't really want to disturb him. He took his job so seriously. For some reason I thought he might be cross with me. I called back just after eleven to give him time in case he was tied up with someone. He was still cross with me. Cross I hadn't said I was in labour when I rang earlier.'

'Did he come straight away?'

'Oh yes, must have broken the speed limit. I had a go at him about that. He held my hand the whole way there apart from when he had to change gear. We got stuck behind an ice-cream van for a while. I've never heard your dad swear like it. Then we got to the maternity hospital and the next thing I know I'm hustled away to the delivery room. In hindsight I should have made your dad leave work earlier perhaps. You only took half an hour. Obviously your dad wasn't there, it wasn't the thing then, like it is now. I could hear him chatting to a new mum in the waiting room the whole time. He was trying to explain interest rates to her. I kept thinking that I would rather be in labour than listening to your dad explain interest rates.'

I laughed.

'And when you first saw me?' I asked.

'You looked like a baby,' she said nonchalantly.

'Oh.'

'You screamed like a hyena. You were so noisy the minute you got into the world, even the midwife said so. Screaming and bawling. It was if you had been storing it up and once you were out, you wanted everyone to know about it. The whole hospital must have heard *you* arrive.'

I don't know why but this makes me happy. I didn't whimper apologetically, I arrived in a fanfare of my own making. That feels good to know. I needed to know that.

'Not at all like Antony,' continued my mother. 'He was much calmer when he was born. He looked thoughtful right from day one.'

'By the way, he's coming to my party,' I told her. 'And Lucas.'

'Really?' said my mum incredulously. 'Coming to a party of yours?'

'Yes,' I said.

'Does he have the time?'

'Perhaps he made the time.'

'Well, if Antony can make the time then I'm sure me and your dad can make the effort. Count us in. Maybe I can get a new outfit with Margaret next week at Meadowhall.'

Maybe it's all the talk of babies and maternity wards that makes me do it. Or maybe it's the fact I just can't bear to head into hospital and have to take the left turn towards the Death Clinic. My feet won't do it. I turn right, despite the fact I'm due to go and give some blood samples in twenty minutes. I turn right and let my feet do the walking until I find myself at the door of the maternity unit.

I can't stop myself. I wander in and, before I know it, I'm sitting on the back row of seats, picking up a magazine surrounded by parents in the various stages of pregnancy glow. I'm submerged in a sea of hand-holding and bump-swiping. Perhaps that's why the younger generation comes out of the womb so tablet-friendly? We are swiping them practically from conception.

'I'm so ready to sit down,' says a woman, easing herself into the chair next to me. 'My ankles are the size of life rings – no, scratch that, *several* life rings. You here for your first scan?'

I stare at her, not knowing what to say. My instinct is to grab her face and kiss her in gratitude for her assumption I'm still young enough to be pregnant. I nod mutely.

'Nothing to be worried about,' she says. 'It's just a bit messy, all that goo on your belly. Looks like… you know, what got you knocked up in the first place.' She lets out a raucous laugh. The hand-holders and bump-swipers turn to glare.

'You on your own too?' she asks.

I nod, not trusting myself to speak.

'This is my fourth,' she says, nodding down to the mound sitting on her knee. 'He asked me if I wanted him to come and I said I rather he stopped at home and defrosted the freezer. So he has, imagine that?' She lets out a rip roar of a laugh again. 'He hasn't a clue what he's let himself in for. There are peas from the Ark in there, I reckon.' She laughs again, good and hard.

She grabs my arm. 'Thank goodness for TENA Lady, eh?' she says, winking at me. 'Or I'd have to do all my laughing on the toilet.'

She laughs again so hard the nurse on reception pauses her phone conversation to look round and see what the disturbance is.

'Your first?' she asks again, nodding down at my non-existent bump. I look down and notice I have a sweater bundled on my knee. There could be a bump under there in its early days, I suppose.

'Yes,' I say steadily. 'We, er, left it quite late.'

'Nonsense,' she declares. 'You're never too old, is what I say. Have you been having trouble conceiving or has it taken you this long to find the right guy?'

I look round nervously. Someone is going to find me out any minute. Several women look away quickly as I look up. All the men are staring into the distance, clearly not interested in any kind of eavesdropping. The women are.

'Both,' I say.

'Aaah, bad luck! That's tough. Still, you managed it eventually, eh? So where's the lucky chap?'

'Oh, he's, er, he had to work. Next time.'

'Oh, that's a shame. A real shame. Look, if you want, I can come in with you. You know, hold your hand and all that. It's a bit scary the first time you do it.'

'Oh no, no, no, that's perfectly all right,' I say. It's time to leave now. Enough of this masquerading as a pregnant woman. What am I doing sitting here? I'm going to get myself arrested any minute if I'm not careful.

'Delilah Hannigan,' a woman in blue and flat shoes announces at a door to the left of the reception desk.

'Ooh, that'll be me,' says my neighbour, starting to pull herself up out of the chair. 'It had better bloody be a girl this time or else I might just kill myself! Four boys in the house, can you imagine? Utter carnage.'

I nod as if I understand completely.

'If you want, you can come with me,' she says, holding out her hand. 'As you've not done it before. See what you're up against. I don't mind. I've had that many doctors and nurses roaming around my bits and pieces they practically have National Park status. Come on. Might just settle your nerves a bit, eh? You look ever so pale, love.'

Somehow following her into the ultrasound room is easier than arguing. I hover at the door, not quite knowing whether to make a run for it or take a seat.

'This is my friend,' Delilah says, before screwing her face up when she realises she doesn't even know my name. She beckons me over to take the seat at her head and grabs my hand and gives it a squeeze.

The next few minutes are as surreal as you can imagine. I wonder if I'm asleep, dreaming of babies and birth in a desperate effort to keep the death wolf from the door. I watch, mesmerised, as the technician squirts on the liquid and rolls the scanner around her belly. I hold my breath then suddenly the sound of the heartbeat fills the room. I'm so happy I could cry. New life is coming. There is new life all around us. Life does go on.

The circus mirror image of a baby emerges on the screen, floating around in blissful limbo. Safe, secure, at the very beginning of everything.

'It looks to me as though you are having a girl,' announces the technician as he goes on to point out indistinguishable shifting shapes that indicate the sex of the baby. Delilah instantly bursts into tears. I can't help but join her.

'Princess dresses and French plaits,' she sobs with joy.

'Yeah,' I say, gripping her hand tightly. 'That's what it's all about. Princess dresses and French plaits. Thank God for daughters!'

Outside we hug. Thankfully Delilah doesn't offer to exchange numbers. Doesn't offer to become my birth buddy for my non-existent child.

I wave her off and perch briefly on a seat at the back. When an adequate amount of time has passed I get up and walk out, trying not to catch the eye of any of the women who have seen me walk in, sit down, attend a scan with a stranger and walk out again. Leave them to ponder that conundrum. Though I do find myself looking up as I go through the door to check for CCTV cameras. I can just imagine my blurred image appearing on the next episode of *Crimewatch*. Thankfully it appears that Big Brother has not been watching this particular mini-drama.

I scurry along back to the Death Unit feeling lighter. Seeing new life on its way has lifted me and given my brain an alternative fixture for a while, keeping the implications of my hospital visit at bay.

'I love your hair,' says the young woman, stabbing my finger with what feels like a blunt needle. She looks about twelve.

'Thank you,' I say, grimacing.

'Very cool,' she adds.

I nod.

'Do you mind me asking where you got it?'

'Got what?'

'Your wig?'

'Actually, it's not wig, it's my real hair.' I say this slowly, reeling at the assumption. Only in the Death Clinic would this be happening. I'm back in reality.

'Oh, I'm so sorry,' gasps the girl. She looks nervously over her shoulder as though concerned someone might have overheard her monumental lack of tact. 'I was… it's just… people ask all the time in here about where to get a decent wig and yours is the best I've seen so I thought I'd ask…'

'It's okay,' I say.

I'd like to be able to reassure her that it happens all the time. Only it doesn't, does it, because hardly anyone knows I have cancer so the chances of anyone complimenting my wig are virtually zero. See, I knew it was the right decision not to have chemo. Who wants the most complimentary thing that someone can say about your appearance to be that you have a good wig?

'I'm really very sorry,' she babbles on. 'I won't make that mistake again,' she says to herself, walking away to file my blood samples.

I sit and listen to her fumbling over equipment with her back to me. She's rattled. I feel for her. Working on the Death Unit must be a minefield of difficult conversations and opportunities to put one's foot in it. You have got to respect anyone who puts themselves through that every day.

Eventually she turns around, looking a bit paler than before, and walks back towards me.

'I need to take some blood from your arm,' she says, a slight tremble in her voice. I watch in horror as she aims a wobbling needle towards a vein in the crook of my arm that I have offered up to her. Just as she's about to stab me, I whip my arm away. She's in no fit state to be putting anything into my body.

She looks at me, distraught. She's so young, I think. She shouldn't have to be doing this. Being polite to the dying.

'Princess dresses and French plaits,' I murmur.

'Excuse me?'

'Princess dresses and French plaits,' I repeat. 'That's what it's all about. Will you give me a French plait?' I ask her.

Her mouth drops open.

'I'm not sure I...'

'Go on,' I say. 'It will make me feel better.'

'Really?'

'Yes, really.'

And it does.

Chapter Thirty-Eight

By the time it gets to Friday I'm a nervous wreck. When the doorbell rings at twenty minutes past seven I nearly faint. The night is so not how I had imagined. But how could it be when you've invited your husband's former best friend over for dinner who he hasn't seen in ages and you're trying to gloss over the fact that said husband has had an affair and might have walked out on your marriage?

Mark arrived home just half an hour earlier and went straight into his office. At least, I hope it's him; either that or we have a very confident burglar currently stripping our assets whilst we sit next door.

I arrive at the front door at the same time as Mark. We nod. I open my mouth, about to thank him for coming, but stop myself. Why should I do that? It's his old mates I've invited over, he should be thanking me. In any case, the only thing I should be thanking him for is having an affair and ruining the end of my life. Still, I must shelve that until later.

'Hi,' I say as I pull the door open. Fixed grins on our faces.

'Good to see ya, good to see ya,' says Tim, stepping in and grasping Mark by the hand. His face glows red from a recent hot shower, contrasting against the glowing white of his shirt collar. He embraces Mark in a bear hug before stepping back and taking in his surroundings.

'So good to see you,' I say, stepping forward and embracing Julie. 'It's been too long.'

'It so has,' she replies. 'We brought you these,' she adds, offering up a bag with bottles clinking inside. 'Not sure what you like so we brought a bit of everything.'

'Well, you didn't need to bring anything at all. That's really kind of you. Thank you.'

'Yes, well, yes, well, we couldn't come empty-handed,' says Tim, glancing nervously at Mark. He hasn't uttered a word yet. Just nodded and looked awkward.

'So, you had a good day, mate?' asks Tim.

'Oh yeah,' says Mark, glancing sideways at me. 'Brilliant. Actually spent all day going through the contract with lawyers on the sale of Brancotec. We're about to change ownership to a private equity firm. Charstone actually. Making sure we screw as much money out of them as we can.'

Twat, I think.

Twat, I see flash through Tim's eyes. This night could be a disaster.

'Right, right,' replies Tim. 'Well, I've been up to my elbows in shit all day. Literally. Blocked drains in Calver Street. Fucking nightmare.'

'It's all right, I made him have two showers,' says Julie. 'Christ, he stank!'

There's another awkward silence.

'Nice place you've got here then,' says Tim eventually.

'Have you never been here?' I gasp.

'No,' he replies, shaking his head. 'I assumed there were strict entry laws. I was beginning to think the only way to get into Oakenthorpe if you were from Checkston was to sneak in on the back of an Ocado van.'

I laugh nervously. There had been much ribbing from Mark's friends when we put our previous house up for sale in order to move to one in the right area that would guarantee entry into a decent secondary school. Mark was determined to get the best education for his children, which involved moving to an expensive suburb and into an overpriced house. In fact I can remember Tim quoting how many extra bedrooms we would be able to buy if we'd stayed in the area where they all grew up. He could understand sinking money into bricks and mortar, but he held no truck with spending over the odds for a house just because it came with a couple of extra GCSEs.

'Well, you're here now,' I say quickly. 'Why don't you give them the tour, Mark, and I'll go and check on dinner?'

He gives me daggers. I turn to head to the kitchen. Off you go, I think. Off you go and show your oldest mate around the house that you said was your dream. I can remember your face when we got the keys: you were as proud as punch. Detached, double-fronted, five-bedroom, on an exclusive estate in the highly sought-after neighbourhood of Oakenthorpe in the catchment area for the renowned Grayspark School. Ofsted reports attached. It was a big moment for you. So show it off to your oldest friend then. The house you were so proud of and never invited him to. The house you are contemplating walking away from.

I nearly burst into tears when I seek sanctuary in the kitchen. It has never looked more beautiful. George is trying out his party menu on us tonight and to get us in the mood he has placed dozens of candles around the room and a blue and white checked tablecloth sits on the kitchen table, taverna style. I'm transported back to 1996 when I'd least expected it. The damn boy has even found some Greek music that tinkles out of a speaker sitting on the dresser. It's too much. I want to be in Greece right now, sitting outside, eating, drinking and being merry. How simple happiness was then and how I took it for granted. I was in heaven and I never even realised it. I walk up behind my son and put my hand on his shoulder.

'I love it,' I tell him when he turns to look at me. I'm grinning despite my watery eyes. He grins back. A proper grin. The grin of an untroubled boy. I drink it in. He'll make it, I think. He is capable of happiness. Occasionally he can grasp it. It will make him hungry for more, I hope, and that will help him. Help him make his way in the world.

'Your dad's just doing the tour, they'll be down in a minute,' I tell him.

'I'll start plating up the starters,' he says earnestly and turns to rinse his hands under the tap.

'Where's the toolbox?' asks Mark, suddenly striding into the room.

'Under the sink in the utility room,' I say. 'Why?'

'Tim's going to fix the leaky tap in the en suite,' he replies, already heading off out of the kitchen.

'Oh,' I say. 'Will you be long?'

'No idea,' he shouts over his shoulder.

George and I raise our eyebrows. The tap has leaked since the day we moved in. Mark had a go at fixing it once and couldn't do it so blamed the 'goddamned tap manufacturer for a stupid design'. We were going to try and get a plumber, but… well, you try getting a plumber to just come out and fix a leaky tap.

I start to unpack the bag that Julie gave me at the door. A bottle of white, a bottle of red and a four-pack of Stella. Blimey, we're in for a session, I think. I'm about to chuck the bag away (sorry, I mean put it in that weird plastic column thing from Ikea with all the other carrier bags; well, I would put it in there but Mark has never got round to putting it up) when I feel something still in there as I scrunch it up. When I open it, I find two miniatures of ouzo. They're a little dusty. I wonder if Tim has had them since 1996? Still, I love them – they make me smile.

I put them on the shelf next to the light-up cactuses. George hasn't switched them on. They clearly don't fit in with tonight's theme. But I do. Their joyful tackiness fits right in. If only we had a stuffed donkey and a sombrero this could be the happiest kitchen in Oakenthorpe right now.

Tim bursts through the kitchen door and dumps the toolbox on the floor, Mark and Julie coming up behind me.

'Jenny, how long has that tap been dripping?' he asks.

'Since we moved in.'

'This dipstick here is trying to tell me it's been a couple of months. Do you take me for an idiot?' he says, giving Mark a friendly punch on the arm. 'I may not understand all that finance crap you do but I know you don't get a brown stain like that from a tap that's only been dripping for a couple of months. And remind me when you moved in?'

Mark doesn't respond so I fill in the gaps.

'Seven years ago.'

'Seven years! You been listening to that for seven years?'

'Well, you know, been busy,' says Mark.

'Too busy for a two-minute job to fix a leaky tap?'

'These things happen,' he shrugs. He looks like George for a minute. His chin is low and his hands are thrust deep in his pockets. He's embarrassed, self-conscious. I can't remember ever seeing him like this.

This isn't going well, I think.

'So this is George,' I say brightly. 'You remember George? He's actually cooking dinner for us tonight.'

'Seriously?' cries Tim. 'Oh my God, you are practically a man! The last time I saw you, you were barely up to my knee and now you're cooking us dinner. Did you hear that, Julie? George is cooking us dinner. Must remember to tell Nathan that George cooked us dinner.'

'If you can get him to listen,' mutters Julie.

'He's such a lazy arse,' explains Tim. 'I've told him I'm throwing the couch out the friggin' window if he doesn't shift his backside off it once in a while and do something, anything. Wait until I tell him you cooked for us, George. He wouldn't know a frying pan from a fondue, I tell you. You been cooking long?'

George blinks.

'Since I started secondary school,' he mutters. 'I want to be a chef.' He turns back round to tend to something on the hob.

'Well, listen to that,' says Tim. 'Ambition, that's what I like to hear. Mind you, it's not surprising, is it, seeing as he's your son, eh, Mark? Sounds like he's inherited your desire for success. You must be proud of this guy.'

Mark nods. 'I am,' he says.

God, I hope he means that.

'So what we having then, George?' Tim asks, stepping up to the cooker and throwing an arm over his shoulders. 'It smells freakin' amazing.'

I watch Mark gaze at their backs. If you didn't know, you'd think they were father and son as George picks up lids and shows Tim what lies beneath. He sounds as impressed and proud as any father would. I glance back over to Mark. He's watching them intently, his brow furrowed. Perhaps seeing George through Tim's eyes could be just what he needs to realise how lucky he is to have him as a son.

'It's a lovely house,' says Julie.

'Well, thank you,' I reply. 'But not very welcoming. I haven't even offered you a drink. What will you have?'

'Oh, whatever's open,' she replies. 'You know me. Well, you *remember* me,' she corrects herself.

'Funnily enough, we were only talking the other day about that night we first met you and went for that tapas meal, weren't we, Mark? Do you remember?'

'Do I remember? I've spent my whole life trying to forget. I still can't believe I threw up in front of Tim's best mates. What must you have thought of me? All I can say is it was the nerves.'

'Not the large carafe of wine?'

'Might have had something to do with it.'

'We weren't that scary, were we?'

'No, you were both great. It's just that Tim had told me all about how you met and how successful Mark was. I'd got it into my head I was going to meet some kind of hyped-up Butlins Redcoat and a brainbox who was going to think I was a blithering idiot. Luckily it turned out you were both, well... normal, I guess.'

'I'll take that as a compliment.'

'It's meant to be.'

★

'That was out of this world,' sighs Tim, leaning back in his chair after he's finished off way more than his fair share of mini kebabs. 'Are you Greek, Georgie?' he booms. 'Is there something you're not telling us, Jenny? Have you been having a bit of moussaka on the side all these years?'

'Of course not,' I mutter, glancing up at Mark. He's relaxed a bit. I've tried pouring lager down him; see if it prompts him to remember how to enjoy Tim's company. He's defrosted slightly but he's still uptight. His mind is on other things and every so often he looks at Tim as though an alien has landed in the middle of his oh-so-middle-class mindset.

He's tried, to be fair, but none of his set pieces are useful in this conversation. Tim wasn't really impressed with how Mark has set up hedged deals with all suppliers, adding double-digit growth to their EBITDA. His response was to tell Mark he had doubled his earnings last year because he took on more work. He took the kids to Disney.

Tim glazed over slightly when Mark tried to explain how he had single-handedly written the five-year strategy for Brancotec, which Charstone had commented was the most detailed they had ever seen. Tim said he didn't see the point in a long-term strategy. In fact his exact comment was, 'What's the point in wasting grafting time on thinking about what you might possibly be doing in five years? We all could be dead tomorrow. Then you'd be mad, wouldn't you? That you'd wasted time thinking about what might happen after you die?'

I must have gasped because Tim turned to look at me.

'Well, Trump is running for president,' he shrugged. 'Who the frig knows where we'll be in ten years' time?'

Throughout, Tim has been his usual jovial self. Making jokes and putting his foot in it here, there and everywhere, which Mark used to be able to laugh at but clearly his sense of humour has left the building. Gone AWOL. When did he turn into a man that didn't find bodily functions funny, I wonder when he fails to raise a smile because I snorted snot down my nose after collapsing in fits of laughter at Tim's story of him lying underneath a bath trying to fix a leak when the husband walked in bollock-naked, after work, not realising he was there.

'No wonder she was shagging the neighbour,' he concludes. 'He had nothing to write home about. Even I came home a bit full of myself, didn't I, love?'

Julie nods.

'He hasn't changed much, as you can tell,' she sighs.

'Remember we used to strip off all the time round the back of the community centre?' Tim says to Mark.

'What?' Julie and I cry.

'We did, didn't we, Mark?'

'Maybe twice,' he says.

'We couldn't get girls to notice us so we'd tell one of them that Ade Tomlinson was going to streak out the back any minute. The girls loved Ade. God knows why, he was a Forest supporter. Anyway, they'd rush out the back of the community centre and, just as they got there, one of us would make a dash across the back naked, but far away so they couldn't tell who it was. We'd take it in turns. Once they were outside we could get them chatting, you see. Ask if they were cold, offer them our coats, that type of thing. Worked a treat.'

I stare at Mark. This doesn't sound like him at all.

'You pulled girls by telling them the class hunk was outside naked?' I ask Tim.

'Basically yes.'

'And you?' I ask Mark.

He nods and finally grins. 'It was my idea actually,' he admits.

'There he goes,' says Tim, reaching over and slapping him on the back. 'The man with the plan. That was our Mark. If we couldn't get something or do something, we could always rely on him to come up with a cunning plan. The best ever was—'

'No, no, no, please…' says Mark.

'No, mate. This was utter genius. I still can't quite believe it.'

'No, seriously, Tim, just leave it.'

'You know when we came to Corfu on holiday?' Tim asks me.

I nod.

'Well, Mark somehow – and to this day I have no idea how he did this – but he managed to get it all half price from his ex-girlfriend who worked for a travel agent. Yes, I did say *ex*-girlfriend.'

All eyes turn to Mark.

He shrugs.

'All I can say is that she dumped me so I asked if she could do me a discount on a holiday because I needed a break with the boys so I could get over her.'

'Fuckin' legend,' says Tim, raising his arms in the air in salute. 'You didn't even like her that much, did you?'

'She was all right,' says Mark. 'I liked her a lot more when she gave us a cheap holiday,' he adds, a smile breaking over his lips.

'She was one of those posh birds you used to be into. You were such a nightmare with them. Do you know what we used to call him at school?' he asks Julie and me.

'Please don't,' begs Mark. He's covering his face.

'The Camilla Catcher,' says Tim. 'He was round them private-school girls like a dose of salts. None of us could understand it. They were good-looking and everything, but Jesus, they were dull!'

'Bethany was all right,' says Mark, emerging from behind his hands.

'Bethany?' says Tim. 'Was she the one who asked me what instrument I played and I told her I played the horn? She told me I was puerile and do you know what I said back?' he asks me.

I shake my head.

'I said, actually I'm Sagittarius.' Tim collapses in fits of laughter.

'I think she dumped me not long after that,' adds Mark.

'Lucky escape, mate. Lucky escape from all of them. Quite frankly his taste in women was dire before you came along, Jenny. God, were we pleased to see you – a hot woman with a sense of humour. What more could a guy wish for, eh, mate?' he says, slapping Mark on the back again. 'To think you could have ended up with that Natalie woman.'

'What Natalie woman?' asks Mark.

'The other one you snogged in Corfu.'

I gasp for the second time that evening.

'Thanks, Tim,' says Mark, glancing at me.

'What? What have I done?'

'You are a moron sometimes,' states Julie.

'What have I done?' Tim looks over at me and clocks my face, then raises his hands in wonder. 'So he snogged another woman in Corfu twenty years ago. He shagged you, several times if I remember rightly. I had to sleep on Shifty's floor, you were shagging so much. I had to buy earplugs,' he says. 'I really don't see what the problem is. If a snog on the first night of the holiday outweighs twenty shags in the second week, well, I don't know what the world's coming to.'

Mark and I look at each other.

'It was twenty-three actually,' he says without taking his eyes off me. I blush. On our first anniversary Mark had given me his boarding card from his flight over to Corfu, which he'd saved. Unbeknownst to me, he had marked on it every time we'd had sex whilst we were there, then saved it. I put it in the 1996 photo album, I'm sure. His version of notches on a bedpost. I must have missed it when I last got the album out. I would have to check.

'Bloody good holiday that was,' says Tim. 'Last lads' holiday we all had, I reckon.'

'Didn't you go away with Shifty and Neil the following year?' asks Mark.

'Oh yeah. But it wasn't the same. We were an utter shambles without you to organise us. I had to be in charge. Took all the fun out of it, if I'm honest. Plus, Shifty paired off with some bird on the second night. Never saw him for the rest of the holiday so it was just me and Neil. Who's going to come and talk to me and Neil? We're like the two ugly best mates without the good-looking one to lure 'em in. Total desert as far as women were concerned. Might as well have gone on holiday to a nunnery.'

'Lucky me, eh?' says Julie. 'Just think, if Shifty hadn't met someone then you might have had half a chance at pulling and she might have been the woman of your dreams and you would have been snapped up before I could get my hands on you.'

'So I have Shifty to blame for you?' Tim asks.

'I guess so,' says Julie.

'I'll kick his arse next time I see him.'

'Did you say kiss?' asks Julie.

'Exactly right, dear,' he agrees. 'But what about you guys? Imagine if we hadn't got the discount from Mark's ex-girlfriend, we never would have gone on holiday to Corfu and you wouldn't have met. So actually, Mark, you owe everything – your wife, your marriage, your children – to the fact that some travel agent woman couldn't stand you.'

'Profound as always,' nods Mark.

'I guess we owe it to all the people who have rejected us,' I find myself saying. 'If it wasn't for the fact that there are members of the opposite sex who just didn't like us then none of us would be in the relationships we are in now.'

'Mmmm,' says Tim. 'If Angela Parsons in Miss Harrison's class at school had liked me then I definitely wouldn't be in the relationship I am in now. Kidding, kidding!' he laughs as Julie takes a swipe at him. 'It's all meant to be, eh, mate?' he says to Mark. 'I don't think we did too badly, do you?'

Mark nods and smiles tightly. It must feel like I've engineered all this but I didn't mean to. I didn't mean for Tim to come round and remind my husband why we got married. I actually wanted Tim to come round and remind him how to laugh. How to have a laugh. That's all. Instead it feels like I've set him up to sit and listen to what a good choice he made when he married me. I don't want to have to convince him of that. This is not going according to plan. Very happy about the fixed leaky tap though – you can't think a day has been terrible if a tap that's been leaking for seven years has been fixed.

I give up on Mark. I was trying to reconnect him to something good. Trying to tether him when all around him is about to change, whatever becomes of our marriage. He'll need someone like Tim to take the piss if he leaves his wife only to find out she's dying. He'll need Tim to crack a joke if he decides to come home only to find he is faced with months of caring for a terminally ill wife. He'll need Tim to get him drunk when he realises he's about to become a single parent and hasn't a clue how to talk to his son. He'll need Tim's hand on his shoulder at my funeral. The hand of the man who has seen him through his past and will be there for him in his future. This is the man to be by his side, I'm convinced of it, whichever road he treads. This piss-talking, bad-joke-cracking, blundering, spanner-wielding idiot is the man for the job. I just wish Mark could see that now, see how much he needs him in his life.

'Did I mention my party?' I blurt.

Mark glares.

'Did someone say party?' asks Tim.

'I'm having a… well, a belated birthday party, next week. There's a sort of Greek theme. You must come. Tell me you can come? It's next Saturday.'

Tim and Julie look at each other. Julie shrugs.

'I'm pretty sure we're free,' she says.

'Of course we're bloody free! A Greek-themed party, with this lady? Hottest ticket in town, surely?'

I grin at him gratefully.

'Do you think Shifty and Neil might be free as well?' I ask, not daring to look at Mark. 'Any of the old gang really. It would be great to see them.'

'Well, we'll find out, won't we? Give Jules here the details and we'll pass the word round. Awesome,' he says, slapping Mark on the back. I'm certain Mark doesn't think it's quite so awesome.

George pokes his head around the kitchen door.

'You ready?' he asks me.

'I think so,' I nod. 'You're going to love this,' I tell Tim.

'What?' he asks. 'He can't produce anything better than he already has? That was epic, mate,' he tells George. 'You're a genius.'

George has his head stuck in the fridge. I hope he can hear him.

'You just wait,' I tell Tim. 'This will blow you away.'

Mark is looking at me questioningly. He's worried I might be overplaying it but I know what's coming. I've been excited about this ever since I came up with the idea.

George turns round to reveal an enormous green and glistening globe in all its glory.

'Is that what I think it is?' asks Jules, a grin already forming on her face. 'I haven't had one of them in years.'

I nod.

'It is, isn't it?' declares Tim, beside himself. 'I think I may have died and gone to heaven. I can't believe it. Tell me it is what I think it is.'

'It's a vodka melon!' I cry, raising my hands in the air. Tim and Jules cheer and clap uproariously as George carefully places it in the middle of the table.

'Would you like to do the honours?' I say, handing the knife to Tim.

'I don't mind if I do,' he says, getting up and poising the tip of the knife at the top of the hard, round melon. 'And may I make a toast,' he adds, starting to push down. 'To old friends,' he says as the knife plunges in.

'To old friends,' I repeat, raising my glass.

Chapter Thirty-Nine

Mark and Tim have rolled their sleeves up and are having an arm-wrestle by the time Ellie comes home. We've cranked the music up and Julie and I are having a dance to a *Now That's What I Call the Nineties* CD I've managed to dig up.

We're in the middle of 'Place Your Hands' by Reef when Ellie appears at the door. I glance up at the clock: it's eleven thirty on the dot. For once she's in on time. That's a relief. No need for a late-night stand-off as I feebly try and punish her for the umpteenth time for staying out longer than acceptable. Her brow is furrowed as she takes in the carnage that now litters the kitchen. The vodka melon looks like road-kill, its innards exploded all over the blue and white checked tablecloth, fragments of red flesh scattered everywhere, including some in Mark's hair and decorating his shirt.

I should have known the vodka melon would be the key. Sinking his teeth into alcohol-drenched fruit finally worked its magical powers on Mark and he caved. Having eaten three slices, Tim carved himself a set of bright green melon teeth and inserted them in his mouth under the table before rearing up next to Mark, causing him to spit melon right in his face.

That was all Tim needed. He leant over and sunk his hand into the half of melon that hadn't been sliced yet, and drew out a handful of rosy red crumbling flesh and threw it in Mark's face. It landed splat on his glasses as he froze and we all collapsed in hysterics. Slowly he raised his hands and wiped the sticky debris away then, quick as a flash, grabbed a handful that had landed on the table in front of him and lunged at Tim, managing to stuff the sticky mess down the back of his trousers.

'You are disgusting,' Tim told him, waggling his bottom, trying to get the lump of goo to drop down his trouser leg.

'You started it,' said Mark.

Tim walked towards Mark, who tried to back away but he wasn't quick enough. Tim swiftly put him in an armlock so that Mark's head was down near his hip. He leaned forward as I pushed what was left of the melon nearer so he could reach it. He dipped his hand in for the second time and rubbed the sticky goo all over Mark's hair until it looked as though he'd gone completely overboard with the hair gel. Mark thrashed about, trying to break free, but Tim is tougher and uglier than him and he had to wait until Tim released him, his hair slick and shiny and sticking up in all directions.

Mark had stood there laughing, trying to catch his breath, when, without warning, his hand was behind Tim's head as he forced it down onto the table straight into the vodka melon. There was a look of pure victory on Mark's face. Jules and I gave him a standing ovation and he managed a quick bow before he allowed Tim to come up for air.

'Fair cop, mate,' said Tim, holding his hand out to shake Mark's. 'I'll let you take that as a victory.'

Mark looked down at his hand suspiciously before offering his own. They were mid-shake when Tim thrust his vodka-melon-dripping face into Mark's neck and wrapped both his arms around him. I watched to see Mark's reaction. He was tense for a moment then softened, putting his arms around Tim and completing the bear hug. They both banged each other's back with fists and eventually pulled away.

'You are such a tosser,' announced Mark.

'Likewise,' replied Tim.

'I could take you any day,' said Mark.

'Arm-wrestle?' enquired Tim.

'Let's do it.'

And that is how Ellie discovers her father late on a Friday night, in a way she has never seen him. Sitting at the kitchen table, vodka melon in his hair and dripping down his face whilst his eyes are screwed up tightly in the sheer concentration of beating his childhood best mate in an arm-wrestle.

'Dad?' she says when he fails to acknowledge her arrival in the room.

'Ellie,' he says, his eyes pinging open. Tim immediately slams his fist to the table and then leaps up out of his chair in victory.

'Get in,' he shouts. 'Best of three, mate? Oh, and who is this gorgeous young lady?' he says, sliding over to the door to take a closer look. 'This cannot be Ellie. Will you just shut up?' he says, turning to Mark. 'Is this Ellie? No one as beautiful as this is coming from your loins. Are you serious?'

'Give it a rest, Tim,' says Mark, getting up to go and stand near his daughter. 'You remember Tim, don't you, love? Are you all right? Did you have a good night?' he asks.

'Er, yes,' replies Ellie. 'Me and Max are just going to sit in the lounge, okay?'

'Max?' asks Mark. 'Who's Max?' He turns to look at me as though I should know.

Max? So this must be the guy I saw her outside school with.

'He's, er…' begins Ellie.

'Hiya,' says a head poking round the kitchen door. 'I just walked Ellie home.'

He grins at the mature adults in the kitchen dripping in vodka melon.

We all stare back at him, not sure what to do. Tim decides.

'Come in then, lad,' he booms, pulling open the door. 'Let's see you then, shall we? Come on, don't be shy, we won't bite.'

'No, it's okay,' protests Ellie. 'We'll go in the lounge, leave you to it.'

But Tim has Max by the arm and is leading him to a chair.

'Hang on,' he cries just as Max is about to take a seat. Tim bends and flicks melon off the chair then pushes him down into it. He perches his own bottom on the side of the table right next to Max. 'You walked her home, you say?' he asks, staring at him.

'Yes,' nods Max. He actually looks a nice boy. I'm not sure he deserves or is ready for this.

'Dad?' pleads Ellie. But for once Mark takes no notice of his daughter as he watches Tim's interrogation of the poor boy who has walked Ellie home.

'You see, I'm talking man to man here,' continues Tim. 'When I was your age I used to "walk girls home".' He makes speech marks with his fingers. 'I know what walking a girl home means and if I find out you have so much as laid a finger…'

'Oh no, Mr Sutton, I wouldn't do that—' begins Max.

'He's not my dad,' cries Ellie, walking over to Max and pulling at his arm. 'That's my dad.' She points at Mark.

'But ditto, what he's saying,' says Mark, pointing at Tim. 'He, er, he's right. She's precious…'

'What he's trying to say is keep your mucky hands off her,' says Tim, walking over to stand shoulder to shoulder with Mark. They both glare at Max like the Tweedledum and Tweedledee of the sad dad world.

Max nods vigorously as Ellie pulls him through the kitchen door to escape.

'In bed by twelve, please,' I shout after her before we hear the lounge door slam.

'Jenny!' exclaims Tim.

'I said "please".'

'I'll go up after them, shall I, and hand out the condoms?'

'Oh, they knew what I meant. Anyway, what's with all the heavy-handed dad thing?'

'Jenny, darling,' says Tim, putting a hand on my arm. 'Me and Mark understand the mind of a teenage boy. We were both there once. Think of your worst nightmare and double it.'

'Do you think we should go in and put *Match of the Day* on or something? I'm not sure I want them to be alone,' says Mark.

'Good idea,' says Tim, grabbing his pint off the table. 'Any melon left?'

Chapter Forty

My hangover is monumental, I conclude as I stand at the top of the stone steps of Shady Grove the following day. Maybe not so monumental as the tapas and carafes of red wine incident, but it's right up there. I'd forgotten the unfortunate side-effects of vodka melon. It looks so innocent. It's mostly fruit after all, isn't it? Sadly it's revealing its inner evil in the glare of the sunlight this afternoon.

Totally worth it though. Best night I'd had in a very long time. And I'm sure that Mark would have agreed if he'd stuck around long enough for me to ask him this morning. He ended up passing out on the sofa before Tim and Julie had even left. I'd put a blanket over him and left him a glass of water and a packet of paracetamol. By the time I got up he'd gone. Empty glass left on the sink alongside an empty packet of pills. No note, nothing.

Karen has just called me on her mobile. She said she should be here any minute, having got stuck in horrendous traffic on the M6. She gabbles on, saying she's had the meeting from hell trying to organise a product launch at The Lowry Hotel in Manchester. Apparently the Brand Manager is stroppy, stubborn and barely out of nappies, whilst the B-list celebrity they want to use in a photo-op has sent a rider as long as your arm. They're demanding a brand of champagne that Karen assumes I have heard of waiting for them in their hotel room.

'Oh,' is my response as she relays all this breathlessly down the mobile phone.

'Can you believe it? I mean The Lowry don't even stock that brand. I remember the days when a decent Dom Pérignon was enough.'

'Right.'

'And it's always the not-all-that-famous people who want the outrageous stuff. I mean, take Kenneth Branagh. All he wanted was a jug of water and some sliced lemon. Lovely man, really lovely.'

'Right.'

'I'm coming off the motorway now – says I'll be with you in ten. See you shortly.'

I hear the buzz of the line hanging up.

She'd rung yesterday and said she'd like to call in and check out the venue for my party on her way back from Manchester. I suspect she wants to know I have everything in hand as she will be remembering my patchy organisational skills from our Corfu days. How she's going to cope with Shady Grove when she's used to high-end hotels I don't know. Its faded grandeur is lovely in the realm of old people's homes but hardly a venue to fill an event company owner with glee. And if she thought the Brand Manager was stroppy and stubborn, then, well... she hasn't met Maureen yet.

Today I decide I should actually make an effort, having already experienced Karen's put-together look. I have coiffed my hair, put on make-up and I'm wearing the knee-high leather boots and brown suede skirt. It's getting a bit loose so I've hidden the gaping waistband under a top, but I think I'm looking okay.

A gleaming silver BMW glides up the drive and my heart sinks. I can't help but compare myself. She has a better car than me. She is better than me. Obviously.

I wave and she sweeps the car round into a visitor spot to the left of the steps. She jumps out, pushing sunglasses onto her head, where they fix perfectly, holding her blonde hair back. Her bright red lips are neatly lined and she has perfected the smoky-eye look. I am in awe.

'For goodness' sake, look at you,' she says, looking me up and down. 'I see where you were going with that dodgy Ginger Spice look now.'

I grin back. 'You look amazing,' I tell her. 'I forgot to tell you the other night.'

'Piss off! I wouldn't be getting this lot in a bikini nowadays,' she says.

'Well, I think you look great.'

'Well, that's very kind of you to say but you, my dear, look incredible.'

We smile awkwardly at each other, not sure what to say next.

'So this is it then,' she says eventually, looking up at the grey stone building. 'Shall we get cracking? I'm really sorry but I haven't got much time. I have to be back by six to pick Sienna up.'

'Of course, this way. I'm sorry it's not The Lowry Hotel.'

Karen stands in the doorway of Maureen's room, looking hesitant. She casts her eyes over the small room with all Maureen's knick-knacks crammed in whilst the unmistakable smell of detergent rams the senses. It's a world away from a meeting room at The Lowry, I imagine.

'Come in, don't be shy,' says Maureen. 'Let Karen sit on the chair,' she continues. 'You and me can sit on the bed.'

She starts to pull herself up from her chair, grabbing hold of her stick for support.

'No, no, please sit there,' says Karen, finally coming into the room. 'I'll, er, I'll, er, sit on the bed.'

Maureen plops back in her chair gratefully.

'Good to meet you at last,' she says as Karen moves a towel to one side and gingerly sits down. 'Jenny has told me so much about you.'

'Has she?' she says, pulling an iPad out of a designer tote bag.

'It's a shame it's taken this to get you back together again,' says Maureen.

I shoot her a warning look. I had an inkling that Maureen might be hostile towards Karen. You know what they say about two's company and three's a crowd? By the suspicious stare that she's giving Karen, I think I might have guessed right.

'Yes, well, life happens,' replies Karen.

'So it does,' agrees Maureen. 'Looks like it's treated you well,' she adds, whilst making a play of looking her up and down.

I'm not quite sure if she is referring to the gorgeous designer dress Karen is wearing, or the expensive bag, or the beautiful shoes, or the ample waistline. At a guess it's the ample waistline.

'I've not done badly for myself,' nods Karen. 'Events Horizon is my own business. I employ five people and we're rated as one of the top events companies in the Midlands.'

'Haven't you done well,' says Maureen, deadpan. I shoot her another warning look. 'Well, I can't tell you how pleased we are to have Jenny here at Shady Grove. It may not have the excitement of running parties but where would we all be if people like her didn't selflessly choose to work in the caring sector.'

What on earth is Maureen drivelling on about? I didn't choose to work here, it was all I could get at the time and then I was too lazy to get out.

'Absolutely,' says Karen. 'She's clearly doing an amazing job. I so couldn't do it.' She casts another dismissive eye around the room. 'I bet she gets you doing some amazing stuff,' she continues. 'Jenny was always the ideas person, I was the organiser. The amount of times I bailed her out because she'd forgotten to book a coach for a trip.'

Karen laughs and fake-punches me on the arm.

And the amount of times I stayed up all night and listened whilst you cried on my shoulder over Sean giving you the runaround, I think.

'Sounds like you had a wonderful friendship,' says Maureen. 'Just marvellous. And now you've found each other again, just in time.'

I shoot Maureen yet another warning glance. What is she playing at? I look at Karen to see if she has registered Maureen's odd comment. Doesn't look like it. She's busy tapping something into her iPad. Karen was good at lists, I wasn't. I thought I could keep it all in my head. The amount of times I would have to ask her if she'd written down some vital piece of information I was supposed to know. She always had. I was the one who came up with the crazy ideas and she was the practical one who made them happen. We were a great team back then.

I feel the pang of two decades of memories lost. I wonder if we would have kept in touch if it hadn't been for Sean. Would we have maintained our closeness despite being hundreds of miles apart, or had we both been glad of the excuse to let it all slip through our fingers? To ease the guilt of not bothering to pick up the phone. What kind of friends would we have been? Weekly calls for gossip or only bothering to get in touch on high days and holidays? Weddings, births, christenings, maybe thirtieth birthdays at a stretch. Would we have gradually slid into each other's past, disappearing from each other's presents? Birthday and Christmas cards until perhaps just a Christmas card with a round robin. Is that what we would have become? From sisterly-level devotion to just a name on a list that maybe gets one of the best cards out of the bumper Christmas charity pack?

Karen and I didn't even manage that. If we had I'm sure her round robin would have been longer than mine – I think she's had more to shout about.

'So shall we make a start?' says Karen, looking up.

'Oh, please do,' says Maureen with a false smile on her face. She reaches over and grabs an old receipt and a pen. She unwrinkles the receipt on her newspaper and turns it over, then poises her pen above it.

'So I've managed to get hold of five sumo suits, three foam guns, and an adult-worthy bouncy castle,' says Karen.

'Wow, that's brilliant,' I say.

'Is that all?' says Maureen.

Karen glances between the two of us.

'It's very short notice,' she points out.

'Of course it is,' I reply. 'I can't believe you got anything, to be honest. Thank you so much.'

'I had to pull a few favours with some suppliers but they know that I'll put more business their way so it worked out fine. Now, do you have access to power and if so, where and what voltage?'

I look at Maureen and she looks back at me. Neither of us has a clue.

'No problem.' Karen keeps tapping on her iPad. 'I'll confirm they need generators. What time can they have access to the site?'

I glance at Maureen, who is still looking blank. She coughs.

'Any time after four, I should think,' she eventually says, scribbling something on her receipt.

'And how long do you want them here for?' asks Karen.

I have no idea. I hadn't thought of any of the logistics of the party, to be perfectly honest. It's only hitting me now just how much is to be done. Maybe I've been in love with the idea of having a party rather than actually organising it.

I look up at Karen, feeling ashamed. I wonder when we should tell her that it's a stealth party, that we are going to have to pretend it's a party for Maureen, even though it's all about me. Karen must have spotted my confusion as next minute she dives into a bag and pulls out a notebook.

'Tell you what,' she says, flipping through the pages, 'shall we go through my failsafe checklist for any successful event and see what needs to be done? It won't take a minute and then maybe we can share the tasks out. I could write us a list each. How does that sound?'

Maureen and I stare in awe at the neat and efficient-looking spreadsheet that Karen is currently unfolding.

'I think that sounds brilliant, don't you?' says Maureen, nodding vigorously. 'I've been telling her we need to do that for days but she wouldn't listen. She talks a good talk, this one, but a little more action and a little *less* talk would sometimes go a long way.'

'Sounds like she hasn't changed a bit,' says Karen, grinning. 'Not in twenty years.'

Chapter Forty-One

Trust my mum to sniff this one out.

Trust her to say the wrong thing at the wrong time in the wrong way. I thought she'd been quiet and then she leaves me this voicemail.

'*Just seen the local paper, darling.*' (She never calls me 'darling' – I should have hung up at that precise moment.) '*Why didn't you tell me about Mark's company? It's amazing news and a fabulous picture of him. You must be so proud of him. Please pass on my congratulations. What a lucky lady you are. Perhaps you will be joining me and your brother in the Caribbean for Christmas now! Wouldn't that be fun? Call me back, I want to know all about it. Bye.*'

I slam the phone down, grab my keys and purse and head down to the corner shop. The local paper is stacked high on the counter, the headline LOCAL FIRM IN MULTI-MILLION-POUND TAKE-OVER screaming out at me. I grab one, folding it up immediately, and throw a fiver down. The paper remains firmly tucked under my arm as I march home – I can't bear to look at it until I'm within the protection of my own four walls.

An hour later and I'm still staring at the double-page spread afforded the successful takeover of Brancotec.

I feel numb. Mark hasn't been in touch since the dinner party nearly a week ago and there he is in full colour, beaming out at me amongst a group of Brancotec employees holding champagne glasses as they stand on a patch of grass on a business park.

So it's finally happened. His 'design for life' came to fruition. He's followed his plan diligently ever since he laid it out for me twenty years ago in Corfu. He's a millionaire Finance Director of one of the Midlands' biggest export companies. It says it there in black and white. My husband. Who'd have thought it?

Only he isn't my husband, is he?

She's there next to him in the picture. I'd recognise that blonde hair and blue skirt anywhere. The caption underneath says her name is Nancy Walker and she's a sales executive.

My husband's next wife?

My children's new stepmum?

No, he said he ended it, and I believe him. But my mind is all over the place.

I have to stop looking, I cannot live in this moment. This moment hurts. I've screwed it all up, I think. Everything. This is Mark's big moment and I should have been at his side. Not to cash in. Not to put my hand out and ask when he's taking me shopping. No, I should have been there to say well done, you did it. I'm proud of my husband. Now I've paved the way to let 'Nancy' do that. They may not be sleeping together any more but I'm sure she's simpering congratulations into his ear. He's hearing the very words he's dying to hear from me from out of those lips and, who knows, it might just turn his head back towards her as they collapse into each other's arms in delirious shared success.

I can't stand this. Think 1996, I tell myself. The party is only a day away now. The party planned to be a reminder of the joy that life can bring. My last hurrah. My last laugh. I have to make the most of this time because after tomorrow this time will be gone. Then I will face the hell of the future, however that may turn out.

I shove the paper in the bin.

I need to do something practical, I need to be busy. I dash out into the hall and decide to move the wall of boxes standing there into the garage, ready to take to Shady Grove tomorrow. A steady stream of deliveries has been arriving all day, courtesy of Karen. I open each box before I move it, delighted to see balloons and streamers and bunting crammed in. Things I would never have thought of, but of course were on Karen's list. Her bloody brilliant marvellous list.

The final two boxes are enormous, but light as a feather. I carefully slit the tape seal and peer inside. A mass of unrecognisable pinkish rumpled plastic appears so I drag it out, laying it out on the hall floor before I finally recognise a squashed sumo wrestler taking shape.

'What are you doing?' a voice says from behind me about half an hour later.

I whizz round and nearly fall over.

Ellie looks horrified, like properly horrified. Even more horrified than when I'd come home with Geri Spice hair.

But I don't stop; I can't stop. If I stop, it might stop being 1996. And I need it to be 1996.

So I carry on. In front of my daughter, in the middle of the kitchen, dressed in a sumo suit, doing the Macarena.

The music is on deafeningly loud, drowning out the bad thoughts. Making me smile. Making me happy.

I dance towards her without missing a step, willing her to smile back. I turn to stand beside her and bump my enormous foam bottom against her side, indicating for her to join me and shake her booty.

'There's another sumo suit in the hall,' I shout at her.

She looks back at me, dumbstruck.

'Don't waste it,' I continue. 'You may never have the chance to dance with your mum to the Macarena, dressed in a sumo suit, ever again.'

Her jaw drops open.

'Fuck it!' I shout right in her face. She takes a step back in shock. 'Go on, say it,' I continue. 'Say fuck it! Fuck it all.'

She shakes her head in confusion.

'Listen to me,' I say, pausing for a moment to grab her arms and look deep into her eyes. Suddenly I know what I need to tell my daughter. What I must make sure she understands before I… before I…

'There's going to be plenty of bad stuff that haunts your memories, Ellie. Loads of crap you've not even had nightmares about yet.'

She stares back at me, petrified.

'So what you have to do, what you absolutely *must* do, is throw yourself into making good memories. Amazing ones. Ridiculously crazy ones. If you do nothing else with your life, spend it making the most crazy-shit memories you can to cancel out the bad ones. Do you understand?'

She nods slowly, her eyes wide.

'This is one of those times,' I say, shaking her. 'Now is one of those times. Do you understand?'

She doesn't move.

'It's your choice. Walk away because you think it's stupid *or* get that sumo suit on and get dancing.'

I release her and resume my Macarena. She stares at me for a moment before she drops her bag to the floor.

'Will you help me on with the suit?' she asks.

Chapter Forty-Two

And here I am on Alice's bench, the late-evening sun on my face. I think how lucky she was that her husband chose this spot for her to be remembered by. Not a cold, grey headstone filed alongside complete strangers. Not a thorny rosebush or a plaque at the bottom of a tree she never laid eyes on, where the living are nowhere to be seen. But here overseeing my party, providing a resting place for the merrymakers as they pause with their drinks and silently mouth Alice's name and the words 'Loved, cherished and remembered' before sitting down and enjoying the view. I wonder what she would have made of the sight in front of her now. I hope she would have enjoyed it, been glad to have been part of it, been glad that her name was uttered time and time again in the midst of such enjoyment.

I'm alone on Alice's bench at last. It's been a complete whirlwind since four o'clock as I tried my best to keep up with the formidable organisational duo of Karen and Maureen.

Our first task had been to get past the fact that this was a stealth party and we only had permission for a quiet gathering on the lawn for Maureen's supposed seventieth birthday party. The fact that she had celebrated this a few years earlier seemed to have escaped Sandra's memory as she signed off Maureen's request to invite several of her friends and family over for an informal drinks gathering on the lawn.

We'd known that neither Sandra nor Nurse Hagrid (our two main party poopers) were ever seen at Shady Grove on a Saturday and the Duty Manager was a bit of a pushover if boxed into a corner. At precisely 3.30pm Maureen gathered her crack team of distractors and gave them a briefing. Jimmy was to go back to his room and pull the emergency cord. This would summon the Duty Manager and a carer. On arrival in his room he was to express concern over the noises coming from his neighbour Bryan's room. The Duty Manager would go next door to investigate and discover Bryan and Gloria locked in a clinch. (This was Bryan's idea. Gloria agreed, but said they must make it look authentic.)

The Duty Manager would go back to Jimmy to explain that it was just Bryan and Gloria in his room together. Jimmy would then act outraged and claim that Gloria had kissed him only last week, how dare Bryan steal her from under his nose. We were then relying on Jimmy and Bryan to keep the Duty Manager fully engaged in a game of room ping-pong as she did her best to arbitrate the love triangle that had suddenly kicked off down on corridor seven (the furthest from the back lawn and with no view of the driveway). It was hoped they could keep her occupied for long enough to provide access to all the vehicles and allow them to start setting up. Once they were on site we were convinced the Duty Manager would not have the gumption to order them off, and Maureen could convince her that it had all been agreed and a bouncy castle and a giant foam machine on the lawn of Shady Grove was nothing to be concerned about.

All had gone smoothly and by four thirty there was still no sign of the Duty Manager or our theatrical threesome. In fact it was nearly five o'clock when a weary-looking Janette emerged and dived straight for the office, shutting the door firmly behind her. Jimmy, Bryan and Gloria came out into the garden, with Bryan looking like the cat who got the cream, his hand firmly in Gloria's.

'How did it go?' I asked.

'Bloody marvellous,' grinned Bryan.

'He said it was love at first sight,' muttered Gloria, her eyes watering.

'During armchair aerobics,' added Bryan.

'He's known all this time,' whispered Gloria.

'And I never dared tell her.'

'Why not?' I asked in wonderment.

'In case she knocked me back.'

'But you're eighty-three.'

'I know, but you never stop fearing rejection.'

'But not today?'

'Not today,' nodded Bryan. 'I just started kissing her and I knew I never wanted to stop.'

I would have cried tears of joy for them if I hadn't promised myself that I would not cry today.

It wasn't until six o'clock that a drained-looking Janette finally appeared and stood at the patio doors, her forehead screwed up as she tried to process what the hell was going on. Maureen grabbed her before she could get too far along the lines of working out that it was unlikely that Sandra would ever agree to inflatable sumo wrestlers being a healthy pastime choice for geriatrics.

'Isn't it marvellous?' I heard Maureen gush. 'It's like a dream come true, really. To be celebrating my birthday like this.'

'What? With a bouncy castle?'

'For the grandchildren, Janette. They'll love it, don't you think?'

'But you don't have any grandchildren, Maureen.'

'Oh you clever girl, you remembered,' she said, giving her cheek a squeeze. 'Some of my friends may be bringing grandchildren,' she added.

'Okay,' Janette nodded slowly, looking unconvinced.

'And what is that?' she asked, pointing at an enormous nozzle attached to an equally enormous pipe.

'Air conditioning,' was Maureen's description of the foam machine.

'Air conditioning? Outside?'

'Yes.'

'Right. And Sandra said this was all right, did she?'

'Of course! It's my dying wish, you see,' Maureen said, looking directly into Janette's eyes. 'To make this happen.' She cast her arm around the chaos on the lawn.

Janette stared back at her, then let out a sigh. She wouldn't argue with a dying wish.

'I'll be in the office if you need me,' she said, before turning away and disappearing for the rest of the night.

It was terrifying how quickly it got to seven o'clock. At six thirty Maureen sent me off to her room to get ready and, as I'd stood in front of her wardrobe mirror in a Union Jack dress, knee-high boots and hair which was supporting a full can of hairspray, I could hear my own heart beating at such an alarming rate I thought I might have a heart attack. It had all been building up to this moment. I had focused all my energy and emotions on tonight and now I wasn't sure my poor heart could deal with the importance of it. Tonight needed to deliver on a scale it is unfair to expect of any event. This was New Year's Eve times a million. My last laugh. My living wake. My last night as me, before cancer me took over.

★

Alice's bench, it turns out, is the perfect view to reflect on one's life as it dances around before my eyes. As I wobble back onto the lawn in my too-high boots and my too-high hair, I hear a ripple of applause coming from my left. There sit all the inmates on the patio wearing the England flag in various guises – on hats, on T-shirts; some even have face-painted tattoos. They all have St George's cross flags, apart from Jimmy, who's sitting in the corner proudly wearing a Scottish shirt and waving a blue and white flag.

'They've come as football supporters from Euro 96,' says Maureen, beaming at her tribe. I laugh. My first laugh of the party and instantly I feel better.

'As long as you don't all start behaving like hooligans,' I joke.

'You just watch out,' says Bryan, still gripping Gloria's hand. 'We're still capable of causing a riot, aren't we?' he adds, hailing all those around him. Some mutter, some cheer.

'I've given them all a shot of ouzo,' says Maureen under her breath. 'Half of them will be asleep inside half an hour. The rest of us will keep going as good and hard as the rest.'

'Okay,' I nod. 'And you have come as…?' I hardly dare ask, taking in the lace confection over her head, lace gloves and black low-necked dress. My best guess is an Italian widow but I can't quite fit that into the nineties theme or the exposure of wrinkled cleavage.

'Madonna,' she states.

'Excellent, good choice,' I nod. It figures, I think. A very smart and talented woman, but completely bonkers. That would describe Madonna, or indeed Maureen, quite nicely.

'We all set?' asks Karen, appearing at my side. She looks almost identical to how she normally looks, apart from the fact she's wearing a black shoulder-length wig.

'Are you getting changed?' I ask.

'This is it,' she says.

I look down at yet another gorgeous designer dress. No clue there. Then she shoves a mug in my face with the words 'Central Perk' written on it in a distinctive logo. I look at her wig again.

'You're Monica Geller from *Friends*,' I roar. 'Of course.'

We used to watch *Friends* complete with subtitles in Corfu. For a long time our greeting when we saw each other was 'How you doin'?' in Greek. We dreamed of Matt LeBlanc showing up at our resort so we could impress him with our bilingual knowledge of the show. I totter forward and give Karen a hug. I used to call her Monica when she was being overly anal about stuff. Wanting to organise me more than I wanted to be organised. I used it as an insult, she took it as a compliment.

And then suddenly we are on a roll. The guests arriving thick and fast, leaving me with no choice but to play hostess with the mostess.

I'm just catching up with Dave who'd arrived whilst I was getting ready and is busy setting his trusty decks up. Seeing him again is like having a rum and Coke for the first time in a while and wondering why you ever stopped drinking it. He hugs me so tight and bounces me up and down, just like any decent drink should. Then he gives me a massive wet sloppy kiss on the cheek and the next thing I hear is him saying, 'Fuckin' hell, who's that?' in my ear.

I whizz round to see who has caused such a reaction and, to my utter astonishment, I watch a bright pink stretch Hummer pull up the drive and come to a stop next to the geriatric England supporters. I have no idea who it is. I mentally scan my guest list, failing to assign any of them with the exuberance, spare cash and audacity to arrive in such a fashion.

For what feels like an age, but is probably just a minute, no one emerges. The footie supporters start to get impatient and stride up to the numerous blacked-out windows and peer in. One raises his stick and taps, but still no one gets out. Then the chauffeur leaps out and commands the hooligans to step back as he holds the door open for his VIPs.

Then before our eyes out pops Posh Spice. A black side-parting falling over the face of Zoe, clutching an open champagne bottle. Then comes Sporty Spice, threatening the crowd now gathered around them with high kicks and flicks, Lisa's face clear and free of make-up poking out the front of a scraped-back ponytail. Baby Spice steps out next in a short pink A-line dress and blonde bunches, giggling and blushing as the chauffeur offers a hand to Emma. And last, but not least, out strides Scary Spice, aka Heather, in a leopard-print jumpsuit and afro wig. It's quite the weirdest thing I've ever seen but she seems to have got herself nicely into character as she growls at the very overexcited Bryan, who is clearly quite beside himself at the glamour that has just arrived at Shady Grove.

'You'll just have to excuse me for a moment,' I say to Dave and attempt a run across the lawn to join my fellow Spices.

'You never said,' I said, breathing heavily when I reach them. 'You all look amazing!'

'Oh darling,' gushes Zoe/Posh, taking a swig from her champagne bottle, 'we couldn't possibly let you be the only Spice Girl here. You needed your girls around you.'

'Girl Power!' shouts Lisa, her foot only just missing my chin. 'I told you we wouldn't let you down,' she adds.

'Girl Power!' says Heather, giving me a 'V for victory' sign with her fingers.

'I can't believe you came as Scary Spice,' I say to her, shaking my head.

'She's a very positive feminist role model,' says Heather. 'Or so my daughter told me.' She grins.

I think it's the first time I've ever seen her grin. She's clearly enjoying stepping out of her flat brogues and into someone else's knee-high boots for a while. Perhaps it will allow her to shake off her intellectual snobbery just for a moment and breathe the normal, mostly-making-a-fool-of-ourselves air that the rest of us mere mortals breathe.

'We've had such a great time getting ready at Zoe's,' says Emma, giggling and rosy-cheeked. 'She got a naked butler in to serve us champagne before we left, can you believe it? And then this car turned up,' she adds, breathlessly pointing at the enormous Hummer.

'What an absolute scream,' I say, for once not minding Zoe's barefaced desire to upstage my party at all costs. She's gone for it, even if it meant throwing a naked man and an obscene amount of money at it, and I'm truly grateful. They all look like they're having the time of their lives and that's what really matters. Maybe, despite the fact we are all very different, we all bring something to the party, and maybe I should embrace their quirks and foibles. They've come up trumps tonight and maybe I should give them the chance to do that in the coming months. Looking at the epic effort here, I'm sure they will.

It's not often that you see the cast of *Toy Story* alongside the Spice Girls, but the next thing I know, Buzz Lightyear looks as though he's doing the conga with Posh Spice. Even more surprising than that, it looks as though Posh Spice is lapping it up. Peering through the plastic bubble helmet, I spot Tim roaring with laughter as he pushes

Zoe around the patio whilst Julie dressed as Jessie the Cowgirl shakes her head in despair.

'To infinity and beyond,' he shrieks when he spots me. He dashes over and lifts me off my feet.

'He's already had a whole vodka melon,' says Julie.

'Bloody addicted,' says Tim. 'Where's that son of yours? I need to go and shake the boy's hand. Vodka and melon? Just genius.'

'He's slaving over the barbeque,' I say, pointing to where George has set up shop on the far patio.

'Come on, peeps,' says Tim, waving over Woody, Little Bo Peep and Mr and Mrs Potato Head. 'Come and meet the child genius Mark has managed to father.'

I hug tightly the collection of Mark's old friends that Tim has managed to muster. They all beam at me as though we have only seen each other last week. I wish we *had* only seen them last week. We've missed out, I can tell, just by looking at them. Their open smiling faces... We would have had fun. There would have been good times, but we stepped away.

I try not to worry about whether Mark will turn up. I very much doubt that he will. The success of the night can't depend on it. I can't let his non-appearance destroy all this. This has to be bigger than just him and me.

The sight I then see makes it all worthwhile. Every bit of it. I look across at the pathway that snakes from the visitor car park and, miserably lolling towards me, is Kermit the Frog. I close my eyes and then open them again, praying I haven't dreamt it. But I haven't. Antony is making his way across the lawn towards me, his frog's legs open wide in astonishment as he takes in the dress code of the other partygoers.

'You said *Muppets*!' he rages.

'Did I? Oh, I think that was the theme when we first started thinking about the party and then we changed our minds to 1996. Did I not tell you?'

'No, you fuckin' didn't.'

'Not to worry. *The Muppets* were around in 1996, weren't they? So it's fine.'

'I'm dressed as a frog!'

'It's brilliant,' I say, almost moved to tears. I lunge forward and embrace him. 'Thank you,' I continue. 'You have no idea how much this means to me.' He looks down at me. We look at each other for longer than maybe we ever have all our lives.

I watch his brow furrow.

'Are you okay?' he asks.

I spring away quickly. He's never asked that. Ever. I'm sure. He looks me up and down. Last time he must have seen me was during the healthy Nutella and Chardonnay years. Plumper and happier. He hasn't watched my slow decline; he is seeing me in stark contrast to his last memory of me.

'I'm fine,' I say quickly. 'Where's Lucas?'

'Already gone to find George,' he says. His lips are moving but his brain is elsewhere, I can tell. His brain is digesting his sister's transformation.

'Brilliant,' I say and look over to see Lucas falling easily into the role of chef's assistant, guided by George. I catch my breath for a moment as I observe my son give instructions confidently and unselfconsciously. I could watch him all night but I need to distract Antony. Fortunately I don't have to as Mum and Dad arrive at their son's side just at that moment.

'Doesn't Antony look marvellous?' says Mum. 'He's such a case,' she laughs. 'Still not sure about that hair, Jenny. Now, where can I put your dad?'

I look at Antony, who raises his eyebrows as if to say, 'And you're making me spend Christmas with this?'

'We've put you some chairs up on the patio,' I tell Mum. 'Look over there, next to Jimmy in the Scottish flag. He's a lovely man, he'll look after you.'

I get them settled with Jimmy, who merrily gasses away to Mum whilst Dad stares at his surroundings. He is calm, which is good; he isn't agitated. Hopefully he will like it here. Then Maureen comes over and gets stuck into my mother.

'You must be very proud of your daughter,' she says bluntly.

My mother blinks at her. 'Who are you?' she asks.

'Maureen. I live here, I'm Jenny's friend.'

'Jenny looks after you?'

'No, she's my friend,' I interject. 'In fact she looks after me more than I look after her.'

Mum glances between the two of us.

'*My* daughter,' she says, staring hard at Maureen, 'likes to be friends with everyone. She always has.'

'I can see that,' replies Maureen. 'Does she take after you?'

Mum opens her mouth and then closes it again. She knows and I know that she is way too judgemental to want to be friends with everyone. Rejection comes more naturally than acceptance. She doesn't know how to reply – Maureen has put her in a corner within seconds.

'Well, it was lovely to meet you,' says Maureen, breaking the silence and offering her hand to shake. Mum stares at it for a moment and limply holds up her own, which Maureen grasps and shakes vigorously before turning and walking off. My mother dismissed within minutes of arriving – I am in awe of Maureen as ever.

'I'd better just go and check on everything,' I say to Mum, Dad and Kermit. 'Will you be all right for a bit? Help yourself to food and drink.'

I turn before Antony catches my eye and demands an explanation for my change of appearance.

★

Maureen is sitting alone on Alice's bench. I sit down next to her.

'Thank you,' I say.

'What for?' she says, reaching over and grabbing my hand.

'For never looking at me as though I had cancer.'

She turns sharply to look at me.

'I thought you were going to thank me profusely for being the driving force behind this shindig.'

'Nah,' I say. 'I'll thank Karen for that.'

'You will not!'

'So easy,' I say, shaking my head.

'What?'

'To wind you up.'

She turns away, looking bothered.

'Of course I was going to thank you for all this,' I say, sweeping my hand over the scene. 'This wouldn't have happened without you.'

'I told you it was a good idea to go to a funeral, didn't I?' says Maureen, turning back to me.

'You did. And I'm glad, sort of. I mean, I'm sad that poor Emily had to suffer to make me realise I needed a damn good party.'

'She wouldn't have minded – she'd have loved the vodka melon.'

'Good.'

We sit in silence for a while watching the array of decorated people, milling around, chatting, laughing, living. I refuse to think about why they are here. That is for tomorrow, today is for laughing.

As if on cue Maureen asks, 'So what happens tomorrow?'

'Shut up, Maureen,' I say. She squeezes my hand.

We sit in silence again, holding hands.

'Can I just say that I've had a really great time planning this with you,' she says.

'Me too,' I nod. I hope she doesn't get all emotional on me.

'Do you think when Madonna takes off her bustier she has cone-shaped breasts?' she asks.

'Definitely.'

'Do you think her nipples reach all the way to the end of the cones?'

'I have no idea, Maureen,' I laugh.

I feel happy. I am actually happy; in this very moment I am happy.

'Ey, ey,' Maureen says, suddenly pulling her hand away. 'Is this lover boy here?'

I open my eyes and to my astonishment see Mark sauntering across the lawn. Hands deep in pockets, eyes shaded by sunglasses. I feel my heart flip over just as it did in 1996 when he'd arrived at the beach in Corfu.

At least, I think it's Mark. He's wearing cool jeans, not his normal weekend accountancy jeans, as I call them, and a dark brown leather bomber jacket. He looks younger, I think, as my heart sinks to my knees. Is it for her, I wonder. In my absence has the bitch already taken my husband shopping with his bursting wallet and restyled him to a version more pleasing to her eye? What's he doing here? Come to show me he's not too old to shop in Topshop?

'I'll leave you to it,' says Maureen, gripping her glitter-sprayed walking stick and heaving herself up.

I'm simmering as he approaches the bench, then I notice that he's somehow grown impressive sideburns in the last week. What's all that about? Nancy likes the hipster look, does she? My head is spinning.

'So did I pick the right costume?' he says, sitting down next to me.

'Costume?'

'Yeah, this is fancy dress, right?'

I turn to look at him more closely.

'Noel Gallagher!' I finally exclaim, slapping my forehead with my hand.

'Of course,' he shrugs. 'Who else?'

The older boyfriend of a twenty-something blonde whose desperate to update him, I think.

'Noel Gallagher,' I repeat, nodding.

It kind of suits him; it kind of *is* him. A lad from the poor part of town who elevated himself to a higher plane through sheer talent, hard work and determination. A funny guy who put his job before his relationships in order to peak in his chosen field. What does life look like when you've made it, I wonder. When your dream has come true. Does the dream match the expectation? Does it override the sacrifice?

'There's another bit to my outfit parked out front,' he says.

'Oh yeah?'

'An Aston Martin. I picked it up this morning.'

'Noel Gallagher can't drive,' I point out.

'Oh.'

We sit in silence for a moment.

'Looks like a good party,' he says, nodding towards the lawn.

He's making small talk? Not in the mood for this. I might just ask him. Ask him right now: what the hell is happening with our marriage?

'He's a nice lad, isn't he?' says Mark before I can get the crucial question out.

He's looking at Max. He's on the bouncy castle with Ellie. They're both covered in foam and laughing hysterically, making foam pies in their hands and trying to shove them in each other's faces. Ellie is dishevelled. Make-up-free, hair scraped back in a ponytail. I couldn't be happier to see her in such a state and I grin to myself at the astonishingly glorious memory of us both dancing in sumo suits the night before. After at least half a dozen songs and an hysterical routine we managed to choreograph between us, we'd cast them aside because we were too hot and she'd told me all about the 'awesome Max'. Max who Ellie admitted she'd never dared talk to before because Phoebe thought he was a 'dweeb'. I asked how Phoebe was. Ellie shrugged and said she didn't know. She said Phoebe keeps calling her but she doesn't feel like talking to her any more. That actually she's discovered that life is better without Phoebe in it. Then she hugged me in a moment of silent mother-daughter bonding I never thought I'd experience and will cherish for ever.

'Is that George?' Mark asks.

George has on chef's whites and is serving out kebabs to my guests as though he's been doing it all his life. His head is up. Really high. His chin must be missing his neck, they've been apart for so long. His eyes shine bright and look into other people's eyes. The only shy thing about him is his acceptance of praise. It is truly a miracle.

'I couldn't do that,' says Mark.

'What?'

'Cook and talk.'

'You never could multi-task.'

'I know. Can I come home, please?'

I look at him. His face is stricken. I don't know what to say. It's what I dreamed of, but... but...

'I fucked up big time,' he continues. 'I don't know what to say, I don't know what to do. All I know is that I want to come home.'

'Can you start by taking off your sunglasses?' I say. I don't want to have this conversation with Noel Gallagher. He pulls them off and puts them in his pocket.

'Why?' I ask. I need to know why; I need to see why in his eyes.

He takes my hands in his and swallows.

'I guess I've been remembering what we had.'

'What *did* we have?' I urge. I need to hear this.

'I don't know how to explain.'

'Try,' I demand.

He raises his head and looks out over the lawn.

'I keep thinking about when we got together when I came to your party in Corfu, you know...'

'In 1996.'

'Yeah. I never dreamed you'd be interested in me, to be honest,' he says, turning to look at me intensely.

I swallow.

'You were so full of life and fun and excitement. I nearly didn't come because I was certain you must have thought I was just a boring accountant. I planned to make sure I got your number and then I'd find you when I'd made it and sweep you off your feet. I thought *then* maybe you might be interested.'

'Whatever made you think that?'

'I don't know. I didn't think I had anything to offer then apart from a vision of who I might become. I was pretty dull really apart from that.'

Wow – how the past plays tricks on us! I'd liked his dreams. I'd liked his focus, but mostly I'd just liked him. I didn't think he was boring. No one with that smile could be boring. And the way he took control, organised me, but not in a domineering way, in a caring way, back in 1996. He looked after me. He made me feel safe; we fitted together like a little piece of jigsaw. I brought the fun and energy and dippiness and he got us there on time and in an orderly fashion. I taught him how to not take life so seriously and he taught me how to take life a little *more* seriously. It was a fair and equal exchange that made us both better people. Before our opposite personalities had time to rub each other the wrong way and develop into opposing ways of living life. When the flush of first love had disappeared and couldn't work its magic on smoothing over the cracks and crevices that develop in a relationship as it wears with age.

'Do you know what I realised this week?' says Mark.

'That you are a dickhead?'

'Yes, obviously. I realised that if we hadn't got together in 1996, and that if I'd gone back to sweep you off your feet with the flash car and the huge bank account, you wouldn't have looked at me twice.'

I think for a minute.

'Correct.'

'It's funny,' he says.

'Oh yes, it's hilarious.'

'Let me finish. When life-changing stuff happens it makes you look back and try and make some sense of it all.'

'Are you talking about the affair or suddenly becoming minted?'

'Both, I guess. I went to collect the car. I ordered it weeks ago and when the deal was getting really stressful I'd look at pictures of it online and it would remind me why I was working so hard. So I picked it up but I felt nothing. I thought it would be the moment, you know, when I'd feel… happy. And I didn't. I felt miserable. It meant nothing without you stood there next to me to take the piss out of me for being so flash. I drove off the forecourt in two hundred grands' worth of car and I never felt so alone.'

'*How* much?'

'You heard.'

I blow my cheeks out.

He gets up abruptly and holds a hand out towards me.

'Will you come and have a look at it?' he asks.

I shake my head. I'm not interested. A flash car has never felt so irrelevant and wrong.

'No, please, come and have a look. You'll like what you see, I promise.'

'I won't,' I say, shaking my head.

'You will. Trust me, please.'

I let him take my hand. I let him lead me over the lawn to the car park. I don't want to see his stupid bloody car. It's meaningless, I want to shout at him. Who needs a sports car when they're dying?

For a moment I think he's brought her with him as I catch a movement on the front seat of his admittedly beautiful car. What on earth is he playing at? I don't have time for this – I'm supposed to be having the time of my soon-to-be-extinguished life.

Mark strides ahead and opens the passenger door. A grey streak leaps out and dashes towards me, jumping up on my Union Jack dress.

'Betsy!' I cry. 'Oh my God, Betsy!'

I sink to my knees and bury my face in her fur. She wriggles and thrashes in delight. It's Betsy right here, alive and kicking right in front of me. I cannot believe what I'm seeing.

I look up at Mark in wonder.

'How?' I ask.

'I drove off the forecourt and… and I just didn't know what to do with myself. I always imagined I'd be coming home and whisking you all off to some fancy restaurant…'

'Please God, not Sebastian's,' I say, shaking my head.

'Then I'd go and treat you all to some serious shopping, but… but… that just didn't feel right and, what with me moving out, I just didn't know what to do. I just wanted to do something to make this moment happy. But I knew money wouldn't do it and this was all I could think of. I've driven all over. I've been to fourteen different dog homes. I thought it had to be worth a shot. In the end it was. They said someone handed her in last week and they knew that eventually someone would come and pick her up. They could tell she'd been loved.'

'You've spent all day driving round dog homes in that car?'

He nods. 'But I do have an admission,' he says, glancing at his feet before looking back up at me sheepishly. 'I think I've agreed to adopt an abandoned Terrier as well. I'm sorry, he just looked so sad and the woman was very persuasive, especially when she saw the kind of car I drove. She said Betsy had really taken to him and that it would be such a shame to split them up now.'

I stand up and lunge at Mark, engulfing him in my arms. I don't think I've ever loved him more than at that precise moment. My husband, the rockstar Finance Director who goes out and rescues a dog the week he becomes a millionaire.

I pull away to look at him. I cup his face in my hands. I breathe him in. My heart is full of joy and love and happiness in a way I never thought would happen to me again. Something I didn't think I would feel before I took my dying breath. How good it feels. Like the sun has come back out after a long and depressing winter. Thank goodness for the sunshine.

'Betsy!' I hear a shriek behind me. 'Betsy,' I hear Ellie shout again. 'Oh my God, it's Betsy! George! George, come quick, Betsy is back!'

I watch as Ellie falls to her knees next to a now beside herself Betsy and wraps her in her arms, only to be removed by George, who runs across the lawn quicker than I have ever seen him move. He literally falls on top of the dog in his excitement.

'Your dad has been round every dogs' home in the area and found him,' I tell our two children.

'Wow, Dad!' says George, looking up at his father in awe whilst Betsy licks his face furiously.

'I could see how desperately you were missing her,' he tells his son. 'I knew I had to do something.'

George gives him a look of confusion. I guess he has never heard his father recognise his feelings because he's always been so busy pointing out his failings.

I look on as George's eyes mist over. Then I watch as he disentangles himself from Betsy and stands up to embrace his dad.

'Thank you,' I hear him mutter into his neck.

'Any time, mate,' says Mark, patting him on the back. 'Any time.'

I'm about to join the love-in when Maureen and Karen appear, both holding clipboards.

'I think we might run out of Prosecco,' says Maureen. 'I've sent Jimmy down to Morrisons.'

'And are you ready for the sumo wrestlers doing British Bulldog with foam?' asks Karen. 'Bloody hell, who's come in this gorgeous motor?' she exclaims.

'Mark,' I say, beaming. 'And you remember Karen, don't you, Mark? From Corfu?'

'Christ, you've aged well!' says Karen, eyeing him up. 'And clearly quite the catch,' she adds, nodding at the car.

'Is that Dad's car?' asks Ellie, suddenly clocking the gleaming specimen she has been next to for the last few minutes. 'I'm so going to enjoy learning to drive in that.'

'You will not, young lady,' laughs Mark. 'Clapped-out old banger for you, I think.'

'Oh, but Dad!'

'Oh, but nothing. You need to earn something like this, then you can drive it. When you've bought it yourself.'

'Quite right,' agrees Karen. 'There's nothing like being able to earn enough money to buy your dream car.'

'You listen to Karen,' advises Mark. 'She's right.'

'What utter dickhead arrives in a car like that!' booms Tim, strolling up, Buzz Lightyear helmet tucked under his arm.

'*This* dickhead,' laughs Mark.

Tim shakes his head at his mate. 'It won't make your penis look any longer, you know.'

'Tim!' I exclaim, nodding towards Maureen.

'I absolutely agree,' she says without turning a hair. 'These cars will do nothing for your sex life, but may I ask, Mark, when can you take me for a ride in it? I do love a fast car!'

'Any time you like,' he says. 'It's nice to hear that someone appreciates it. You name your date and time and we'll go and do doughnuts on the industrial estate.'

'Now that's the best offer I've had all year,' she replies beaming. Everybody laughs.

'I'm so glad you're all here,' I suddenly gush, looking around me. 'So bloody glad!'

This is the crack team that will pull us all through this, I'm sure. Or more importantly, will pull Ellie and George through this. What with Maureen and her no-nonsense attitude to George, Karen's role-modelling for Ellie and Tim's piss-taking to boost everyone with a laugh and a joke, this family will have half a chance of making it through this alive after I'm gone. The relief is enormous.

George suddenly jumps up. 'My kebabs might be burning,' he declares. 'I'd better get back to them.'

'We'll be over in a minute,' Mark tells him. 'Can't wait to try them.'

George grins then turns and runs back across the lawn to his post behind the barbeque.

'I'm taking Betsy to meet Max,' says Ellie, getting up and dragging the dog after her. 'Make sure she likes him.'

'And what are we all standing here for?' asks Tim. 'There's one hell of a great party going on over there, you know.'

'Will you just give us a minute?' asks Mark. 'Just need to ask Jenny something.'

'Well, we'll be waiting by the bouncy castle,' he replies. 'And you know I don't like to be kept waiting by a bouncy castle!'

Maureen squeezes my arm before she takes off back down the lawn, followed by Karen still checking her clipboard.

I turn towards Mark trying to make sense of the sudden sense of euphoria that is gushing through me but he is shoving a piece of paper under my nose that clearly he needs me to give my attention to.

'Look at this,' he says. I'm vaguely aware of a picture of pure blue azure sea and a white building.

'Let's buy a holiday home in Greece,' he says, pointing vigorously at the paper. 'I had a look online. There may be some red tape but we could do it. There are some amazing properties for sale out there, right near where you used to work, and it's actually a great investment. What do you say? Imagine being able to fly over at the drop of a hat and have our own balcony overlooking that. And the kids would love it, wouldn't they? I was thinking we should get one with at least four bedrooms, then they could come over with their mates and stuff. And, who knows, one day we might be entertaining husbands and wives and even grandkids. How about that? What amazing new memories we could create in the future if we bought a house like this one. Can you imagine bouncing your grandchildren on your knee in that glorious sunshine?'

I blink back at him, glancing between his face and the piece of paper. I'm felled. This isn't supposed to happen. Tonight is about now, living today, and then beginning to deal with the treacherous road to the future tomorrow. Mark has painted my future in glorious technicolour, in colours I never even dreamed of, where I would live out my days in utter bliss. This is cruel, so cruel. I want to scream. How can life be this evil? This is a horror story.

'What's the matter?'

Tears are streaming down my cheeks. I can't stop them. I want to; I don't want to be here now. Today is about living, I'd promised myself that. Tomorrow the dying will commence.

'I knew it,' I hear a voice interrupting my sobs. 'Why the hell didn't you tell me?'

I look up through waterlogged eyes as Antony, still dressed as Kermit, bears down on me.

He knows, I think. He's worked it out and now the sight of me sobbing has confirmed his theory.

'It's nothing to do with you!' interjects Mark, looking angry at Antony's interruption.

'She's my sister,' replies Kermit fiercely.

'Oh yeah and you've always been there for her, haven't you? A great brother you've been.'

'I can't help it if I live three hours away. I had no idea what was going on. Why didn't you tell me?' he says, poking his frog's leg in Mark's chest.

'Like I said, it's got nothing to do with you. We've dealt with it.'

'But I'm a doctor, for fuck's sake! I might have been able to help.'

'Oh, I'm sorry. I forgot that you were a doctor. Of course you're some kind of god who can solve all ailments, including your brother-in-law's infidelity. Is there an operation for that these days? Of course you could really help by castrating me. Is that what you want to do?'

'What?'

'You heard.'

'You're having an affair. Whilst she's—'

'Not any more. It's over,' Mark shouts back.

Antony looks at me in disbelief.

'Just stop,' I shout. 'Stop it, both of you. I want to hear no more about any of this tonight. This is my party and you're not going to ruin it. Understood?'

Mark is looking at the floor and Antony is staring at me open-mouthed.

'Understood?' I repeat.

'But—' says Antony.

'But nothing,' I reply, giving him such a glare he takes a step backwards.

'Time to dance,' I say, stuffing the piece of paper back in Mark's pocket and grabbing his hand. 'Let's just dance, shall we? It's time to dance right now.'

Chapter Forty-Three

Everyone's arms are in the air. The crowd sways as one, singing 'Champagne Supernova' at the very tops of their voices.

I'm high on life once again.

Epilogue

It's the last thing I remember. The swaying and the singing, then nothing. I just crumpled into a heap on the floor apparently. Right there in the middle of 1996 amongst the cast of *Toy Story*, *Friends*, the Spice Girls and the odd Muppet.

Jimmy pulled the emergency cord just inside the patio door and the night duty nurse came running, but Antony was already on his mobile calling for an ambulance. Mark said they had another confused conversation as he told my brother that I was probably just drunk and wouldn't need an ambulance whilst he shouted at him for hiding our secret. It wasn't until Maureen took them both to one side and sat them down and told them what had really been going on that the light dawned. She told me when she came to visit that Mark couldn't speak. He was in total shock whilst Antony was jumping round the patio muttering, 'I knew it.'

Mark was by my bedside in hospital when I came round, still wearing his Noel Gallagher sideburns. He was holding my hands. The minute I opened my eyes he began to weep. His head dropped on the pillow beside me and he sobbed and sobbed. Huge, wracking man sobs that are impossible not to add your own to. We held each other so tight for a long time without words, the pain and the sorrow of the news ebbing and flowing between us.

He asked me why I didn't tell him, of course. I confessed that I found out the same day as I found him having sex in his office. Distraught, he paced the room with his head in his hands, unable to find any light that reflected well on his actions. So I also said that I was glad I hadn't told him. That I wanted the chance to keep living just a little longer, and not telling him had allowed me to do that. I was grateful for the time I'd had without everyone looking at me like I'd changed into a different human being overnight. It also meant I would now die knowing he picked me. That he was here because of me and not the cancer. *I* got my husband back, my disease didn't do that.

Doctor Death looked mightily relieved to see Mark when he came to visit me on the ward later that day. He shook his hand vigorously and squeezed mine as if to say, 'Well done, you need this man'. The nurse insisted that Mark should push me in a wheelchair over to Doctor Death's office, which was fun, I have to say. I got him to do wheelies, which he didn't want to do, but it made us both laugh.

Mark asked for some paper and he wrote a lot of notes whilst the doctor again described my condition. I listened to some of it. Some of it went over my head but it didn't matter because I knew Mark would have picked it all up. Just as I was wondering how old the doc was, I became aware of them both looking at me: they were clearly expecting me to say something but I had no idea what. Maybe I was still high on whatever drugs they had given me.

I raised my eyebrows at Mark, willing him to answer for me. He reached over and squeezed my hand and then asked the doctor if we could come back on Tuesday and then make some decisions. Apparently we needed to spend some time together and talk it through. The doctor had sighed but agreed as long as Mark promised to bring me back with a plan.

When I put my toes in the water I thought my heart would burst with joy. I felt happy. How weird.

The doctor discharged me and that night we were on a flight to Corfu with George and Ellie. God knows how Mark had managed to swing it but I bet there are a lot of strings you can pull with money and a dying wife. We told the kids it was a big treat to celebrate their dad's deal. They seemed surprisingly willing to accept that as a viable reason for the crazy urgency of having to go that day. George did keep casting me worried glances on the plane though. He knows we're hiding something, but we have decided to tell them both the truth after we get back. When we have decided what will happen next. When Mark and I have come up with a plan that will ease them through this as best as possible. We'll tell them together then.

We sat on the beach on the last night and Mark held my hand as he took his notes from our meeting with the doctor out of his pocket.

'We'll do this together,' he said.

'Okay,' I whispered as my consent to listening and starting on the road to my dead end.

He explained what the doctor had said in my language. Slowly and carefully.

'So we have options,' he said in his concluding arguments. 'We can follow Mr Randall's chemotherapy plan. You heard what he said, the treatment should prolong your life. And that's what you want now, right? Now you've done what you needed to do. You want to be around as long as possible, don't you?'

I hesitated and was alarmed to see a look of horror spring to his face.

'Ellie and George and I *need* you to be around as long as possible,' he said, grabbing my hand. 'You do know that, don't you?'

'Of course,' I replied, nodding. 'Of course I will do whatever it takes to be here as long as I can.'

'Good, good,' said Mark, gathering himself and glancing back down at his notes. 'But I do think it would be worth also looking at other options. Get a second opinion, investigate trial drugs. Don't you? There is hope.'

I looked at him – I hadn't been expecting this.

'Be rational, Mark,' I sighed. I don't think I have ever said this to him. Him to me many times.

'The numbers are stacked against you, I admit.'

'Have you done a spreadsheet?'

'No,' he said.

This was not good news. He hadn't done a spreadsheet because he knew he wouldn't like the answer.

'I haven't done one because everything's based on probability. Probability strikes me as the wrong measure to use in this instance.'

'Are you trying to be my husband or my accountant?'

'I love you,' he said and we cried for a while.

★

'So listen,' he says when we are finally able to speak again. 'You could have a very high probability, say ninety-nine per cent, of something happening to you but you could still be the one per cent that it doesn't happen to. When you're talking life or death, haven't you always got to believe you could be the one per cent?'

I look out to the sea. I feel the waves lapping over my toes, I feel the summer sunshine on my back. He's asking me to have hope. Against all the odds, he's asking me to still hope I'm the one per cent.

'Come on,' he says. 'You decided you were going to live as though you didn't have cancer. You decided that, you made that happen. You can also decide whether you're going to live as though you are in the ninety-nine per cent, *I'm going to die* bracket, or in the one per cent, *I have hope* bracket. Which is it going to be?'

'How can you make something so irrational sound rational?'

'Because that's the only way I can live through this.' The tears threaten his eyes again. '*I* have to live in hope.'

I look at him for a long time. He has never felt more solid, more real, more alive, and neither have I. Never have I lived more in the moment than at this very moment. I am alive now, right now, and with the man I love.

'You're right,' I agree, grasping his hands. 'I decided how I was going to live the last few weeks. It was my choice. And I can decide again. We can live however we want. So let's do it, let's live in hope for however long we have.'

A Letter from Tracy

I want to say a huge thank you for choosing to read *The Last Laugh*. If you did enjoy it, and want to keep up-to-date with all my latest releases, just sign up at the following link. Your email address will never be shared and you can unsubscribe at any time.

www.bookouture.com/tracy-bloom

I hope you loved *The Last Laugh* and if you did I would be very grateful if you could write a review. I'd love to hear what you think, and it makes such a difference helping new readers to discover one of my books for the first time.

I love hearing from my readers – you can get in touch on my Facebook page, through Twitter, Goodreads or my website.

Thanks,
Tracy

 tracybloomwrites

 @TracyBBloom

www.tracybloom.com

Acknowledgements

Thank you to my husband Bruce, my agent Madeleine Milburn, my editor Jenny Geras, the marvellous Peta Nightingale and my friend Joanna Courtney, who were all early readers of this book and without whose encouragement I would never have got to the end.

Thank you to my sister Helen, who does an amazing job as a nurse. She very kindly offered advice on all things medical. Any errors are entirely mine and not hers.

Mostly I would like to acknowledge everyone out there who help and support those who are faced with the terrible knowledge that their life is going to be cut tragically short. To put yourselves in a position where you face people in the worst of circumstances is bravery on the grandest scale. Many thanks to Tony for nominating Sue Ryder Care, who provide fantastic hospice and neurological care for people facing frightening, life-changing diagnosis, who will receive ten per cent of my earnings from this novel.

Finally, thank you, Gemma – I hope you would have approved. I have tried my hardest to be at my absolute best, just as you always did. So happy to have had you in my life – miss you always. Xx

Lightning Source UK Ltd.
Milton Keynes UK
UKHW02f1829090218
317591UK00002B/109/P